The Madness

ALISON RATTLE

HOT KEY BOOKS

First published in Great Britain in 2014 by Hot Key Books
Northburgh House, 10 Northburgh Street, London EC1V 0AT

A CIP catalogue record for this book is available from the British Library.

ISBN: 978-1-4714-0103-9

1

This book is typeset in 10.5 Berling LT Std using Atomik ePublisher

Printed and bound by Clays Ltd, St Ives Plc

FSC

Hot Key Books supports the Forest Stewardship Council (FSC),
the leading international forest certification organisation, and is
committed to printing only on Greenpeace-approved FSC-certified paper.

www.hotkeybooks.com

Hot Key Books is part of the Bonnier Publishing Group
www.bonnierpublishing.com

The
Madness

For Daisy, Ella, Riley, Paul. My reasons for it all.

'Love is merely a madness, and, I tell you, deserves as well a dark house and a whip as madmen do.'

William Shakespeare, *As You Like It*

Clevedon, Somersetshire

1868

Clevedon (so called because of the cliff or cleve here terminating in a dun or valley) is a pleasant watering-place on the south side of the Bristol Channel. The sea coast presents features of romantic interest, in some localities being indented with wild and craggy bays; in others furnishing a parapet of rocks over which the sea dashes in sheets of foam. The place offers the usual accommodation for sea bathing.

The Illustrated London News

I

A Mermaid on the Beach

By the time she was fourteen years old, Marnie Gunn could swim like a fish. Hardly a day went by when her flannel shift was not hung out by the fire to dry. Often as not, it was still damp in the morning when she pulled it back on and went to the beach with Ma to attend to Smoaker Nash's bathing machines.

It was Ma that'd made Marnie go in the sea every day to begin with. 'The best cure in the world,' she said. 'Make you strong and hearty, it will.' Marnie was only five at the time and thought Ma was trying to drown her. She would yell and hit Ma with her small fists, and kick at her with her one good leg. But Marnie was only little and no match for her mother. Ma would put Marnie under her arm and carry her down to the iron-grey sea. She would grip Marnie tight around the waist and plunge her under the freezing waves again and again. Marnie's voice would shrink to nothing with the shock of it.

'I won't have no cripple for a daughter,' Ma would say. Marnie soon learned not to protest. For worse than the piercing cold of the ocean was the hot sting of the horsewhip that Ma would crack over the backs of her legs to 'harden her up'.

Marnie had no choice but to learn to love the ocean. After a while Ma began to loosen her grip and Marnie was astonished to find she could swim. It was easy and natural.

Soon, Marnie couldn't imagine life without her daily bathes. It was true what Ma said. She did grow stronger every day, and while she was in the water, she didn't have to use her stick or think of her twisted leg or the cruel taunts of the village children who would spit and laugh at her because she was different.

When the children gathered on the lane to trundle their hoops or play tip-cat, Marnie would hobble past as quickly as she could. Sometimes, she would thrust her stick out into the path of a rolling hoop and send it toppling into the hedgerows. It felt good to spoil their silly games. She let their angry cries and nasty words wash over her as she hurried down to the sea. *'Imbecile!' 'Muttonhead!'*

Marnie didn't care. She had something they didn't. She had the sea and its soothing whispers and comforting embrace. She could swim for further and for longer than any of them. When they hoiked up their skirts and rolled up their britches to splash in the shallows, Marnie would swim far out, past the breakers, where the screech of the gulls and the idle sighs of the waves were the only sounds she could hear. From that distance, the village children looked like nothing more than stray dogs and Marnie could see the bathing machines spread out along the shoreline and the figures of Ma and the other dippers standing solidly in the water.

Ma was the best dipper in the whole of Clevedon. Ladies came from all over to take the sea-cure and they all wanted Ma to dip them. She had a way about her that had the ladies laying in her arms like docile babies.

The ladies didn't look anything like Ma. Ma smoked a pipe for one thing. She was broad and stout with arms as thick and brown as the blacksmith's. She was almost as strong as the blacksmith too, and could stand up to her waist in the sea most of the day, holding the ladies afloat on the waves.

The ladies came on the train from Yatton Junction. They brought huge leather trunks with them and piles of fancy bandboxes. All the ladies were pale and fragile-looking, like they'd never seen a bit of sun or wind. Marnie thought they wore far too many clothes. They were covered in layers of velvet and lace, with tight jackets and huge skirts that seemed to take up the width of the esplanade. They wore close-fitting bonnets decorated with frills, ribbons, flowers and stuffed birds. Their hands were enclosed in tight white gloves, even on the hottest of days. Marnie thought she would die if she had to wear that many clothes.

Marnie liked to watch the ladies, though. She would stand bare-foot at the top of the beach steps and stare wide-eyed as the pale creatures glided along the esplanade twirling frothy parasols in their gloved hands. Although she wasn't aware of it, Marnie's raw beauty drew the stares of the visitors too. With her yellow hair hanging down her back like thick ropes of tangled seaweed and with eyes as startling and blue as hedgerow cornflowers, she could have been a creature of myth washed ashore in a storm.

But then the visitors would glance down and spy her stick and twisted leg. They would recoil and move away to the other side of the esplanade, as though by being too close they could catch something nasty. A long time ago, the stares of the ladies used to hurt Marnie, like being struck by sharp stones. But now she was used to it and the disgust in their eyes bounced off her salted skin without leaving a mark. She had learned not to cry. It didn't change a thing. Instead she would stick out her hand towards the ladies, making them back away even further. 'Spare a penny, madam?' she would ask, trying not to smile as they spluttered and blushed. On occasion she would be rewarded with a few coins and would treat herself to the biggest pastry in Miss Cranston's shop window. She would eat her prize slowly, licking the cream from the centre and letting the buttery pastry melt on her tongue. It tasted all the sweeter if the village children walked by and saw her; she relished the greed and envy in their eyes more than the delights of a dozen of the creamiest pastries.

Marnie always made sure her lips were free of crumbs before she went back home to the cottage. Ma would have beaten her black and blue if she ever caught wind of her tricks.

It was a warm June morning and Clevedon was busy. The guesthouses were full to bursting and Miss Cranston's Tea House was doing a roaring trade. Smoaker Nash's bathing machines were fully booked now the tide was at its highest. Marnie knew she couldn't go in for another swim, not now the water's edge was packed with the machines. Ma had told her time and time again that the ladies needed their privacy. She couldn't go over to Byron's Bay either. That's where the men bathed naked and now that Marnie was fourteen, Ma said it was high time she practised modesty.

Marnie was bored. She didn't want to go and help Smoaker in his proprietor's hut, although she knew Ma would expect her to. She was too hot and listless. She usually liked collecting the sixpences that each bather paid for a half-hour use of a machine. She liked to drop the silver coins through the slit in the top of Smoaker's tin box and hear them rattle to the bottom like small pebbles. She liked to help clean out the bathing machines too, after the horses trundled them back up the beach and the bathers emerged, fully clothed again, but shivering and bedraggled.

Marnie would climb up the wooden steps of the machines and into the snug interiors that smelt of damp wood and the flowery scent of perfumed ladies. With the doors at either end shut it was dim inside, the only light coming from tiny windows set high up on the sides of the machines. After Marnie had gathered up damp towels, she would sweep wet sand from the floors and look under the benches that ran the length of the machines to see if anything had been left behind. Once she'd found a fancy button that shone like the inside of a shell. Another time she'd found a hair comb with broken teeth. It was carved with swirls and curls and looked as if it was made out of bone that had been washed by the sea. Marnie had put these treasures in the pocket of her frock and hidden them under an old firebrick in the backyard of the cottage in Ratcatcher's Row.

But Marnie wasn't in the mood for treasure hunting now,

nor did she want to be carting about heavy armfuls of wet towels. She wanted to be back in the sea, cooling herself in the clean, bright water and imagining herself to be all alone; just a dot in the middle of the wide, wide ocean.

Marnie sighed. She wandered away from the esplanade and back down to the beach; she didn't want Smoaker to spy her if he poked his head out of his hut. Marnie was tired of the busy season now. She couldn't wait for the ladies to pack up their trunks and go back to Yatton Junction to catch their trains home. Then the sea would be all hers again for a while, and she wouldn't have to share it or put up with anyone's pitying stares.

Above the noise of the lapping waves, the heavy crunch of horses' hooves on shingle and the creaking and rumbling of bathing-machine wheels, Marnie heard the din of voices. She turned to look and saw a small crowd gathered on the slipway outside Smoaker's hut. There seemed to be an excitement in the air. People were pausing from their usual business and turning their heads.

Marnie held up her hand to shield her eyes from the sun and saw two footmen, dressed in gold livery coats, black breeches and white stockings, carrying something heavy on to the beach. Their powdered hair had come loose and was sticking to the sweat on their foreheads. There were several maids in black dresses and starched white aprons running to and fro, flapping their hands about, and a boy in a blue suit standing very still in the middle of it all.

Then there was Smoaker, marching down the slipway towards a bathing machine that was being towed into the sea. He called to the attendant to stop and banged on the side of the machine, shouting, 'Time's up! Time's up!' He pulled open the door and there was a shriek from inside. Smoaker stuck his head in the doorway and a moment later a red-faced lady clutching a bonnet to her chest with one hand and carrying a pair of boots with the other stumbled down the steps and shrieked again as her stockinged feet trod on shingle. The horse was turned, and the empty bathing machine was pulled back up the beach towards the footmen. Marnie saw then that the thing that had been carried on to the beach was a bulky Bath chair, and reclining in its depths was the most beautiful lady Marnie had ever seen.

She was swathed in layers of creamy lace and pale golden hair trailed in curls from under her huge straw bonnet. She had smooth ivory skin that shone like a polished pebble and her eyes were the deep green of the sea on a stormy night. Marnie wondered if she might not be a mermaid that had been stranded on the rocks. She watched closely as the footmen lifted the lady from the Bath chair and carried her into the bathing machine. Was she being returned to the sea? Marnie looked carefully, trying to catch a glimpse of a fishtail or the shine of scales under the layers of lace. But there was nothing. Two maids followed the lady inside the machine, and then the footmen came out and shut the door.

The fuss in the air calmed then, as the bathing machine was towed down to the water's edge. The footmen and the maids sat on rocks at the bottom of the slipway, gossiping quietly and dabbing at their faces with handkerchiefs. It was only then that Marnie noticed the boy in the blue suit again.

13

He had moved away from the rest of them and he was on the beach, standing with his back to the sea. He had his hands in his pockets and he was staring right at her.

2

The Journal of Noah de Clevedon

Clevedon. JUNE 15th 1868, Monday

We arrived in Clevedon last night. The journey here was tedious. Mother was unwell for the most part and had to resort to her smelling salts on several occasions. The servants went ahead of us last week to prepare for our arrival, but despite the fires they have lit, it still feels cold and damp in the old manor. My bed sheets have the tang of mildew about them.

I miss the noise of London already. It is far too quiet here. I wish I could have stayed with Father. I don't see that I can be of any use here. Mother has Clarissa to look after her and the servants to run the place. But Father's wishes are to be obeyed, and he is busy with pier business, so here I am. I don't know what I shall do with myself. At least I have Prince to keep me company. He won't mind being here with the endless countryside and countless rabbits!

Mother went to take the sea-cure this morning. We caused quite a fuss on the seafront with our army of servants and Mother in her Bath chair! The cure is said to be most beneficial. I can only hope it lives up to its promises and that Mother gets well as soon as possible, so that we can return to London.

There was a strange girl on the beach. I could not help but stare at her. She looked a wild little thing, with a tangle of dirty yellow hair. But she had the most beautiful face I have ever seen. I am sure she cannot belong in this place. Though I suspect I shall have plenty enough time on my hands to find out more about her.

I dined with Clarissa this evening as Mother took to her bed early.

3

Inside a Seashell

Ma was full of it. All that evening she could hardly sit still. 'Can you believe it, Smoaker? Lady de Clevedon back at the manor after all these years! Is Sir John come home too, I wonder?' She bustled around the kitchen, carving chunks of bread for the supper table and stirring the thick pea soup on the stove. She stopped now and then to glug from her pot of beer and to top up Smoaker's pot from the jug on the table. 'This'll be the making of us, Smoaker! Soon as word gets round I've been asked for special by the *Lady* herself, they'll be coming from all over. Reckon we can put our prices up, don't you think, Smoaker?'

Smoaker Nash never said much about anything as a rule. But he was as excited as Ma was and he patted Ma's behind and pinched her cheek between his thumb and forefinger, as though she were a chubby baby in napkins.

'I reckon you might be right, Mrs Gunn,' he said.

'She hardly weighed a thing, you know,' Ma continued. 'As

light as a gull feather. She almost floated by herself. Quite lost her breath when I dipped her, mind. She was only strong enough for the once under.'

Smoaker nodded knowingly. 'A proper lady. Fancy that, Mrs Gunn. We've got ourselves a proper lady.'

Marnie chewed on her bread and tried to feel excited too. But she couldn't help being disappointed that the beautiful lady in the Bath chair hadn't been a mermaid after all.

Ma ladled the soup into bowls and Marnie sipped at hers while Ma's chatter filled up the room. Marnie broke a piece of crust from her bread and held it under the table for Nep. The cat snatched at it, then ran to the corner of the kitchen where it swallowed the bread in two bites. Nep was Smoaker's cat, through and through. It sat on his lap most evenings and Smoaker would stroke its back, tickle its chin and whisper, 'Who's Papa's baby?' in its ears. It would never sit on Marnie's lap. It knew she wasn't quite right, and like everybody else, the cat didn't want to come near. The only way Marnie could ever catch its attention was by offering titbits. Usually Ma would have scolded her for wasting her supper on a cat, but she was so taken up with the day's events that she didn't notice.

Smoaker belched loudly and mopped up the last of his soup. He was as small as Ma was large, with a huge belly that hung over the belt of his trousers. Tufts of grey hair grew behind his ears, but the rest of his head was bare. The sun and the wind had roasted it reddish-brown, like the thick crackling on a Sunday leg of mutton. Nep jumped on Smoaker's lap and purred noisily as it licked its paws. Marnie was envious of the cat. She hated that it had a Pa when she didn't. She wished every day she had a pa to dote on her like Smoaker doted on Nep. She wanted to know what that would feel like.

Ma had told her often enough that Smoaker wasn't her pa. He was just 'a dear, dear friend'. Marnie knew he was a *dear friend* to Ma because sometimes Ma didn't come to bed at night and Marnie would hear thuds and the squeaking of bedsprings from upstairs in Smoaker's room. This made Marnie feel left out and empty. It was as though Ma, Smoaker and Nep were the real family and she was just a visitor.

Whenever Marnie asked about her pa, Ma's face would go all tight, like someone had tied a knot in the back of her head. 'You don't have a pa,' she would say as she tapped the bowl of her pipe. 'I found you washed up on the shore, I did, curled up soft and pink inside a seashell.' Marnie knew that wasn't true, of course. She knew she must have had a pa at one time. She wasn't daft. She knew that a man had to have shared in the making of her. He was out there somewhere, she was sure of it. She dreamed about him all the time. He was a fisherman with a dark-brown leathery face and yellow hair. He smelt of the sea at low tide; of warm fish and seaweed. If Marnie squeezed her eyes shut tight and held her breath for a moment, she could conjure up a memory of a rough woollen gansey pressed against her cheek and a pair of strong arms holding her. Marnie imagined her pa had gone out in his fishing boat one day and got caught in a storm while chasing a shoal. She never believed the sea would have taken him away from her, though. He had just got lost somewhere and was sailing around the world right now, trying to find his way back to Clevedon. She was certain he would come home one day, and she wanted to be the very first thing he saw when he pulled his boat up on the beach.

When Marnie went to bed that night, Ma and Smoaker were still up drinking beer, smoking their pipes and celebrating their good fortune. Marnie knew it would be one of those nights when Ma never came to the bed they shared. The bed felt big and lonely. Even Nep wouldn't come and curl up on her feet. She closed her eyes and listened to the shush of the sea and the rasping noise of shingle being dragged by the waves and flung back on to the beach. She tried to breathe in rhythm with the ebb and flow of the tide.

In, out . . . in, out . . . in, out.

She slowly drifted to sleep. She dreamed her feet were cold and wet. She was shivering, her skin was damp, and she could smell the fishy tang of seaweed and the salty air. She stood on the edge of the sea looking out at Pa in his wooden boat. Green paint flaked from the hull in long curls, like peelings of sunburned skin, and waves rocked the boat backwards and forwards as though it was an infant's cradle. Pa stood underneath the cotton sails, beckoning to her with a raised hand. But as hard as she tried, Marnie couldn't move. Then she looked down at her feet and her twisted leg, and saw instead a golden fishtail. A wave swept over her and pulled her into the sea and suddenly she was swimming through the water, faster and faster, whipping her tail through the foamy waves. But no matter how fast she swam, Pa never got any nearer. He stayed just out of reach, beckoning her and beckoning her with his outstretched hand.

4

The Rat-Catcher's Boy

The following morning Marnie went out to the backyard to find Ambrose peering over the wall. 'What you doing, Marnie?' he asked, sniffing a slug of snot back up his nose. Marnie ignored him and picked up the metal pail that stood by the back door. The copper over the fire needed topping up and Ma had sent her to fetch water from the pump at the end of the lane.

Marnie didn't like Ambrose. He was the rat-catcher's boy from next door. He was always following her about, asking questions and telling her things she didn't want to know. He was a skinny, bony thing with a mean face and shiny black hair that sat on his head like a flattened crow. Marnie had never seen him without his scabby rat-terrier or without snot hanging from one nostril or another. When he was with the other village children, he would join in with their taunts as they walked behind Marnie, laughing and dragging their legs in imitation of her gait.

'What you doing?' he asked again. 'You should've seen the

size of the rats me and Pa caught yesterday! As big as the dog they were!' he shouted after Marnie as she hurried out of the backyard gate. She hoped he wasn't going to follow her. She just wanted to get her chores finished so she could get to the beach before it got busy. Ambrose never came to the beach. He had a fear of the sea and that was another reason Marnie didn't like him.

Marnie knew that Ma felt sorry for Ambrose. His pa was as cruel as they come and his ma wasn't much better. Ambrose could never please either of them. He often had purple bruises across his cheeks or streaks of blood mingled in his snot. Sometimes, when the windows were left open on hot summer nights, Marnie would hear his thin sobs breaking through the night air. Still, she couldn't bring herself to like him.

Marnie waited her turn at the pump and after she'd filled the pail, she walked back home slowly. Ma was sweeping the kitchen floor and humming to herself as Marnie set the pail down by the fire.

'That's a full one, I hope,' said Ma without turning to look.

'Yes, Ma,' said Marnie. She could still feel the sting of Ma's hand across her face from the days before she had learned to balance herself against her stick in a way that kept the water steady in the pail. Marnie never spilled a drop now and Ma had no excuse to touch her. Marnie grabbed a chunk of bread from the bowl on the table and walked quietly to the door.

'Mind you help Smoaker today, my girl!' Ma shouted after her. 'It's going to be a busy one!'

'Yes, Ma,' said Marnie quickly, and she picked up her stick and left the cottage, stuffing the bread in her mouth as she went.

It was another glorious day. Marnie could already feel the heat of the sun on her skin and smell the sweetness of baking grass. She hobbled across the lane and sat on top of the embankment above the esplanade. As she slid down the slope on her behind, the long tufts of yellowed grass whipped her bare legs. When she reached the bottom, Marnie used her stick to push herself up to standing and stepped on to the esplanade. She was pleased to see it empty, save for a pair of early strollers heading towards Byron's Bay. The beach was empty too, and the tide low enough to have exposed the pink sand that lay hidden under the waves at full tide. Marnie stopped to take a deep breath of the warm morning air.

'Marnie! Hey, Marnie! Wait for me!'

She turned at the sound of her name and saw Ambrose scrambling down the embankment after her, with his rat-dog at his heels. Marnie groaned. What did he want? If she hurried to the beach, perhaps he'd go away. He'd never dare come near the water.

Marnie limped as fast as she could to the beach steps, her stick tapping loudly on the ground. She took the steps one at a time, biting her lip in concentration, and hopped down on to the beach. She made her way across the rocks and on to the shingle, then glanced behind to see if Ambrose had gone. He was still there. He'd climbed down the steps too and was standing on the rocks staring all agog at the waves tumbling on to the shoreline.

'That's right, rat-boy. You stay where you are!' shouted Marnie. 'See how wild it is out there?' In truth, the waves were little more than gentle curls; just as Marnie liked it. Ambrose wouldn't come any closer. Marnie was sure of it.

She pulled off her frock and set it down on the shingle with her boots and stick. Then, wearing only her old flannel shift, she walked across the shingle till it turned to thick, wet sand that oozed between her toes. She walked straight to the water's edge and caught her breath as the first wave broke over her legs. The water was cold enough to make her skin burn. A shudder of pleasure ran through Marnie's body. She waded in until her shift billowed around her waist and her feet left the ocean floor. It was all perfect; just as it should be. Nothing else mattered now. It was just her and the sea and Pa.

'Where are you, Pa?' she shouted into the sea breeze. 'I'm here again! I'm waiting for you!'

But the horizon was empty.

Suddenly, another sound broke through the noise of breaking waves. Marnie turned her head and saw the rat-boy's dog paddling furiously beside her, yapping every time a wave broke over its snout.

'Go away!' she hissed and splashed it with the back of her hand, making it yap even louder.

'Here, boy! Here!' Ambrose's voice sailed over the water.

Marnie saw him standing on the shoreline, hugging himself with his skinny arms.

'Get 'im for me, Marnie! Get 'im!'

Marnie clenched her teeth. Why did he have to go and spoil it all? Why couldn't he just leave her be?

'Get him yourself!' she shouted.

'Please, Marnie! Please! Me pa'll kill me if he's lost.' Ambrose was doing an urgent little dance, hopping from one foot to

24

another. Marnie almost felt sorry for him. He'd get a thrashing for sure if he went home without the rat-terrier. But the dog wasn't in any danger. It was a swimmer and would find its own way back to shore. Ambrose could worry for a while longer, she decided. Serve him right for being so nasty.

'What's the matter, rat-boy?' she taunted. 'Scared of a bit of water?' She turned her back to him and dipped under the waves.

Ambrose's shouts were silenced as the weight of the ocean fell around her ears. It was delicious to be alone in her own place; to feel her arms pull strongly against the water and to feel the air tight in her chest. She opened her eyes to see the watery world around her blurred in greens and blues; black thickets of seaweed stretching slimy tentacles towards her and the rocks on the seabed crusted with barnacles. When her heart began to pound in her ears and her lungs burned hot, Marnie swam to the surface and swallowed deep gulps of air. She rubbed the salt from her eyes and looked towards the shore. Ambrose had gone. There was no sign of his dog, either. Good, thought Marnie. He'd gone back home to catch some rats, hopefully. Back to the dark, dirty places where he belonged.

The sun was growing hotter by the minute. Marnie felt it warming the back of her head. Light bounced off the top of the waves, and further out, beyond the waves, the surface of the sea shone bright as a newly polished spoon. Marnie wanted to stay there all day. But she knew that soon enough the ladies would start to arrive, bathing machines would crowd the beach and she would have to spend the rest of the day helping Smoaker. She closed her eyes. Just a while longer, she thought. She wished she could stretch time so it never ended.

Her thoughts were interrupted by the sound of barking. She opened her eyes and looked towards the beach. The rat-dog was back. It was running into the sea and back out again. Marnie paddled with her hands and looked around for Ambrose. He couldn't be far away. He wouldn't leave his dog. As Marnie watched, it seemed that the dog was trying to pull at something, but every time it got a grip the sea pulled it away again. The dog's barks were becoming more and more frantic. Curious now, Marnie swam back towards the shore. As her feet touched the sandy bottom she saw the dog was nipping at something large. A clump of seaweed perhaps, or a log or a piece of driftwood? She waded closer. The dog began to bark at her now, urging her to hurry. Marnie took her time. A thought was forming in her head that made her belly flip like a floundering fish. She screwed up her eyes against the sun and scanned the beach, half expecting to see Ambrose running back to fetch his dog. But all she saw were figures on the esplanade and the first of the bathing machines being hitched to horses. She moved closer to whatever was worrying the dog, daring herself to look.

The first thing Marnie saw was Ambrose's hair, spread out like black feathers in the shallows. He was lying in the water, his legs pointing towards the horizon. His head was being bobbed about by the waves and he was staring right into the sun. Seawater had filled his britches and shirt, so he looked all blown-up and fat. The rat-dog was pulling at Ambrose's shirt, playing tug-o-war with the sea. Marnie prodded Ambrose with her foot, but he wouldn't stop staring.

Despite the heat from the sun, Marnie shivered. She'd only

ever seen one drowned person before. When she was nine, she and Ma had found a woman washed ashore at Byron's Bay. She'd still had on her bonnet and mantle, but part of her face had been eaten by fishes. Ma had said the woman must have got tired of living and had walked into the sea on purpose.

Now, in the blink of an eye, Ambrose had drowned too.

Ma had always told Marnie the ocean couldn't be trusted. That even on the calmest of days it could send up a strong wave that could drag a person or fishing boat down to its depths. Marnie had never believed her. The ocean was the one thing Marnie did trust. She knew its colours and its moods. She knew when it was feeling gentle and she knew when it was angry. She knew when she was welcome and she knew when to stay away. But always, it made her feel better about herself.

But Ambrose hadn't trusted the ocean; he'd been frightened of it. And now look what had happened to him. Marnie looked down at Ambrose's pinched and mean face. It served him right, she thought. He should have stayed away.

Marnie left the rat-dog pulling at Ambrose's shirt and limped along the beach to fetch Smoaker.

5

A Tart and Some Gingerbread

Marnie was amazed at all the fuss that was made of Ambrose after he'd drowned. Like he'd suddenly become someone important. His ma had wailed for hours and his pa had slit the rat-dog's throat and thrown the body on the beach for the gulls to pick at.

Marnie watched as the village women trooped along Ratcatcher's Row with pans of stew, loaves of bread and packets of bacon. Miss Cranston brought along a pretty-looking tart and a basket of spicy-smelling gingerbread. What a waste, thought Marnie. She was quite sure that Ambrose had never eaten gingerbread in his life.

Ambrose was laid out on the rat-catcher's kitchen table now, in a white nightgown with his hands folded neatly across his chest. Marnie had been made to go and look, 'to pay your respects', Ma had said.

Ambrose's hair had been brushed all tidy and his eyes were closed tight. It was the first time Marnie had ever seen him without snot hanging out of his nose. Ma made her step up close to Ambrose. 'Say a little prayer for him, Marnie,' she said. But Marnie could think of nothing to say. She didn't want to be there, pretending to be sorry. She didn't like it in the rat-catcher's cottage. The curtains had been drawn and candles were burning on the mantelpiece. It was hot and stuffy and smelled faintly of fish guts rotting in the sun. Marnie couldn't breathe properly.

More people crowded into the room. It seemed to Marnie that the whole village was in there. Some of the women muttered prayers under their breath. The men took their caps off and twisted them round in their hands. Marnie moved away from Ambrose to make room for them and stood at the back of the room, waiting for Ma. They had paid their respects; surely they could go now?

Marnie thought the village women were still praying as they filed past her to make their way outside. She heard them mumbling. But when she looked up at their faces she saw they were glaring at her, like a gaggle of angry geese.

'Always in the water, that one.'

'Cursed child.'

'Not right, it isn't.'

'What do you expect from a bastard?'

'Marked by the Devil, she is.'

'Strange one.'

'Lured him into the sea.'

They hurried out of the room and Marnie was left with a feeling in her belly that she didn't like. She was glad when Ma grabbed her hand and took her away.

'Don't listen to their tittle-tattle,' Ma said. 'It'll all blow over soon enough.'

Back at home, Ma gave Marnie some bread and jam for supper. There was no butter because, as Smoaker kept saying, 'a drowning's no good for business'. He was right. Not a single bathing machine had been hired since Ambrose had drowned.

'It's only been two days,' Ma said. 'You know those London ladies. They'll have taken fright, that's all. It's what folk are saying round here we have to watch out for.' She glanced at Marnie, then leaned towards Smoaker and whispered something in his ear.

Marnie licked the jam off her bread and thought of the basket of gingerbread and the pretty tart. She wondered if they were still on the doorstep next door, or if the rat-catcher's wife had already taken them in.

'Now, Marnie,' said Ma as she came over to clear the table. 'Me and Smoaker think it's best you keep out of the sea from now on.'

The lump of bread Marnie had been chewing on shot to the back of her throat. She coughed hard.

Ma thumped her on the back. 'We're not saying you had anything to do with the accident Marnie, but all the same . . . You know what folks are like round here with their superstitions and the like. You'll be blamed for every storm and every bad catch.'

Marnie swallowed the lump of bread. What did Ma mean, she couldn't go in the sea any more? It wasn't her fault the stupid rat-boy had drowned.

'But . . . but I need the sea,' Marnie said quietly. 'How will I ever be cured if I don't bathe?'

Ma sighed heavily. 'Don't be daft, girl! The sea's not going to cure you of the polio! It's made you strong and healthy, but it's not going to stop you being a cripple. You're stuck with that leg, Marnie. You're old enough to understand that now. There is no cure.' Ma looked relieved, as though she had got rid of a particularly vexing problem. 'Now, mind what we tell you and no more bathing. It's the business we have to think of now.'

Marnie heard Ma's words but she couldn't make sense of them. No cure? Stuck with being a cripple for ever? She felt as though a hand had gripped her around the throat and was squeezing harder and harder. It was Ma who believed in the sea-cure. It was Ma who had told her the sea would make her strong and healthy. It was Ma who had made her believe a miracle might happen.

Had it all been a lie?

No, thought Marnie. She couldn't believe that. It had to be true. Ma was scared, that's all. She was scared of the other village women and their vicious gossip. She shouldn't listen to them. What did they know? They'd called Marnie a bastard when it wasn't true. Ma couldn't mean what she was saying. After all, why would all the rich ladies come from London to take the cure if it didn't work? They all believed the sea would rid them of their ailments. Marnie believed in the power of the sea too. It *would* cure her one day. She knew it. Bit by bit, day by day, her leg would grow straighter and stronger until one day she would throw her stick away for ever and run as fast as the sea winds across the beach.

31

Later that evening, Marnie went outside to use the privy. After she'd finished, she poked her stick into the pile of ash that she'd just soiled. Then she crept around to the rat-catcher's back doorstep and stuck the end of her stick into the large pan of soup that had been added to the offerings. Lastly, she swiped at the basket of gingerbread and sent the squares of cake rolling along the dusty ground.

6

A Twisted Leg

Tucked under the blanket that night, with Ma snoring loudly at her side, Marnie tried to remember a time when she'd been like everyone else. She hadn't always been this way. She knew that.

'You were only five,' Ma used to say to her in rare gentle moments. 'It was the worst of times. I thought you were going to be taken from me for ever.'

Marnie squeezed her eyes shut and saw a bed in a room with yellow walls. It was cool in the room; the shutters were never opened and a candle burned all day and all night. She remembered heavy, aching pains; in her head and neck, under her arms and in her legs. She remembered cold wet cloths on her forehead and the hot stench of herself when she soiled the bed. She remembered a plain-faced woman in a black dress and lace collar with her hair coiled tightly at the back of her head. On days when the pains weren't so bad, the woman would bring books into the room, and a slate and some chalk. Although Marnie's fingers could barely hold the chalk, the woman taught her how to scratch out letters on the worn black slate.

It seemed like a dream to Marnie. A muddled dream full of hovering people, words she didn't understand, voices she didn't know and pains – always pains. It was a long, long dream that could have lasted for days, weeks, months or years.

Then finally there was a day when she sat up in bed and the pains had gone. The woman with the coiled hair came into the room and opened the shutters. The bright sunlight hurt Marnie's eyes and made her cry. Then Ma came and told her to get out of bed and Smoaker Nash brought her a little walking stick he had whittled himself. Marnie had wondered what it was for. Then she'd pushed back her blanket to see two thin legs sticking out beneath her nightgown. One leg, her right one, was shrivelled away to bone and the foot was twisted at a strange angle. Had it always been like that? She had no idea. The shrivelled leg was useless anyway, and it had taken her ages to get used to Smoaker's stick.

Marnie soon realised it was a bad thing to have a leg like that. She couldn't run along the lanes with the other village children. She was shooed away from their doorsteps like a mangy cat. People stared at her as though she'd done something wrong and they called her bad names. Mostly, though, they ignored her altogether.

But then Ma gave her the sea and everything changed. Once Marnie had learned to swim, she didn't care about the village children and their silly games any more. She had something much finer. She had the greatest friend of all. She had the sea, and she spent every minute she could bathing in its reassuring depths. When she was in the sea she could forget about being different. She could forget about being a freak. When she was in the sea she knew somehow that she was better than everyone else. And she'd be right there when her pa came home too, and he'd put his arms around her and she'd bury her face in his rough warmth.

7

The Boy in Blue

June melted into July, each day growing hotter than the last. A fresh batch of London ladies arrived in Clevedon from Yatton Junction. Knowing nothing of the drowning, they wafted down to the beach with pink faces and glittering eyes in search of a cure for their various maladies. Once again the bathing machines were in demand. The dippers lined up ready in the sea, their skirts floating round their waists, and the horses trundled up and down the shingle with sweat foaming on their flanks. Marnie was stationed in Smoaker's hut, collecting the sixpences and handing out clean towels, while Smoaker himself supervised the harnessing of the horses and counted the coins that clinked with pleasing regularity into his tin. Marnie could only watch the sea twinkle in the distance and smell its warm saltiness on the discarded towels left behind in the bathing machines.

Each day lasted an eternity. It was torture to wake every morning and see the sun hanging limply over the glassy sea, and to know she was forbidden to swim. Her leg throbbed and ached and seemed to grow heavier each day. She felt as dry and shrivelled as the heart of an old crone. Still Ma wouldn't allow her to bathe.

'They think you're strange as it is, Marnie. They think it's your fault Ambrose drowned right next to you. Let's not fan the flames. You were born on land, my girl. Not in the sea.'

'It's not right, Pa,' Marnie said out loud as she walked into the village to fetch a loaf for Ma. 'Don't let them take the sea from me. Come back now and tell them. Please come back now.'

She tried not to take any notice of the way the village women nudged each other as she hobbled past. When Marnie waited in line at the water pump, they stood with their arms folded over their bosoms and watched with eyes as sharp as fish hooks as Marnie filled her pail.

'*Look at her,*' they hissed. '*Dares to show her face after what she did.*'

'*Might as well have killed him with her bare hands.*'

'*It's a wonder her mother keeps her under the same roof.*'

'*The rat-catcher must wish he'd slit her throat instead of the poor dog's.*'

Once, one of them spat into her pail so she'd had to empty it and start all over again. And another time, the shoemaker's wife had nudged her so hard that she'd fallen to the ground and the water in her pail had spilled and been sucked away by the dry dust. She hadn't refilled her pail that day and Ma hadn't understood one bit.

'Don't you shame me any more, my girl,' she'd said. 'I won't have them looking down their noses at us!' She made Marnie go back to the pump. 'This time you bring back a full pail or I'll have the whip to you!' Marnie knew that Ma didn't want a cripple for a daughter. She would beat it out of her if she could.

Marnie hid herself in the sweaty shadows of Smoaker's hut and counted away the days. There didn't seem to be a reason to get up in the mornings any more. She wished more than ever she had a pa to look out for her; someone to protect her and love her. When the bathing machines weren't crowding her view of the horizon, Marnie would stare out to sea for hours at a time, hoping to conjure up a small wooden fishing boat with torn sails and a hoary fisherman with a yellow beard grown to his knees who could be no one but her pa. But as hard as she tried, she could never make anything appear.

'WHERE LADY DE CLEVEDON HERSELF TAKES THE CURE!' Smoaker Nash announced proudly as he stood outside the hut greeting every new customer. Marnie grew sick of hearing it. Lady de Clevedon had only been the once, but to hear Smoaker, you'd think she was bathing from morn till dusk. But the words seemed to have an effect on the ladies. The nervy ones calmed down and handed over their sixpences without trembling, and the excited ones chattered even more, their cheeks aflame with colour and self-importance.

Marnie's throat was tight with envy as she took their money and handed out fresh towels. If she was a rich lady from London she would hire a machine for the whole day and only come out of the water when her skin was as wrinkled as an old apple. She remembered Ma telling her once that the Queen Victoria had her very own beach on the Isle of Wight and her very own bathing machine that was like no other. It didn't need a horse

38

to pull it down to the water, but was sat on rails that ran right down into the ocean. It was a palace on wheels, Ma said. What a thing! To have your very own beach, thought Marnie. She sighed and looked out of the window at the machines lined up at the water's edge. But what was she thinking? She did have her own beach. *This* was her beach, whatever Ma or anybody else thought. Although she wasn't big and brawny like Ma, she was as tall and her arms and shoulders were hard and strong from years of ploughing through the waves. Soon, when the gossips had grown bored, she would be allowed to go in with Ma and help her do the dipping. No one could tell her to keep out of the sea then. Marnie couldn't wait. She would be the best dipper ever. Better than all the other dippers in Clevedon. Better even than Ma.

Queen Victoria herself would come to know the name of Marnie Gunn.

'Marnie!' Smoaker came panting through the door. His face was as red and sticky as jam beneath his battered straw hat. 'Quick, girl! The Lady de Clevedon is on her way! Find the newest towels. The whitest ones. Make sure they're spotless!'

Marnie blinked hard. Her daydream disappeared; a fragile cobweb swiped away. 'What?' she asked dully.

'Towels!' growled Smoaker.

At the back of the hut was an old wardrobe that Smoaker had carted down to the beach years ago. Inside it smelled of mothballs and damp and was filled to bulging with towels. Most of them were frayed and had seen better days. The Mistress Miles, who took them in to wash, was frayed around the edges

39

herself and had definitely seen better days. The towels often came back more grubby than they went. Ma had given up on complaining since there was no one else willing to take in such a daily load. Marnie hunted through the wardrobe and pulled out the thickest, whitest towels she could find. She shook out the sand – no amount of washing seemed to get rid of it – and folded the towels neatly. Smoaker was hovering by the door, hurrying her with his hands.

There was a clamour of voices on the slipway outside. The gold-liveried footmen, the huddle of maids and the Bath chair containing Lady de Clevedon had arrived. Marnie smoothed her frock and straightened her shoulders. She'd never spoken to proper gentry before. What should she say? Should she curtsey? Would she have to speak at all? But Smoaker was there already, nodding his head, handing a footman the towels and showing him the way to the last available bathing machine. Marnie's shoulders slumped. She wasn't needed after all. She'd been daft to think Smoaker would let *these* customers see the cripple in the hut. She looked out of the window and saw him running down the beach. Off to tell Ma the Lady de Clevedon had come again.

It was stifling in the hut. Marnie's skin was sticky and the back of her throat bone dry. Outside on the slipway, the maids had settled to gossiping and the footmen were lurching on to the beach with the Bath chair.

Marnie couldn't bear it any longer. It wasn't fair. No one will notice, she thought. No one will notice if I'm gone for five minutes. I'll just dip me toes in and splash me legs. I'll be back before anyone knows I'm gone.

40

Marnie stepped outside the hut. Lady de Clevedon's arrival had brought the whole of the beach and the esplanade to a halt. Everyone's eyes were on the progress of the Bath chair and the milky skirts that spilled over the sides. Everyone's eyes but those of a boy in a blue suit. Marnie flushed. He was looking straight at her. It was the same boy she remembered from the last time the Lady had bathed. He was standing apart from the rest of Lady de Clevedon's household party with his hands in the pockets of his blue striped britches. A large slate-grey wolfhound sat at his heel. Marnie paused, unsure whether to continue. Sod it, she decided. Who was he anyway? He wasn't anything to do with her. What she did was none of his business.

It was hard to move quickly along the beach with her stick sinking into the shingle with every step. Marnie felt the boy's eyes following her as she made her way along the rear of the bathing machines. She knew what he would see: a spit of a girl with a withered and twisted leg, hobbling along like an old woman.

'Never seen a cripple before?' she wanted to shout.

Marnie walked past the bathing machines and along the shore for a while. If she kept right to the water's edge, the bathers wouldn't see her. She knew to keep away from the machines. She knew the laws well enough. They were pasted on the wall of Smoaker's hut. Anyone coming within fifty yards of a person bathing from a machine should be made to pay a penalty of forty shillings. Ma had drummed it into her.

'They pay for their privacy, Marnie. And it would be a scandal to be sure, if anyone but a dipper were to see a lady in her bathing gown!'

41

Even the fishing vessels had to keep their distance.

Marnie tugged off her boots. Already her toes tingled in anticipation of the cold froth of seawater. There was a sound behind her. The crunching of shingle and shells. She turned quickly, afraid that Ma or Smoaker had seen her and had come to thrash the back of her legs and drag her back to the hut. She stumbled in surprise. It wasn't Ma or Smoaker at all, but the boy in the blue suit, walking right towards her with a shy smile on his face.

'Hello,' he said. 'I've seen you here before, haven't I?'

Marnie nodded slowly, readying herself for a sneer and a nasty taunt. Close up, she saw he was older than her. Sixteen, maybe? Or seventeen? His pale complexion was shaded by a wide-brimmed hat trimmed with a band of blue ribbon to match his jacket and waistcoat. There was something strange about his eyes, though.

'You're the dipper's daughter, aren't you?' he asked.

Again, Marnie nodded slowly. She saw then what it was with his eyes. The left one was blue, while the right one was grey, like a rain cloud had passed over an early-morning sky.

'I shouldn't be here,' Marnie said quietly. She bit her lip and peered over her shoulder. She felt cornered. She wanted to wade into the sea right now and swim away from this stranger. But she knew she couldn't. What was he going to do next? Usually the taunts came straight away, but this boy seemed to be looking at her kindly. It was a cruel trick, she was sure. Any minute now he would spit on her and push her to the ground.

'Where should you be, then?' he asked.

Marnie looked down at her bare feet. She tried to move her

42

twisted foot behind the other to hide it. The boy didn't seem to notice. There was no sign of mockery on his face.

'Where should you be?' he asked again.

'In the hut.' Marnie pointed across the beach. 'I take the charge. For the bathing machines.'

The boy kicked one foot gently at the shingle. 'My mother is taking the sea-cure now.' He nodded towards the bathing machines. 'Lady de Clevedon,' he added.

Marnie didn't answer. What was there to say? She thought she'd better hurry back before Smoaker missed her. But how could she go without appearing rude?

The boy bent down to ruffle the head of his dog. 'My name is Noah,' he said, 'and this is Prince.'

Marnie looked at the dog then back at the boy, unsure of what she should say or do.

'Does it work?' asked the boy.

'Beg your pardon?' said Marnie.

'The sea-cure. Does it work? Mother is very frail, you see.'

'It's very healthful,' said Marnie hesitantly. 'They come from all over to take the sea-cure.' She paused. 'The London doctors . . . they recommend it to all their patients.'

'Thank you,' said the boy. He sighed. 'I expect you will be seeing us here most days from now on.'

He wasn't going to taunt her, thought Marnie. He hadn't glanced once at her leg. 'I'm sure your mother . . . Lady de Clevedon will benefit,' said Marnie. She chanced a smile and a ribbon of delight slipped down her back when the boy returned her smile. She bent to pick up her boots. 'I have to go now,' she said.

'Of course,' said the boy, and he stepped aside, gesturing with his arm for her to pass. 'But before you go . . . what is *your* name?'

'It's Marnie,' she said. Then she took up her stick and turned away from him.

This time, as she walked back up the beach, she didn't mind the feel of his stare needling into her hot back. She didn't mind one bit.

8

The Journal of Noah de Clevedon

Clevedon. JULY 7th 1868, Tuesday

The days are getting hotter. But it is quite pleasant up here in the orangery where I am sitting now with a glass of iced ginger beer by my side. Father left for London this morning. His business with the other directors of the Pier Company is finished now. It is all settled and building of the pier will begin soon. It has been good to have him here this last week. I begged him to take me back to London with him. But it is not to be. He said that at least here in Clevedon we are free from the stink of the Thames. I would rather the stink of the Thames than the dreary stink of boredom. But Mother has not improved yet, so I must stay.

We went to the beach again this afternoon for Mother to take her dipping. The strange girl was there again. She was walking towards the sea carrying her boots. She looked so feral with her bare legs, loose frock and with her hair falling freely down her back. I followed her to the shoreline and amused myself in a short conversation. She is the daughter of Mother's dipper and her name is Marnie. She is lame in one leg but seems quite full of character. Her eyes are like nothing else I have ever seen before. They are the bluest of any blue you can imagine. It was hard for me to tear my gaze away. For some reason, I am sure this will not be the last I see of her.

Father left me a new book to read. It is called 'Uncle Tom's Cabin' and it is causing quite a stir, apparently. I shall start reading it tonight.

9

Goose Pimples

Ma's excitement at having the Lady de Clevedon to dip again knew no bounds. She preened herself like a milk-soaked cat and, although she was too heavy to prance as such, she seemed to have gained a certain amount of lightness to her step as she went about the kitchen preparing supper.

'Oh, Smoaker,' she laughed. 'The Lady told me she thought she should never recover from the plunge I gave her! But when she'd got her breath back, she said it was the most delightful experience and she felt herself all aglow. "I will bathe as often as it is safe." Those were her very words!'

Smoaker sat in his chair by the fire and frowned. Nep was curled up on his lap and Smoaker had stroked the cat's black fur to a shine. ''Tis good news,' he said. 'But I'm afraid we have a new concern upon us now.'

Marnie looked up from the tallow candles she was trimming and listened harder.

'A pier is to be built,' said Smoaker. 'I heard at the inn that

Sir John de Clevedon has formed a company and put up the money himself.'

'A pier?' said Ma. 'Whatever for?'

'To bring more visitors to the village, they say. There'll be paddle steamers too, going from the end of it to Wales and back.'

'Good for business, then?' said Ma. 'Plenty of new bathers, I'd say.'

'Maybe . . . ' said Smoaker sullenly. 'But what will we do in the meantime? While the pier's being built?'

Ma paused in stirring the supper pot; her face paled. 'What do you mean?' she asked slowly.

Marnie knew the answer before it came out of Smoaker's mouth and she felt her belly drop into her boots.

'The beach'll be out of bounds,' said Smoaker. 'There'll be cranes and ironworks and an army of workers . . . ' He left his sentence unfinished. Silence filled the kitchen as the news sank in. Marnie's mind was racing to find something good to latch on to. But there was nothing but a horrible emptiness.

'That's why they came back,' Ma muttered. 'That's why the Lady and Sir John came back to Clevedon then. To build a pier.' Her voice rose in sudden panic. 'But what about us? What will we do? How will we put food on the table?'

'It'll take months to build,' said Smoaker, his voice growing high with indignation. 'We'll lose all our winter visitors. And what about the horses? They'll still need feeding even if they're not being worked.'

Ma came to the kitchen table and sat heavily in a chair. She put her face in her hands and began to moan. 'We're done for, Smoaker. We're done for! The Lady de Clevedon!' she spat.

'The haughty bitch! Never said a word to me about no pier when I dipped her today. Taking advantage of our services, knowing all along they're going to be the ruin of us!'

Marnie thought about the boy on the beach. He'd said nothing about the pier either, though he must've known what his father was planning. She wished she'd never been so polite to him now. She looked at Ma's stony face and at Smoaker angrily jabbing tobacco into his pipe. Why was everything slipping away? The world was shifting beneath her feet and there didn't seem to be anything left for her to hold on to. Marnie's chest tightened. The sea. The beach. They were all she had. They were what made her feel part of the world. Without them she was nothing, a nobody.

'What'll happen to us, Ma?' she asked carefully. But her voice was lost in the noise of Ma's whining and grumbling.

Marnie took a deep breath and put a hand to her breast to calm the clattering of her heart. It wouldn't be for ever; a few months at the most, she told herself. But she couldn't stop the heat that rushed through her and made her mouth dry. The walls of the kitchen closed in on her and suddenly there wasn't enough air to fill her lungs. She was suffocating. She needed the sea right now, if only the sight of it.

Neither Ma nor Smoaker noticed when Marnie slipped outside.

Marnie's skin stiffened with goose pimples as the evening air wrapped itself around her. She hurried as fast as her leg would allow, down the embankment and across the esplanade to the railings that ran alongside the beach. She took deep breaths, gulping in the air as if that too was going to be taken from her. She stared out into the dark expanse of ocean. Was that a light far out to sea? A fisherman's lantern wavering yellow in the darkness? She gripped the iron railings tightly. Was it Pa, come home at last? She stared for a long while, hope and longing burning through her insides. Was it her imagination or was the light growing larger as it moved its way towards the shore? Marnie blinked and strained her eyes to see more clearly.

'Pa!' she shouted into the glittering darkness. 'Pa! I'm over here!' Then a sad laugh choked its way out of her throat. Was she so daft? It was only the reflection of the moon she saw floating in the sea. She was a great soft lump to think it was anything else. She turned and slumped back against the railings. Then a terrible thought struck her. What would happen if Pa came back when the workers were building the pier? How would Pa land his boat if the beach was out of bounds? What if he came and went away again and she never knew a thing about it?

It didn't bear thinking about.

10

A Blue-Trimmed Straw Hat

Marnie was dancing with her pa on sand as soft as velvet. She had two solid legs, as straight and strong as young saplings. She could jump and twist and turn and twirl. Pa was laughing at her gently and telling her he'd never seen anyone as light on their feet.

'Get out of bed, you idle lump!'

Ma's voice broke into Marnie's dream and shattered it into hundreds of droplets of sea spray. Marnie opened her eyes to see her dream evaporate into the bright light that was pouring through the bedchamber shutters.

'Idle hands are the Devil's workshop, my girl!' Ma shouted through from the kitchen.

Marnie pulled the blanket over her head. What was the point in getting out of bed when every day was as miserable as the next? But the morning sun seeped through the worn weave and teased her with its dazzle. *Get up, get up*, it whispered. Even when she closed her eyes again, the light played and

51

swam on the insides of her eyelids. Marnie sat up and pushed herself off the bed. She wished she could leave this place. She wished she could find a shell on the beach big enough to curl up inside. She would hide herself away in its pearly centre and be swept out to sea, across the horizon to a faraway shore where Pa would be waiting for her.

Ma poked her head around the door. 'If you think you'll be getting any breakfast, then think again! Don't know what's come over you these last weeks. Get dressed, we're going now!'

Marnie picked her frock off the floor where she'd dropped it the night before. She pulled it over her head and pushed her feet into her boots. She didn't care about breakfast. She had no appetite anyway.

Ma led the way, stomping off ahead towards the beach. As Marnie followed, the pointed glares and sharp words of the rat-catcher's wife and her neighbour, Mrs Munsey, jabbed at her all along Ratcatcher's Row.

'Walking around, bold as brass.'

'No good will come of it.'

'Little fiend.'

'Devil's child!'

Ma turned, her face flushed with shame, and she gestured for Marnie to get a move on. Marnie glared at the two women. They could think what they liked. Marnie didn't care. If they thought she was the Devil's child then she'd act like the Devil's child. Marnie locked eyes with them and scowled until she saw a flicker of fear cross their faces. Then she laughed.

'Marnie!' Ma hissed. Marnie threw the women one last glare and hurried after Ma. She could tell by the set of Ma's broad shoulders that her face would be dark with rage. Marnie swiped at the ground with her stick. The morning hung heavy and hot around her. It hadn't made her feel any better glowering at the women like that. It hadn't given her any satisfaction either. There was no comfort to be had anywhere. There was only the blaze of Ma's anger and the scorch of the July sun quivering and boiling in the blank blue sky. Day after day of the unforgiving heat had turned Marnie's skin nutmeg brown and sucked the juice from her very soul.

With work on the new pier due to start in September, Ma and Smoaker were making the most of the few weeks they had left on the beach. The weather had brought in new crowds of visitors from Bristol, Bath and London. They thronged the beach, all anxious for a dip, and the air thrummed with chatter, the squeals of paddling children and the barking of dogs. The bathing machines had never been so much in demand, and Ma and the other dippers spent every daylight hour up to their waists in the sea.

Marnie stayed close to the hut, walking backwards and forwards to each bathing machine to remove damp towels. She felt she was melting to nothing in the heat as the noise of the sea filled her head with a confusing muddle of longing and resentment.

'Hello, again.' The voice was loud inside the wooden walls of the hut.

Marnie started. She looked up from the towels she was folding to see the boy again. He was still wearing his blue-trimmed straw hat, but this time he was dressed in a pale cream linen suit, the sleeves rolled up to his elbows.

'The Lady de Clevedon on her way, is she?' asked Marnie. Her tone must have been brusque, as the boy's smile faltered for a moment. Marnie didn't care an inch. This boy's father had ruined everything with his fancy plans for a pier.

'No,' he said. 'It is too hot for Mother today. But I thought I would take myself and Prince for a walk.' He paused and put his hands in his pockets. 'They say it is the hottest July in living memory.'

'Do they?' said Marnie. She wasn't interested in his small talk. The boy was looking at her intently. She remembered his eyes; one blue, one a cloudy grey. His hound came around to her side of the counter and snuffled at her feet. She nudged it away irritably. Why this boy was bothering her, she didn't know. The way he was looking at her made her feel like a freak at a sideshow. Well, she was used to that. Let him quench his curiosity if he wanted; it made no difference to her.

'I have taken the waters in Bath,' said the boy. 'Mother was very fond of it. But I have to admit I have never seen the appeal in sea-bathing.'

You wouldn't, thought Marnie scornfully.

'Perhaps you could persuade me to change my mind?' he said. 'I could hire a machine, maybe?'

Marnie glanced up at him. What game was he playing? She wished he would go away and leave her be. 'The bathing machines will be moved off the beach soon enough,' she said. 'To make way for the pier.' She glared at him. 'In any case, it's Byron's Bay you'll be wanting. That's where the men bathe.'

'Ah, yes. Of course,' said the boy.

54

Marnie was pleased to see a pink blush spread across his cheeks. 'But I'm sure I wouldn't bother if I were you,' she said. 'The men at Byron's Bay are mostly hardy types who bathe for pleasure, and without attendants. Maybe paddling the shallows would suit you more?' Marnie knew she was being rude and disrespectful, but she couldn't help herself. It warmed her insides to see the flutter of shock cross the boy's face. He had most likely never been spoken to so bluntly before. He would chastise her now, or complain to Smoaker, she was sure. But at least he would leave her alone, which was all she wanted right now.

To her surprise, the boy began to laugh. 'You are probably right,' he said. 'I would be no match for hardy men and strong waves. But maybe, when you are not so busy, you would consider teaching me the ways of the sea? Or at least introduce me to the pleasures of paddling?' He tossed Marnie a smile so full of easiness that she was too stunned to reply.

Then he whistled to his hound and the both of them were gone, out of the door. Marnie looked down at the pile of towels in front of her and realised she had folded and unfolded the same one at least a dozen times.

II

The Journal of Noah de Clevedon

Clevedon. JULY 21st 1868, Tuesday

I stayed for a long while at breakfast this morning and ate three boiled eggs for want of anything else to do. Mother has ordered in The Times newspaper (although she never reads it herself) and I felt quite the gentleman as I breakfasted alone while flicking through its pages. The only item worth noting was the weather report. This July is one of the hottest ever recorded. It has not gone unnoticed. Everyone and everything is wilting! It is too hot even for Mother to take the sea-cure. The strength of the sun is too much for her to bear.

Despite the heat, I felt in need of some life outside these stone walls, so I took Prince for a walk into the village and along the esplanade. I have never seen so many people crowd the shore.

I saw the girl, Marnie, walking back and forth from the bathing machines with armfuls of towels. I could not help but go and speak with her. She is certainly fierce! She seems not to care at all that

56

I am the son of Sir John de Clevedon. For some reason I like that about her. She intrigues me. I will try to persuade her to teach me to swim. It will give me something to do, at least.

Dined with Clarissa again tonight. At least the food was agreeable (pork cutlets and baked pears). Clarissa says Mother is refusing to take even a little broth. I wish she would just have something. I will take a tray up to her in the morning. Maybe she will eat for me.

I must write to Father now and ask him to send me more books.

12

A Scrap of Scarlet Ribbon

After supper that evening, as Marnie sat in the shadow of the old stone wall in the backyard at Ratcatcher's Row, she remembered the boy's name. She wasn't even thinking about him when, suddenly, the name *Noah* announced itself. She shook her head, trying to get rid of it. She didn't want to think about him.

She was looking at the treasures she'd collected over the years that were hidden under the old firebrick. Things that had been left behind in the bathing machines: lost objects, broken objects, things that might not ever be missed. Did a young lady from London ever notice she'd lost a carved-bone comb? Did a starchy old matron from Bristol ever miss a mother-of-pearl button? Did a frail governess from Wales mean to leave a scrap of scarlet ribbon behind? Marnie was thinking all these things as she tried to cool her skin in the shade of the old wall. The heat of the day seemed to have sucked all sound from the world and Marnie thought she might be the only person left breathing. She felt small and lonely. In a strange way she even missed Ambrose and his mocking sneer. She'd known what to expect from him, at least. His half-cocked taunts had been a familiar part of her day. Now he was just another piece of her life that was missing.

Noah's name came into her head again. Tap, tap, tapping behind her ears and pushing its way in front of her other thoughts. Marnie groaned with annoyance. He didn't deserve a name; he only deserved to be thought of as 'the boy'. Why did he and his family have to come back to Clevedon and ruin everything? A pier? Marnie snorted. Who needed a pier anyway?

But despite trying her hardest not to think about him, Marnie couldn't help remembering how it had been in the hut that morning and how his smile had made her feel. A flicker of warmth sparked in her belly. It was as though the boy – Noah – had known somehow that she had always wanted to be smiled at like that.

But no. She wouldn't think of him any more. She never wanted to see him again. Not when it was his fault that everything was being taken away from her. Marnie was surprised to feel hot tears slipping down her cheeks. She wiped them away angrily. She hadn't cried for years; not since she was a little girl, unused to the cruelties of the world. She sniffed hard and pushed her shoulders back. There was no room for that sort of nonsense.

Marnie sat with her back pressed against the wall. The cool dampness of the stones spread across her shoulders like a soothing cloak. She pulled her knees to her chest and held them tightly. The wall was solid against her back; it felt like it was the only thing holding her in place. She thought if she moved too much she might float from the ground and not be able to get back. She might float higher and higher into the sky until she reached the place where the gulls glided and screeched and they might peck at her hungrily and tear her into bloody little bits. Just like they'd done to the rat-dog. Marnie had never felt so adrift and fearful. She couldn't imagine what would happen to her when the workers arrived to fill the beach with ironworks and cranes. 'What will I do, Pa?' she whispered. 'I think I might die without the sea.'

Marnie stayed out in the backyard till the sky eventually darkened and the closeness of the night fell around her like an unwanted embrace. There was no noise coming from the cottage. Ma and Smoaker must have taken themselves to bed. No one had come to find her; no one had noticed she was missing. Like all the things left behind in the bathing machines, Marnie was lost and no one was looking for her.

She uncurled her body from against the wall and struggled to stand. Her leg was worse, she was sure of it. Without the sea to nurse her, the old pains were returning. She felt the disease inside her waking up and stirring; like a nightmare returning to haunt her.

It was dark inside the cottage and Ma wasn't in their bed. Marnie heard the low murmur of her voice up in Smoaker's room. Once, when she'd been no more than ten, Marnie had woken in the night to find Ma gone from the bed. Marnie had turned cold with fright at first, convinced that Ma had vanished the way that Pa had done. Then she'd heard voices from upstairs. She'd heard Ma's laugh and Smoaker make a noise that sounded like he was in pain. Then she'd heard Smoaker laugh and Ma shush him with a smile in her voice. Marnie had pushed herself up the stairs on her backside, anxious to be included in whatever was going on. She'd sat outside Smoaker's room for a while, listening to the unfamiliar sounds. They were playing a game, Marnie decided, and she wanted to join in too.

When she'd pushed the bedchamber door open, it had creaked loudly and Marnie had found herself looking straight into Ma's eyes. Ma had stared at her hard with a look so full of hatred that Marnie had bumped back down the stairs so fast she had bruises on her behind for days. Marnie never forgot the way Ma had looked at her, nor the glimpse she'd had of Smoaker kneeling in front of Ma with his britches round his ankles and Ma sitting on the edge of the bed with her large breasts hanging bare over the top of her bodice.

Marnie shuddered now, at the memory. She hated Ma for doing things like that with a man who wasn't Pa.

Marnie sat in Ma's chair by the kitchen fire and watched as the glow from the embers grew dimmer and dimmer. The noises from upstairs stilled and Marnie was left alone with the night.

As she stared into the dying fire, she wondered how things had come to this. Why had it all turned to ashes? Had she been so foolish to believe that everything would always be as she wanted it? That the sea was hers for ever? That Pa would come back? That one day she would be cured and would be like everyone else? She didn't want to let any of that go. She couldn't let it go. She clenched her fists tight. It was all their fault, she thought. The de Clevedons. With all their money and grand plans, they didn't give two hoots about the likes of Marnie. She hated them and what they were doing, and if she ever saw the boy Noah again, she would tell him so.

She sat in the deepening gloom, not bothering to light a candle. In the distance, Marnie heard the sighs of the sea. It sounded as though it was missing her as much as she was missing it. It was so close, only out the door and a short walk away. It would be so easy . . . so easy.

It was then that the idea struck her. Such a simple, gleaming idea that she gasped out loud at the wonder of it. She could go now. Right now. Ma and Smoaker were asleep, they would never know she'd gone. The village was in darkness; no one would see her creep down to the beach.

Blood rushed through Marnie's ears in a tide of excitement and she laughed to herself quietly. Not even Nep the cat saw the kitchen door close quietly behind her.

It was exactly as she imagined. The night air still held the warmth of the day, the beach was empty and the light of the moon had turned the sea to liquid silver. Marnie stripped naked, so as not to wet her shift. She entered the sea slowly, savouring each delicious sensation. The water gripped her ankles and held tight. Then it crept up her legs and swallowed her hips. Finally, when cold tongues licked at her chest, Marnie sighed and gave herself up to the rocking motion of the waves. She swam and swam, a wild energy filling her limbs. She whooped out loud. 'I'm back, Pa!' she shouted into the dark horizon. It felt so good. She knew she would stay there all night if she could. She was where she belonged and would never stay away for so long again.

13

The Journal of Noah de Clevedon

Clevedon. JULY 24th 1868, Friday

The last few days have been so hot and tedious, I think I am going quite mad. I dreamed of the girl Marnie last night. I dreamed of her tousled hair and sun-kissed skin and the piercing blue of her eyes. When I woke this morning I was tangled and wrapped in my sheets and covered in an unpleasant sweat. Why I dreamed of her I do not know. I can only imagine it is the boredom and heat setting my imagination on fire.

I felt more settled after I had Hetty draw me a cool bath and I joined Mother in the shade of the orangery for a light luncheon. I told Mother she must at least have a little fruit and cheese if she is to be strong enough to take the sea-cure again. 'I will eat for you,' she said. 'You are such a comfort to me.'

I am not sure which takes longer to pass here: the interminably hot days or the endless evenings.

14

Salt and Fish

It was the last Saturday of July. Marnie was woken early by the sun pouring bright through the shutters and resting ribbons of warmth across her face. She rubbed the sleep from her eyes and rolled on to her back. It was quiet in the cottage. Ma and Smoaker must still be asleep. Ma had slept in Smoaker's room again last night and it suited Marnie just fine. She had been able to slip away once more, down to the beach, to swim her fill in the night ocean. Marnie lay still now and listened to the soft hush of morning and the distant, muffled breath of the sea. She hugged herself. She could cope with the long, hot days now she knew the sea was waiting for her after dark. She wished she could tell someone her secret. She wished she could share what she was feeling. But there was only Pa, and he wasn't here.

'You'd be proud of me, Pa,' she said. 'I won't let them take the sea from me, you know. I've found a way. Even when the workers come to build the pier, I won't let it stop me.'

Marnie brushed a straw-yellow curl from her face. She was

glad to feel that her hair had dried in the night. But it was still sticky and stiff with salt. She sat up and dragged her fingers through the mass of tangles. She couldn't have Ma noticing anything and becoming suspicious.

'You'd understand, wouldn't you, Pa?' said Marnie as she climbed from her bed and pulled on her shift and frock. 'I know you'd understand.'

'Understand what?' Suddenly Ma was in the room and Marnie flushed.

'Nothing,' she muttered.

'You keep talking to yourself like that, my girl, and you'll end up in the madhouse.' Ma glared at her. Marnie tossed her hair over her shoulders and caught the faint scent of salt and fish. She bent to pick up her boots, hoping that Ma wouldn't catch the smell too.

Instead Ma grunted at her. 'When you're finished dressing,' she said, 'you can go down the village and fetch me an ounce of baccy.' Ma plodded from the room. 'How I ended up with one like that I'll never know,' Marnie heard her say.

For such an early hour, Clevedon was as busy as Marnie had ever known it, with villagers scurrying about their business before the day got too hot, and visitors taking an early stroll along the esplanade before going back to their guest houses for breakfast.

There was a queue outside Mr Tyke's the grocer, and Marnie joined the back of it. She liked Mr Tyke's. It was always very dark and cool inside his shop, and you could buy anything from a pin to a pound of bacon. Mr Tyke wore a long apron over his pot belly and tiny round spectacles on the end of his nose. Marnie didn't mind Mr Tyke. He treated her like everyone else, rubbing his hands together and asking, 'And what can I do for you?'

He was saying this now to the girl in front of Marnie who had reached her turn at the counter. The girl was small and dressed neatly in a dark frock and a clean white apron. Marnie looked at her closely. She didn't recognise her from the village, but she couldn't be a visitor either. They never came into Mr Tyke's.

'A half pound of butter and five ounces of yer best tea, if you please,' said the girl.

Mr Tyke nodded at her. 'Coming right up! And how's things up at the manor, then?'

The manor? Of course, thought Marnie. The girl must be a maid from up there. Marnie remembered the maids she'd seen on the beach the other day, with the Bath chair and the footmen.

'Cook's 'aving a fit,' the girl was saying. 'Master de Clevedon's asked for pancakes for 'is breakfast and we've run out of butter.'

Mr Tyke chuckled. 'Well, I'd better wrap this up as quick as I can then. We can't have the Master impatient for his breakfast, can we?'

Marnie watched as Mr Tyke weighed a cut of butter and wrapped it quickly and expertly in a sheet of paper. She watched as the maid placed the package in the basket she had hanging over her arm. So the boy Noah was having pancakes for breakfast, was he? Marnie laughed out loud. The maid turned to look at her and Mr Tyke glanced up, puzzled.

'Something tickled you?' he asked.

'Sorry,' said Marnie. 'I was just thinking, that's all.'

Mr Tyke gave the maid an apologetic look and went back to weighing her tea. 'There you go,' he said. 'I'll add it to the manor bill.'

The maid turned to leave, making sure she gave Marnie a wide berth. Marnie stared after her. She was itching to follow and trip the maid with her stick. She wanted to see the butter fall from the basket and roll out of its packaging and get ruined in the dust of the lane. See if the boy got his breakfast then. But Mr Tyke was rubbing his hands together.

'And what can I do for you?' he asked.

Later in the day, as Marnie half-heartedly swept sand from a bathing machine, she saw the footmen from the manor carrying the Bath chair on to the beach again. A knot of maids were hanging around outside Smoaker's hut and Marnie recognised the one she'd seen in Mr Tyke's that morning. It was a pity she hadn't managed to spoil the butter. She would have liked the thought of Noah de Clevedon having to wait all morning for his pancakes. Without wanting to, Marnie found herself searching the beach for him. He was sure to be here if his mother was. Marnie passed her gaze quickly over the array of bonnets and parasols that seemed to cover the whole beach. She saw his hound first, sniffing its way across the shingle. Then, a few steps behind, there he was. The boy; strutting along like he owned the place.

Marnie felt a bubble of anger rise in her throat. She swept the last of the sand from the machine up into a furious cloud, then clambered down the steps back on to the beach. Smoaker was by the hut now, fawning over Lady de Clevedon. She knew that Ma would simper over the Lady too, at least while she was dipping her. What was wrong with them? Why did they have to pretend, when Marnie knew that later, back at the cottage, Ma and Smoaker would both be ranting?

Well, she wasn't going to pretend, Marnie decided. She wasn't going to act like everything was fine when it wasn't. She wasn't going to bow and scrape to the bleedin' de Clevedons. Not when they'd come back and turned everyone's lives upside down and ruined everything. Given the chance, she'd tell the boy exactly what she thought of him and his rotten family.

He was walking towards her now. A wide smile stretched across his pale face. Marnie glared at him and gripped her broom tightly in her hand. She wished her heart wasn't knocking so loudly in her chest.

'Marnie!' he said. 'I hoped I might see you here.'

'Why?' said Marnie. She kept her voice hard. 'I thought you'd have better things to do with your time than waste it on a poor dipper's daughter.'

'Oh,' said Noah. He stopped. 'I beg your pardon. I was only being polite.'

'Well, don't waste your breath on me,' Marnie spat back. 'I shan't be being polite to you or your family!'

Noah lowered his eyes. His hound nuzzled into his leg and growled low in its throat. 'Hush, boy,' said Noah. 'She didn't mean to be so unfriendly, I'm sure.' He fondled the hound's ears. 'Perhaps we shall catch you in a better mood next time.' He glanced quickly at Marnie before turning on his heel and walking away.

'Don't bother with a next time!' Marnie shouted after him. But her heart wasn't in it and her voice tailed away into the clamour of the beach. Marnie groaned. She didn't feel like she'd thought she would. She didn't feel glad to have spoken to him like that. Part of her had wanted to talk to him properly. Part of her had wanted him to smile at her again.

Marnie kicked angrily at the shingle. She wished the boy wasn't a de Clevedon. She wished she didn't have to hate him. She wished she could just have a friend.

15

The Journal of Noah de Clevedon

Clevedon. JULY 25th 1868, Saturday

What a dreadful day. It did not begin well. I passed a restless night, plagued by dreams of the girl Marnie again. They were pleasant enough dreams. But that is the problem. Should my thoughts be taken up by this girl? Should my thoughts not be of dear Cissie back in London? As a consequence, I woke tired and confused and more world-weary than ever.

Then I had a fancy for pancakes at breakfast, which did not arrive until almost mid-morning, by which time my fancy had evaporated and it was time to go with Mother to the beach for her to take the sea-cure.

As I suspected, and secretly hoped, I saw Marnie working by the bathing machines. She looked as beautiful as in my dreams and I went over to greet her. It seems she has taken against me, though, and was exceedingly rude. I was, I admit, shocked that she would speak to someone of my station in such a way, but to my shame it has only made me more determined to speak to her again.

As a final insult to this doomed day, Mother did not take well to her dipping. It did not revive her senses. Indeed, it seems she has taken leave of her senses and had to be taken back to the manor and put to bed at once. I would seek out a local doctor, but Mother will not entertain the idea. So I have had to send word to Doctor Russell instead.

And so this day cannot end quickly enough for me. The sun has eventually crept to bed and it is a relief to feel a small breeze come through my chamber window. I will stop my ramblings now and hope for a peaceful night.

16

Like an Empty Pocket

Things were not good between Ma and Smoaker. Marnie could tell by the way Ma thumped Smoaker's bowl down in front of him at supper time. She could tell from the thin silence that quivered in the air, just waiting to be broken. She could tell from the bitter whispers that passed between Smoaker and Ma, after Marnie had taken herself to bed and blown out her candle. Most of all, Marnie knew things were not good when Ma stopped going to Smoaker's bed. Ma's hot, heavy form lying next to her at night disturbed Marnie's sleep and tainted her night excursions to the sea with a maddening danger.

Marnie knew it was all to do with the pier, of course. She knew Ma was scared and didn't know what to do. She'd only ever known being a dipper. While the pier was being built there would be no bathing and no money to be earned. Ma seemed to blame everyone for the pier; she blamed Smoaker, she blamed the de Clevedons and she blamed Marnie.

Marnie hated it in the cottage. Nothing was certain any

more and nothing was fixed. Only the sea was always there. When she was floating on its surface she could forget Ma's moods and the dark worry that creased Smoaker's brow. She could forget the black shadow of the coming pier that filled her dreams. She could forget how her life had been turned inside out like an empty pocket. When it was just her and the sea, she could let her thoughts wander where they liked. She could talk to Pa with no one to hear and she could let her hopes for his return rise up high on the crest of every wave.

But it wasn't so easy to get away at night now. Only when Ma had supped heavily on beer and was a dead weight beside her could Marnie chance leaving the cottage.

It was worth every flip of her heart though, and every creak of the floorboards and doors for Marnie to feel the wet shingle on her bare toes and the first lap of the sea on her ankles.

She'd tied her hair high on her head tonight. It was easy to dry bare skin but she couldn't risk Ma questioning her over sea-soaked hair.

It was a good, calm night. A cloudless sky patterned with stars stretched like a silk cloak overhead as Marnie paddled lazily on her back. 'It'll be all right, won't it, Pa?' she said. 'As long as I have you and the sea, nothing can be too bad, can it?' She imagined that no matter how far away Pa was, her voice had travelled in the breeze and reached Pa's ears, so that at this very moment he had turned his sails towards her.

Marnie thought of the boy again and how she'd spoken to him the day before. She had wanted him to feel bad. She had wanted him to know that just because he was the son of

Sir John de Clevedon, she wasn't going to bow and scrape to him like everyone else. She should have felt smug that she'd been so rude. But she didn't. Instead she felt a strange regret gnawing at her insides. 'I did right, Pa, didn't I?' she said, as she tried not to think of the hurt look in Noah de Clevedon's eyes. 'He got what he deserved, didn't he, Pa?'

The night breeze flitted gently across her face and touched the small circle of her belly, poking naked above the water. Marnie sighed deeply. She was content now. Pa was answering her in the only way he could.

17

The Journal of Noah de Clevedon

Clevedon. JULY 26th 1868, Sunday

Doctor Russell has arrived from London to attend Mother. She has weakened dramatically. I questioned him as to the benefits of sea-bathing. He said, and I quote, 'A healthy plunger would feel a considerable shock or chill, a contraction of the skin and ringing in the ears. On leaving the water a general glow should succeed and the spirits be raised. But when bathing does not produce a glow, the chilling sensation continues, the spirits become languid and the appetite is impaired, it may be assumed that the bathing is doing more harm than good.'

So he advises that Mother desists from dipping, but that we remain here in Clevedon where the soft, mild air will benefit her more than the fog of the city. He is also worried that several new cases of cholera in London might indicate the return of the epidemic that killed so many thousands when I was but a babe in arms. So there is still no chance of us returning to London yet.

Doctor Russell is a kindly man, albeit somewhat pompous. But at least I had someone other than Clarissa to converse with at dinner. That damn girl Marnie is still playing on my mind. Codfish with egg sauce, and summer fruits for dessert.

18

Not One for Gossip

August drifted by in a haze of heat. Marnie was barely aware of the passing of the days. They were just a stretch of time she endured until night fell and she could escape to the sea. Ma and Smoaker were on better terms now and so busy with their new plans that Marnie found, if she was careful, she could come and go unnoticed; like a cat out on its nightly prowls. Smoaker had signed up for work as a labourer on the pier and Ma had finally decided on a new way to earn a crust. She was to set herself up as a laundress and when the workers arrived to build the pier, she was to take one of them in to lodge.

'He'll have our bedchamber, Marnie,' she said. 'You can make do with sleeping in the kitchen.' It didn't have to be said that Ma would go in with Smoaker. Whoever the lodger was, he would no doubt assume Ma and Smoaker were wedded.

The news that she was to sleep in the kitchen came like a gift to Marnie. No more waiting with her heart beating fast to see if Ma was going to Smoaker's bed. No more holding her breath as she slid from under the blanket on the nights that Ma stayed put. She would have a mattress by the fire, a space of her own and a whole night, every night, to come and go as she pleased.

As the end of the summer season approached, demand for the bathing machines grew less and less and Clevedon gradually emptied itself of visitors. And this year, for the first time, there would be no autumn or winter visitors to replace them. Marnie found herself looking out for the Bath chair and Lady de Clevedon and the entourage from the manor. But none of them came. They must have gone back to London. She told herself she was glad of this. It meant she didn't have to see the boy Noah again. She tried to put him from her mind and not think about how kind his eyes had been, even after she'd been so rude to him.

Marnie was surprised then at how her heart lurched when she saw the young maid from the manor come out of Mr Tyke's early one Saturday morning. She was so surprised that before she knew what she was doing, she had smiled at the maid and wished her a good morning. The maid smiled back and although Marnie didn't need anything from the grocer's, she found herself pushing open Mr Tyke's door.

'Ah,' said Mr Tyke, looking at her from over the rim of his spectacles. He rubbed his hands together. 'And what can I do for you?'

'I . . . I was just wondering,' Marnie began. 'Up at the manor? Have they all gone back to London?'

'I should hope not,' said Mr Tyke. 'They haven't settled their bill with me yet!' He looked closely at her. 'But what's that to you, Marnie Gunn? You're not usually one for gossip.'

'It's just that . . . that . . . ' Marnie thought quickly. 'We haven't had the Lady de Clevedon for a dipping lately. And I just thought . . . I just thought it was because they'd all gone back to London, that's all.'

'Well now.' Mr Tyke leaned over his counter and beckoned Marnie forwards. He rubbed his hands together again. 'That's because, young missy, the Lady de Clevedon is ill in her bed. She didn't take to the sea-cure by all accounts and has had to have a London doctor attend to her.' Mr Tyke smiled and licked his lips, like he'd just eaten one of Miss Cranston's cream pastries.

'Well, it weren't the sea that made her ill!' Marnie snapped.

Mr Tyke shrugged. 'Just telling you what I heard, that's all. Now, anything else I can do for you?'

Marnie shook her head and mumbled a thank you. She stepped outside and stood in the lane watching the back of the maid disappear up the hill towards the manor. It was strange, thought Marnie, how she kept thinking about Noah de Clevedon. It was stranger still that she should feel glad he hadn't gone back to London. There was a chance now that she might see him again, and somehow that made a difference.

Even the breeze that blew in from the sea was charged with a new kind of hope and anticipation. The villagers were buoyed by the idea of the new pier. It was all they talked about. As Marnie waited her turn at the pump the next morning, the village women let her stand there in peace. They had more important things on their minds now. A crippled girl and a drowned boy held little interest for them against the notion of a village full of strangers and an unimaginable iron structure that was to be built in their midst.

It was a new feeling for Marnie, to be able to go about her business and look up and around at the world without meeting a hostile eye or hearing the sharp words of a bitter tongue. She liked the feeling. It was something she'd never had before. 'You see, Pa?' she said as she walked back to the cottage. 'You see how they don't bother me any more? Things are changing round here. It's time you came back now. Ma'll be glad to have you. I know she will. Smoaker doesn't need her any more now there's no dipping. We can get a cottage, just the three of us. I'll come out in the boat with you, Pa. You know I'm not afraid of the sea. I'm like you, Pa. I belong there.'

Marnie stopped at the bottom of Ratcatcher's Row and stared out at the horizon. 'I'll never stop looking out for you, Pa,' she said. 'I know you'll come for me one day.'

19

The Journal of Noah de Clevedon

Clevedon. AUGUST 28th 1868, Friday

I have not had the time nor inclination to write this journal for the last few weeks. Mother has been dreadfully ill. Worse than I have ever known her. Doctor Russell stayed for the first two weeks of August and even Father came back for a few days at the doctor's urgent request. We all thought we should lose her.

But for whatever reason it is not her time yet. She has rallied, and we are all so very thankful. I do not know what I shall do when she does finally leave this life. I do not love another in the world like I love her and I know there is no one in the world who could love me as much either.

I have stayed by Mother's bedside night and day and I admit to being exhausted by it all now. I have been reading to her at all hours. Sometimes from the Bible, sometimes from her favourite novels. Today she requested Mary Barton again. I have read this one so often to her, I feel I know the Bartons and the Wilsons as well as if they were my own family!

It has been far too hot to venture outside of late. The days have passed cruelly slow. It is as if the world outside of the manor has come to a halt. I don't think I can stand another day cooped up inside these ancient walls. I need other company now. I think of my dear London friends often, and if it were not for my letters from Arnold I would think the whole world had forgotten me. He writes to me of the parties he has attended and, most maddeningly, of the ones that Cissie Baird has attended too. I know he tells me to excite my jealousy, but I shall not fall for his games. There will be time enough for me to woo the splendid Cissie when – eventually – we return to London. But for now, alas, I must make the best of my situation here in Clevedon.

I confess, the dipper girl Marnie has never been far from my thoughts. She has aroused something in me that I cannot put into words. I know I should put her from my mind. I know this place is playing tricks with my imagination. But can it harm me to have some measure of amusement and company other than Clarissa and Mother?

There is the bell again. Mother is ringing for me.

20

A Change in the Air

By the beginning of September stacks of ironwork began to appear in Clevedon, stored in huge piles along the beach and esplanade. The beach was officially closed and Smoaker took the bathing machines up to Eccles Farm, a rambling place up on the main road that ran out of the village towards Yatton. Smoaker had worked there as a boy and the old family were still fond of him, so they let him stow the bathing machines in an empty barn and put the horses out to pasture.

With the bathing machines and horses dealt with, there was only the hut left on the beach. Marnie went with Smoaker to help clear out the towels and bathing gowns before he dismantled the wooden frame and carted it off to Eccles Farm. The beach was unrecognisable. The piles of ironworks cast giant shadows across the shingle; even the sea crept timidly up along the shoreline, unsure of this strange, new place.

Marnie went into the hut and began to push towels into large sacks and to sort through the bathing gowns, putting to one side those that were in need of repair. Outside, Smoaker balanced on a ladder and cursed loudly as he tried to pull nails from the roof of the hut.

Marnie felt the change in the air, like right before a storm when the sky grew tense and the air sparked and prickled at her skin. A mix of fear and excitement rumbled through her insides like distant thunder.

Once the hut was gone, Marnie knew things would never be the same again. It made her belly churn to think of it. Part of her wanted everything to stay exactly as it always had been. Another, much smaller part was glad things were changing, and she itched to walk into the unknown. Marnie brought a towel to her nose. She sniffed the scent of Mistress Miles's soap and, underneath, the faint whiff of salt and wet bathers. She sighed. As long as she could escape to the sea at night she didn't really care what happened next.

A dog barked in the distance. Smoaker banged and pulled at nails. There was a loud clank as something dropped on to the slipway. 'Damn thing!' shouted Smoaker. 'Marnie! Come and get me my hammer!'

Marnie put the towels down and stepped outside. She hoped she could go back to the cottage soon. The thought of having to stay and watch Smoaker take the whole hut to pieces made her groan inwardly. She picked up the hammer and stretched up to pass it to Smoaker. He grabbed it from her without offering a word of thanks. He had only managed to loosen one section of the roof and already his forehead was glistening with angry sweat. He was an idiot, thought Marnie. How he was going to help build a whole pier, she couldn't imagine.

As Marnie turned to go back inside something large and heavy rushed past her and knocked her off balance. She fell hard against the wall of the hut, her breath pushed out of her chest in a sudden burst.

'Mind yerself, girl!' Smoaker shouted, as his ladder shook.

Marnie steadied herself and gulped down a lungful of air.

'Prince!'

Marnie turned. Noah de Clevedon was running towards her. She took another gulp of air as her heart jumped into her throat. Noah ran past her to the beach, where his wolfhound was cocking its leg at the base of a pile of ironwork. He slipped a leash around the dog's throat. 'Sorry!' he shouted back at Marnie. 'Are you hurt?'

Marnie shook her head. 'I'm well enough.'

The hound galloped towards the sound of Marnie's voice, dragging Noah behind. Noah's feet skidded through the shingle as he pulled on the leash with both hands and his straw hat fell from his head. 'Beastly hound!' he shouted.

A laugh slipped unbidden from Marnie's lips. Her hand flew to her mouth, but it was too late. Noah stopped in front of her and smiled widely. He ran his fingers through his hair. It was damp and fine wisps of it, the colour of toast, were stuck to his cheeks. He was flushed a deep pink and Marnie felt something inside of her soften.

'I see you have full charge of your animal,' she said lightly.

'He has not been out for days,' said Noah. 'I think the freedom has gone to his head. Still now, boy. Still.' The dog sniffed at Marnie's ankles and out of habit she tried to hide her bad leg behind her good one. 'He's as gentle as they come,' said Noah. 'I'm sorry he knocked you.'

Marnie shrugged. 'I'm still standing, aren't I?' Then, fearing she had been too sharp, she held out her hand and the dog licked at it eagerly with a tongue that was as hot and rough as sun-baked sand. They stood in silence for a moment, watching the hound. Then Noah, having got his breath back, looked around as though seeing where he was for the first time.

'Oh,' he said. 'Of course. I didn't think.'

'Didn't think what?' said Marnie.

'Your business,' said Noah. 'You cannot trade while the pier is being built.'

Marnie snorted. 'Did you think it would be otherwise?'

'I . . . I didn't think at all,' said Noah. 'Is it so very bad? What will you do?'

'Oh, don't worry your head,' said Marnie, feeling the hairs along her arms bristle. 'It's all arranged.'

'But how? Where are your bathing machines?' Noah's face was so full of concern that although Marnie wanted to throw all her anger at him, she found that it had fizzled out.

'They are up at Eccles Farm. In the big barn,' she said.

'So you will go back to the business when the pier is finished?'

Marnie nodded. 'I expect so. We are to take in a lodger in the meantime, and Smoaker . . . ' Marnie tilted her head towards Smoaker at the top of the ladder, ' . . . will labour on the pier.'

'I am glad,' said Noah. He looked up at Smoaker and lowered his voice. 'He is your father, I presume?'

Marnie felt her face flush. 'No! He . . . he's just a friend of Ma's.'

'Oh, I see.' Noah looked at her.

'Me . . . me pa is a fisherman,' said Marnie quickly. 'He . . . he's away fishing now. Gone for months at a time, he is. But he'll be back any time soon.' She licked her lips and looked Noah in the eye.

He smiled at her. 'He sounds like my own father. He is always away on business. I never know when I might see him next.'

The hound had lost interest in Marnie's hand and began to tug at its leash and pull Noah back up the slipway, away from the beach. 'Whoa, boy!' said Noah. 'I am sorry,' he said to Marnie. 'I had better take him back to the manor before he gets me into any more trouble. I hope everything turns out well for you and your family. The pier will be the making of this place in time! You'll see!'

Marnie didn't know why she said what she did next. It came out of her mouth before the words had entered her head. Perhaps she just liked the way Noah talked to her. Like she was the same as him somehow. Or maybe it was just the change in the air.

'Still want me to teach you how to paddle, then?'

Noah held tight to the hound's leash and looked back at her in surprise. He laughed. 'Indeed I do! But we shall have to wait until the pier is finished now, won't we?'

Marnie shook her head. She stepped towards him and lowered her voice. 'If you want to see the ocean at its best, meet me on the beach tonight, at eleven.' She pointed. 'Over there, beyond the ironworks. The tide'll be just right.'

Noah laughed nervously. 'Tonight? After dark? Will that not be dangerous?'

Marnie raised an eyebrow. 'No more dangerous than your

great lump of a hound on the loose.'

Noah laughed at her cheek. 'But it will be cold,' he said. 'And I usually take to my bed by ten o'clock.'

'And where's your bed?' asked Marnie. 'Still in the nursery?'

Noah opened his mouth to protest. Then shut it again. 'I'll see what I can do,' he murmured. 'Eleven o'clock, you say?'

Marnie nodded. 'I'll be there anyway,' she said. 'Whether you dare to come or not!' She turned and went back into the hut, her hands shaking slightly as she picked up the last of the towels.

There was a ripping sound and a shower of wood dust fell on Marnie's head and shoulders. She looked up to see that Smoaker had pulled the first plank off the roof and was peering down at her through the space.

'What did *he* want?' he asked.

'Nothing,' said Marnie carefully. 'He was just poking his nose around.'

'Huh! Well, he can bleedin' well keep his toff's nose out of our business! Caused us enough trouble already, that family.' Smoaker grunted as he began to prise the next section of roof off.

Marnie blinked the dust from her eyes and hurriedly finished packing the towels. She wanted out of the hut quick, before the whole lot fell down around her.

21

The Journal of Noah de Clevedon

Clevedon. SEPTEMBER 5th 1868, Saturday

This morning, a slight breeze blew in through my chamber window and woke me up. There were clouds in the sky too that, at long last, softened the brutal blue of these past weeks. I somehow knew today was going to be different. A change at last from the damnable routine of late.

I breakfasted well, then waited until Mother took her mid-morning nap before taking Prince – who has been confined to the grounds for far too long – for a walk down to the village.

I was not altogether prepared for the sight that met my eyes down on the seafront. The place is transformed! The esplanade and beach are barely visible beneath the vast amount of materials that have arrived for the pier. Father will be pleased to hear that progress is being made.

I was hoping to bump into the girl Marnie, but not quite in the way that I did.

Prince's spirits were high and he escaped his leash and ran down the slipway towards the beach, almost knocking the poor girl to the ground. Luckily, she was quite unharmed. She was also much changed in her manner. She was actually pleasant to me! We talked freely for a few moments and she even teased me lightly. There was no coyness about her at all. She is a strange creature, but all the more fascinating for it. She reminded me how I'd asked her to teach me to swim and has dared me to meet her on the beach tonight, after dark!

I know I should not go. It is against all that is proper. But I also know that nothing will stop me from being there.

I did not mention her to Mother when she questioned me about my day.

22

White Silk Stockings

Marnie was having second thoughts. She wasn't at all sure why she'd asked Noah to come to the beach. She was mad at herself, if the truth be told. Her night swims were her one precious secret; the only thing she had managed to keep hold of that meant anything to her. Now she had invited a near stranger to share it.

As Marnie lay at the edge of the bed listening to Ma's breathing, she thought that maybe she shouldn't go at all. Let the boy turn up if he wanted to; she would stay right here. She turned on her side with her face pressed into Ma's arm. Ma's skin smelled of stale sweat, tobacco and old bacon. Marnie closed her eyes and willed sleep to come. Ma grunted and for a moment Marnie imagined herself in bed next to a fat, sweating pig. She shifted around on to her back, but it was no better there. Ma's breath, warm and vinegary with beer, seeped into Marnie's nostrils. Marnie tried breathing through her mouth, but that was no good either as she fancied she could *taste* Ma's breath. It was thick enough to bite. Why couldn't Ma have gone to Smoaker's room tonight?

It wouldn't be many days before the lodger arrived, Marnie remembered. Then she would be blissfully alone at night next to the kitchen fire. Ma's snores rattled through Marnie's thoughts. Marnie sighed and turned on her other side with her back to Ma. She heard the bells of St Andrew's on the Hill strike half past ten. She wondered if the boy Noah was on his way to the beach. Would he have torn himself away from the comfort of his bed, or had he waited patiently, watching from a window as the sky grew darker and darker? Don't be foolish, Marnie thought. A proper young gent like him would never risk such an adventure. Especially not with the likes of her. He is certain not to come. With these words circling round her head like aimless gulls, Marnie grew more fidgety by the minute. It was no use; she was never going to sleep now. The sea heaved and breathed softly through the night air and Marnie could no longer resist its pull.

The bedchamber door creaked as she slowly opened it. Ma murmured at the noise and turned over, the bed-frame protesting loudly. Marnie waited, still as can be, until the air settled around her again. Then she limped through the dark kitchen and out of the cottage, her heart beating faster with every step. He wouldn't be there. It was the maddest notion to think that the son of Sir John de Clevedon would be down on the beach waiting for her.

She didn't see him at first. The heaps of ironworks had altered the appearance of the beach. Like scars running across a face, something once familiar had now become quite strange. Marnie had not yet grown used to the change and she stumbled on small rocks she hadn't expected to be there. Even the large rocks that had sat in the same place all her life looked unfamiliar with the harsh shadows of the ironworks cutting across their shapes.

'Marnie!'

She jumped at the sound of her name as it hissed through the thin sea mist. A figure rose to standing from the nearest and largest rock. 'Marnie!'

She dug her stick into the shingle and steadied herself. 'You came, then?' she said, watching him as he ambled towards her with his hands in his pockets.

'Yes,' he said. 'My nursemaid was kind to me and let me out of the nursery. But I must be back by midnight for my cup of warm milk.' He smiled at her wryly, with one corner of his mouth. Marnie felt a small trickle of pleasure run down her back. She shivered slightly.

'I told you it would be cold,' said Noah.

'I'm sure you don't know what proper cold is,' said Marnie tartly. 'And I'm sure your nurse will have put a bed warmer between your sheets for when you get back.'

'I am sure there will be one waiting for me,' said Noah. 'Only it is Hetty the parlour maid's duty these days. My nursemaid, sadly, left me years ago, after I finally learned to dress myself.'

Marnie tossed her head. Noah was looking at her expectantly and suddenly she couldn't think of anything clever to say. What was she doing here? What was *he* doing here?

'Why did you come?' she asked quietly.

'Because you dared me to,' he said.

'Have you nothing better to do?'

'Yes,' he said. 'I could be sleeping in a warm bed.'

'Perhaps you should return to it then and leave me be?'

'Indeed not! You challenged me to come and here I am! Now, your part of the bargain was to teach me the ways of the sea, if I remember correctly?'

Marnie hesitated. Could she truly do this? Could she trust this boy and let him into her private world? She looked into his face and saw nothing but an earnest innocence. Was this it, then? Marnie's insides turned over. Was this what walking into the unknown felt like?

'As you wish,' she said. She bent to take off her boots and motioned for him to do the same.

He had on a fine pair of brown leather boots which he carefully unlaced and took off to reveal white silk stockings. Marnie sniggered. 'You'd best take off your hose too. And roll up your britches.'

His bare feet shone white in the moonlight and he winced as he stood on the shingle.

'Your skin is too soft,' said Marnie.

'Unlike your manner.' He smiled as he said this and suddenly Marnie didn't mind him being there at all.

'Come on,' she said. 'Let's get our toes wet!'

She led the way to the water's edge and Noah followed, padding gingerly, like a cat on broken glass. Marnie lifted the skirt of her frock and walked straight into the water. The shock of cold ran through her body and she closed her eyes to savour the sensation.

Next to her, Noah squealed like a young girl. 'You do this for pleasure?'

'Hush,' said Marnie. 'Wait for the waves to come to you. Wait for the sea to get to know you in its own time.' Marnie stood still and let the waves wash over her ankles; the bigger ones leaped up her shins and wet the hem of her frock.

Noah stayed silent and watched as each wave poured over his feet and dragged the sand back from under them. 'Whoa!' he exclaimed. 'I am going to fall!' He reached out and grabbed on to Marnie's arm to steady himself. 'My feet are sinking!'

'Don't look down,' said Marnie. 'It'll make you giddy.' She let him lean on her for a while and they stood in silence looking out into the darkness of the ocean.

'It is beautiful, isn't it?' said Noah. 'It is full of stars. I cannot tell where the sea ends and the skies begin.

'I'm glad you like it,' said Marnie. 'If you listen hard you can hear it whispering.'

'Listen hard? But I can hear it quite clearly. It is filling the air with its noise.'

'No. Not that sound,' said Marnie. 'The sound underneath it all. The whispering.'

Noah stood silent for a moment. Then he shook his head. 'It is no use. I can hear nothing but the crashing of the waves.'

'You are new to it,' said Marnie. 'In time, once you get to know the ways of the sea, it will let you hear its voice.'

'Is that so?'

'You don't believe me?'

'All I know is, my feet are numb and there is sand scratching my toes.'

'You think that's bad?' said Marnie. She bent to the water, scooped up a handful and threw it at his legs.

He yelled loudly. 'That is unfair!' He kicked at the water and sent a shower over Marnie's head.

Marnie didn't flinch. Instead, she scooped up two handfuls of water and threw them straight in Noah's face. He gasped. 'You mean to start a war?' He kicked at the water again and sent a small wave over Marnie's skirts. Soon, they were both splashing furiously, sending spray after spray of the icy sea over one another. Moments later, Noah was laughing breathlessly. 'Stop!' he begged. 'I am near soaked through!' His britches clung wetly to his legs and his hair lay flat to his forehead and dripped water down his face.

'Have I won the war, then?' asked Marnie. She had never felt so good. She had thought she would hate to share all this with anyone else, but to her surprise, having someone there with her had made it all the more wonderful. She wanted to tear off her frock and plunge into the sea. She wanted Noah to follow her in and taste the true delights of the night ocean. But she sensed he wasn't ready yet. She would have go careful with him.

'Yes! I concede. You have won the war this time!'

This time? Did that mean there would be another time? Marnie felt her skin glow and was glad the night shadows would conceal her flushes.

They walked back up the beach. Noah shook the water from his hair, tossing his head from side to side like a wet dog. Marnie laughed. 'I see your wolfhound has been teaching you

96

some tricks.'

'Yes indeed!' Noah smiled. 'Prince would have loved it out here tonight. But I am afraid his barking would have woken the whole village!'

'Have you had him for long?' asked Marnie.

'He was a gift for my fifth birthday. From my father. I have grown up with him. I can't quite imagine life without him now.'

They walked in silence for a while. The wet skirts of Marnie's frock turned cold against her legs. 'I hope you do not mind me asking,' said Noah. 'But how did you come to be lame? Were you born that way?'

Marnie stiffened. Nobody had ever asked her that question before. She swallowed down the shame that suddenly filled her mouth.

'I am sorry,' said Noah, when she didn't reply. 'I did not mean to offend you. I did not mean to pry.'

'You're mistaken,' said Marnie. She wouldn't let him know she was ashamed of her affliction. 'You haven't offended me. You got your wolfhound for your fifth birthday . . . I got polio for mine.'

Noah stopped walking. He touched her on the arm. 'I . . . I am so sorry.'

'Don't be,' said Marnie. 'It doesn't matter. I do well enough.'

'Yes,' said Noah, taking his hand away. 'I think you do.'

They climbed up the beach steps on to the esplanade. 'Well, thank you,' said Noah. 'I should be getting back to the manor. To see if my bed has been warmed!'

Marnie nodded and turned to go.

'Will I see you again?' said Noah.

Marnie carried on walking. She hoped he couldn't hear her heart banging loudly under her damp frock. 'Come to the beach Sunday next.' She tossed the words over her shoulder. 'Same time. Same rock.'

23

The Journal of Noah de Clevedon

Clevedon. SEPTEMBER 6th 1868, Sunday

I had the strangest few hours of my life last night. Marnie is quite extraordinary. I have never met anyone like her. She was so natural with me and seems to have little sense of her place in the world. It is a pity she is lame, for she really is such a beauty. When I first saw her standing on the beach in the moonlight, she quite took my breath away. Dressed in a proper gown, with all the manners of society, she would put most of the young ladies of London to shame (excepting Cissie, of course!).

I confess I have never felt so free as I did last night. It was as though I had been released from heavy shackles. I did not have to think what I was saying or mind my manners. Marnie will be a most amusing distraction for me while I am forced to stay here. It is wise that we meet at night, though. I cannot risk being seen and having the servants' tongues set to wagging. Father would be most distressed to hear I had struck up a friendship with a local wench, no matter how innocent it is.

Mother was too ill to attend church again today, so I accompanied Clarissa. I prayed as usual for Mother's speedy recovery and nodded a greeting to the band of curious locals who gathered after the service in the churchyard.

I must let Prince out now, for his last turn around the grounds. It is past ten and I am worn out from the adventures of last night.

24

Soiled Washing

The following morning the lodger moved into Ratcatcher's Row and took up residency in Ma and Marnie's bedchamber. He was a tall, thin man with broad, bony shoulders and a patchy black beard. 'This is Eldon Cross,' Ma said, when Marnie returned to the cottage with the morning pail of water. Marnie nodded a greeting to the man and decided at once that she didn't like the way he looked at her; as though he had been given a plate of hot stew and dumplings that he knew was all his to eat.

Smoaker seemed to like him, though. The two of them sat on the doorstep smoking their pipes before they took themselves off to the beach to join the other labourers.

The first bundles of soiled washing had arrived and Ma was anxious to begin at once. 'We'll start as we mean to go on, Marnie, and do this proper. Mistress Miles thinks she's got it all sewn up, she does. Reckons herself a proper *laundress*. She never did too well by our towels, mind, did she? We're up against it, Marnie. We've got to prove ourselves, we have. Get this laundry spick and span.'

Marnie looked in dismay at the oil-stained shirts and britches that Ma had spread out on the kitchen table. There was flannel underwear too, in all sizes, with a variety of unmentionable stains staring her in the face.

'Right! First things first, Marnie. More water. That lot in the copper's hot enough now.'

All morning Marnie lugged pails of water back from the pump. Ma had set up the wash tub in the backyard and the whites were put to soak in shavings of lye soap. Marnie was set to removing the worst of the stains. A hot coal wrapped in a rag to melt off hardened wax, chalk rubbed on grease marks and milk dabbed on to the yellow piss stains that patterned the fronts of underclothes. Ma grunted as she twisted the dolly stick round in the tub. 'Through the wringer with these lot,' she instructed Marnie.

By early afternoon, the bushes out front were decorated with the results of their efforts. Marnie's arms had never ached so much and her hands were red raw and itchy with the lye. 'I'm fair worn out now,' said Ma. 'Keep an eye on the washing while I go for a lie down. And don't forget to turn it.' She took herself off to Smoaker's room while Marnie wandered across the lane and sat down gratefully on the grass embankment. She saw the horizon in the distance; a hazy blue where it met the sea. It was familiar and calm. Unlike the beach. The tide was out and what little of the beach Marnie could see swarmed with men and strange machinery. A vast steam-crane swung a length of ironwork out towards the shoreline. Smoaker had said there was three hundred and seventy tons of ironwork to be put in position. Marnie couldn't imagine what that meant. The roar of scraping metal, the thud of tools and the hiss of steam had silenced the sea. Marnie couldn't hear its voice any more. She only felt the ground beneath her shaking and trembling.

Marnie pulled her knees to her chest and thought back to the night before. All day she had wanted to do this. But she'd held the memories in the back of her head, bundled up like a net of squirming fish, until she could be alone with them. She let them go now, and shook them out so they darted around fast, challenging her to catch one.

Noah de Clevedon. She said his name out loud. She said it slowly, feeling the way her lips curved around each sound. He'd come to the beach to meet her. He'd been kind to her. They'd laughed and talked and he hadn't minded when she'd thrown water in his face and soaked him through. He'd made her feel safe in a funny sort of way. He didn't seem to mind who she was or what she was. Marnie liked this new feeling that was bubbling around inside of her. She liked Noah, she realised. She didn't hate him at all. She felt warm and soft all of a sudden. She'd never liked *anyone* before this. She stood up and laughed out loud and hollered into the afternoon air. Was this what having a friend felt like?

If it was, it was almost as good as jumping the first wave on a hot summer day.

As she turned to go back to the cottage, Marnie saw two of the village women staring at her from across the lane. 'What are you looking at?' Marnie shouted. 'You never seen anyone happy before?' Then she raised her stick in the air and hollered even louder.

25

The Journal of Noah de Clevedon

Clevedon. SEPTEMBER 12th 1868, Saturday

At long last, Mother's health seems to be improving. Doctor Russell's tonics are obviously working. She even took her evening meal with me and Clarissa last night. It is so good to see some colour back in her cheeks. She is still too weak, though, to make the arduous journey back to London. It seems I must endure this place a little longer.

Autumn has suddenly crept in around the edges of the days and it is bleaker here than I could have imagined. With only myself and Mother in the house, not all the rooms have been opened. There is an eeriness to the place that I do not like. The servants tiptoe about so as not to disturb Mother and they have all taken to talking in whispers. It is all so tedious and lonely. I miss the London house with its bustle and noise and constant visitors. I miss my friends. Although I did receive another letter from Arnold yesterday. But his tone was so jolly and his news so full of incident (he spoke with

Cissie Baird at a fancy-dress ball a week gone and she sends her regards to me!) that I felt worse than ever after reading it. I am sure the poor fellow did not mean it to be so!

I will write back and tell him of my clandestine meeting with Marnie. He will be scandalised, of course. I will impress upon him the nature of her rare beauty in the hopes of securing his envy!

26

The Lodger

The week passed by in a blur of suds and stains. Marnie quickly grew used to the new rhythm of the days and the odour of wet wool and sour piss that rose from the steam of the washing tub and settled on her skin.

The weather was dry and blustery and the scrubbed garments dried quickly out on the bushes. In her spare moments, when Ma had gone for her lie-down, Marnie would wander down the lane and watch the progress on the pier. She didn't mind being at the cottage all day, not now she was bedded down in the kitchen at night and was free to escape to the beach after dark whenever she fancied. The nights were growing colder, but Marnie savoured the touch of the hard, icy waves as they washed her clean from the stench of the day. Creeping past the night watchman stationed in the workmen's hut and the makeshift shacks of the workers who had chosen to sleep on the beach only added an extra thrill.

It was Sunday now and Smoaker and Eldon Cross were sat

in the kitchen supping beer and enjoying their day of rest. Eldon had taken a shine to Marnie. She could tell by the way he kept looking at her. Like now. He was staring at her over the rim of his beer pot. Marnie wanted to poke her tongue out at him. He was so *old*. At least thirty, give or take a year. And he was ugly with it. Bony face and piggy eyes. He'd be hard pushed to find a girl to look once at him, let alone twice. Marnie knew why he was ogling her. He thought she was like him; an outcast that no one would ever want. Well, he would soon find out how wrong he was. She had a friend now. And not just any old friend. Noah de Clevedon, the son of Sir John de Clevedon, no less. And she was going to meet him on the beach again. Tonight. Stick that in your pipe and smoke it, she thought. She glared at Eldon Cross, then turned her back and busied herself with the supper pots.

The shadows were lengthening outside the kitchen window. It wouldn't be long now. Ma yawned and heaved herself from her chair to light the candles on the mantelpiece. They'd all be to bed soon, thought Marnie. Soon as the sun went down.

'Fetch your old pa another beer, Marnie,' Smoaker said. 'And one for Mr Cross too.'

Marnie pulled a face. 'Coming,' she sighed. For reasons of propriety, Ma had instructed Marnie to address Smoaker as Pa, at least while Eldon was in earshot. But Marnie was damned if she would ever do that. Smoaker wasn't her pa and she wouldn't pretend he was.

Marnie fetched the beer jug and topped up Smoaker and Eldon's pots. 'Ta,' said Eldon. 'She's a good girl, i'nt she?' he said to Smoaker.

Smoaker grunted. 'Not bad,' he said. 'Could be worse I s'pose.'

'Nah, you're a lucky man. I'm telling yer. To have a daughter like that.' Eldon winked at Marnie.

Marnie would have loved to have tipped the remains of the jug over his head. Instead she turned to Ma. 'More beer?' she asked.

'Not for me,' said Ma. 'I'm off to my bed now. See to the fire, won't you?' She untied her apron and threw it over the back of her chair. Then, with a nod to the men, she thumped up the stairs.

Marnie took the jug back out to the pantry. She was glad of something to do. Her insides were jittering around like wasps in a jam jar. In the week since he'd arrived, Eldon had always taken himself off to bed first. But he was growing more comfortable now. Sitting there yarning with Smoaker. Marnie prayed Eldon wouldn't take it upon himself to be last to bed. She didn't want to be alone with him in the kitchen. She wanted them all to bed and the time to pass in a wink. She wanted to be on the beach. And to see Noah again.

Marnie dawdled outside to the privy. With any luck the men would have finished their beers by the time she got back. After she'd squatted over the ash pit, she paused in the backyard and looked up at the sky. It was going to be a clear night. There was a nip in the air, but it was still. There was no wind to speak of. It would be perfect down on the beach. She wondered if she could get Noah right in the sea this time. Give him a proper dip. Her belly squirmed in anticipation. This was the worst bit. The waiting.

She thought of Pa. Out there somewhere in the world. Was he any closer to coming home? What would he make of it all? she wondered. A new pier. A new friend. 'You'd like him, Pa,' she said. 'I know I didn't at first . . . but I was just angry about the pier. He's kind to me, Pa and . . . and I've told him about *you*. I've never told anyone about you before.' Marnie turned back to the cottage. 'So you'd better hurry back so he knows you're real,' she finished quickly.

Marnie held her breath as she walked back into the kitchen. Her heart lifted. There was no one there; only two empty beer pots on the kitchen table. She let her breath out, slow and long, and crept to the pantry to fetch her bedding. She had sewn an old sheet together and Smoaker had brought her some new straw to stuff it with. It smelled good and fresh. With her blanket tucked around and with the dying warmth of the fire to lie in front of, Marnie was as cosy as a rabbit in a burrow. She blew out the candles and settled down.

The cottage creaked. She heard Ma turn heavily in bed and Smoaker complaining under his breath. She looked across the kitchen at the door to her and Ma's bedchamber, where Eldon was sleeping. There was no light coming from the crack underneath. Good. He was settled too. Now all she had to do was rest awhile and listen out for the bells of St Andrew's to strike half past ten.

27

The Journal of Noah de Clevedon

Clevedon. SEPTEMBER 13th 1868, Sunday

I have just returned from the beach. My hair is damp and stiff with salt. My sea-logged clothes are lying in a heap in the corner of my room and, despite my dressing gown, I am shivering with cold from head to toe. I fear I may have left puddles all through the hallway downstairs.

But I have never felt so exhilarated! My blood is rushing hot around my veins. Even the tips of my hair seem alive. I don't know how Marnie persuaded me in. She just seemed so at ease, with her skirts billowing out around her and her hair trailing on the surface of the water. I took off my frock coat, silk vest and boots and before I knew it, I was up to my knees in the sea.

'Just a little at a time!' she called out to me. I waded out to her, my breath ragged with the shock of the cold. She swam around me; glided, almost. She was so graceful. 'Shall I dip you?' she asked. I was about to decline when I felt her hands on my shoulders and

all at once she pushed me right under. I cannot express the great fear that took hold of me in that moment. It was like nothing I have ever experienced before. I thought I should never breathe again. But then she lifted me to the surface and, once I had filled my lungs and recovered my senses, I was overcome with the most wonderful feeling of well-being.

Then she apologised. She said it was something that had to be done quickly before I had too much time to think on it. She said she hoped she hadn't offended me. She looked so serious, I could not help laughing. It was a ridiculous situation; the both of us wet and bedraggled and acting so polite! She soon saw the fun in it too.

She says she will teach me to swim next time, and I am to bring a dry set of clothes. It was most unpleasant having to walk back to the manor looking and feeling like a drowned sailor.

I will sleep well tonight. I know it.

28

Clevedon Manor

By the end of September the weather turned bleak. It was too wet for the washing to go outside any more, so it was hung around the kitchen on string that was nailed to the ceiling beams. It took an age to dry and sent Ma into the foulest of tempers. Marnie kept out of her way and worked quickly and quietly, willing the hours to pass. The never-ending damp of the cottage got inside her head, settled on her hair and skin and made her own clothes reek of mould. Even the straw inside her mattress had begun to rot. But Marnie barely noticed. She had her weekly meetings with Noah to look forward to now. And at long last it was Sunday again.

Marnie lay in front of the dying fire listening out for the church bells. The wind had whipped up outside and it crossed her mind that Noah might not come out on such a night. But she didn't dwell on the thought. Instead she imagined how wild the sea would be. Churned into a frenzy of spitting waves. She loved it like that, when it was full of life and anger. It made her feel like she could do anything in the world. She wanted Noah to see it too, and to feel what she felt.

Over the last couple of Sundays Noah had taken so well to the sea that he could manage a few strokes in the shallows now. He had got into the habit of bringing a flannel shirt with him, which he would change into behind a rock. *Their* rock; the one he always waited by.

Marnie thought about last Sunday. It had been the best so far. She and Noah had got carried away in the joy of it all and had forgotten to be quiet. They'd made so much noise, whooping and hollering in the waves, that they'd woken one of the workers. He'd come out of his shack, waving a lamp across the beach and shouting, 'Who's there?'

Marnie and Noah had ducked down in the water so the waves lapped their chins. The lamplight crossed inches in front of their faces. They gripped each other's hands under the water and stifled their laughter until eventually they heard the man's footsteps crunching back up the beach. Then they snorted water from their nostrils and shushed each other as they waded back to shore. They'd dressed quickly, Noah behind one rock and Marnie behind another. They didn't speak until they were back on the esplanade.

'That was close,' Noah had said, his face flushed with excitement. 'Imagine if he had seen our faces peering at him from between the waves! He would have thought we were a two-headed sea monster, or a couple of lunatics from Bristol Asylum at the very least!' He giggled like a small child.

The adventure had warmed Marnie through to her bones. She knew Noah felt the same way too. His eyes had sparkled at her. 'You are so different when you are in the sea, Marnie,' he said. 'I have never seen anyone look so alive. It is as though you were born to it.'

Marnie looked at him solemnly. 'But I was born to it.'

Noah laughed and bowed deeply. 'Indeed! Now, I must go. And so must you.'

Marnie watched him as he walked away. She rested on her stick, her heart full of something she couldn't name. Then Noah had suddenly stopped and shouted back at her, 'Are you sure your father didn't catch you in one of his nets, little mermaid?' She heard him laughing to himself as he strode off back to the manor. She stayed, gazing at his figure until it disappeared into the distance.

Marnie turned to face the sea. 'Is it right what he said, Pa?' she had whispered, careful not to wake another worker. 'Did you catch me in one of your nets?' She liked the thought of that. She liked that Noah talked of Pa too. It made him seem real, and it made Marnie more certain than ever that he would be coming back to her soon. Pa would come home. She just knew it.

The distant toll of the church bells brought Marnie back to the present. She lay still on her mattress, counting the ten strikes. Not long to go now. All was quiet in the cottage and she knew she would have no trouble sneaking out.

It was wild down on the beach. The towering steam-crane creaked as the wind battered its body and the workers' shacks shivered in protest. As she walked past the half-built pier she spied the dark figure of Noah, his hands buried in the depths of

114

a long overcoat. Her hair lashed across her face as she hurried to meet him.

'Not a night for swimming, surely?' he shouted to her above the roar of the wind.

'Maybe not!' she agreed. 'It's best to leave the sea be when it's in this mood.' She turned her face to the sea-wind and the full force of the elements took her breath away. 'See how magnificent it is!' she hollered.

Noah came to stand by her side. 'You are quite mad!' he said, laughing. He held his arms out and the wind caught under his coat and blew it open. It sailed behind him like a cloak. 'Whayyy!' he shouted. 'I feel I am riding an unbroken stallion!'

They stood in silence for a while, and Marnie marvelled at how much her life had changed. Having a friend like Noah made everything seem so good. He didn't care about her leg. He seemed to like her for who she was, not what she was, and that meant everything to Marnie.

Noah nudged her. 'Come back to the manor with me.'

'What, now?' said Marnie.

'Why not?' said Noah. 'It is time you saw something of my life.'

It was an effort for Marnie to walk up the old road that led to the manor. It wound uphill, out of the village, and was strewn with small rocks and peppered with potholes. After she'd stumbled a couple of times Noah came to her side, and without saying a word, he offered her his arm. Marnie wasn't used to being helped and although she was grateful, she couldn't bring herself to thank him. They walked in silence.

An owl hooted in the distance and the wind blew through the trees that lined the road.

'It is not far now,' said Noah. 'Look. Can you see the light burning in the south porch?'

Marnie looked up, and sure enough there was a yellow haze glowing softly through the trees. They walked through an open pair of tall iron gates. Marnie saw the bulk of the manor in front of her, silhouetted against the night sky.

'We will go around the side. To the servants' entrance,' said Noah. 'The Grand door will be locked by now.'

Marnie saw a couple of lights burning in the upstairs windows. 'Who's up at this hour?' she asked.

'That will be Mother,' said Noah. 'She has trouble sleeping these days. She is most likely reading.'

'And the other window?'

'Clarissa. She is Mother's lady's maid. She won't be sleeping if Mother is not.' Noah pointed to a bigger window in the centre of the upper floor. 'And that is my bedchamber,' he said. 'I have the best view of any room. I can see over the village and right out to sea..If I had a spyglass, I imagine I could even see you on the beach.'

It was a strange notion and Marnie fell silent again. She could scarcely believe she was about to enter the mysterious Clevedon Manor. The de Clevedons had lived at the manor for hundreds of years, although it had lain empty for as long as Marnie could remember. Until Noah and his mother had come back, it had been many years since any of the family had paid a visit. Marnie knew of no one who had ever been inside. The manor's servants were sent to the village for goods, but kept themselves to themselves and never gossiped with the locals. The villagers talked of the de Clevedons in hushed tones, as if they were royalty or something. Marnie was awestruck. She felt as though she was about to enter the palace of Queen Victoria herself.

Marnie followed Noah to a small wooden door, set deep in the old stone walls. He opened it and motioned for her to follow him. Marnie held her breath. She pictured velvet curtains, carved oak furniture, huge fires and jewelled treasures; riches beyond her wildest dreams. It was pitch black inside. The air was musty and cold and Marnie's stick clicked on the stone floors. She shivered. It wasn't how she imagined it at all and disappointment flooded through her. Then, as if he'd read her thoughts, Noah whispered to her, 'This is only the screens passage. The oldest part of the manor. It leads to the kitchens and the buttery and the larder. But I will take you through to the Great Hall first.' He pushed open a door to his side and Marnie immediately smelled a change in the air; a smoky warmth of candle wax and burnt logs.

'Wait here and I will see if there are enough embers in the fire to light a spill,' said Noah. She heard his footsteps cross the hall and as she peered into the shadows she saw a flickering light growing bigger and bigger. Noah's face, lit up by the flame of a thick creamy candle, came towards her. 'Come in,' he said. 'Come and see the Great Hall!'

Marnie saw nothing at first but shadows and shapes. Then, as Noah busied himself lighting more candles, the Great Hall gradually revealed itself to her. It was vast; the vaulted ceiling so high, the top of it disappeared from view. There were beautiful

117

tapestries hanging down the walls and a whole gallery of portraits. The stern faces of dozens of men and women stared down at Marnie from within their gilt frames.

'Who are all these people?' she asked in a whisper.

'Mostly my family,' said Noah. 'My grandfather, great-grandfather, even my great-great-grandfather! Some of their wives too, and cousins, of course. There are some friends here too. Have you heard of Tennyson, the poet, and William Thackeray, the celebrated writer?'

Marnie shook her head.

'You have not heard of *Vanity Fair*?'

Again, Marnie shook her head. 'What's a Vanity Fair?' she asked. 'Is it like a May Fair?'

Noah laughed. 'No, you silly thing! *Vanity Fair* is the title of Thackeray's great novel. He is famous throughout the whole of England for it.'

Marnie flushed furiously. 'Well, he's not famous here, is he? And why should I care about such things as that, anyway?'

Noah's eyes danced with amusement. 'Calm yourself,' he said. 'I only answered your question as to who is in these portraits.'

Marnie turned away from him and walked towards the fireplace. She hadn't meant to be sharp with Noah, and it wasn't his fault she'd been made to feel stupid. She wasn't sure what to feel at the moment, or how to act. All of this had stunned her and knocked the wind from her sails. Being inside the manor was astonishing enough, but seeing all those faces looking down at her, and knowing that Noah had such a family, filled Marnie with envy. What must it be like to go all

118

the way back in time and know exactly where you came from and who you belonged to? Marnie wished she had a picture of her pa. The tiniest miniature would do. Just so she could look into his face.

Marnie stood in front of the fireplace. It was so huge that the remaining embers in the fire basket looked lost. She swore the fireplace was bigger by far than the whole of a bathing machine. She could walk into it and live inside quite comfortably.

'Shall we go to the kitchens?' Noah's voice beside her made her jump.

'The kitchens?' said Marnie.

'Yes. I need to check on Prince and I think we could both do with a hot drink, don't you?'

Marnie followed the light of Noah's candle back into the screens passage. As they walked along, Marnie smelled the history seeping from the stone walls. She held out her hand and touched the cold stone and imagined how many others had laid a hand on the same spot. Was she the very first?

'Here we are,' said Noah. He swung open a heavy wooden door and light flooded out into the passage. 'Hetty. You may go to bed now,' Noah called out.

'Yes, sir. Thank you.' Marnie heard a girl's voice and the scraping of a chair.

After a moment Noah turned to her. 'Come. We have the kitchens to ourselves now.'

'Who was that?' asked Marnie as she followed Noah into the kitchen.

'Hetty,' said Noah. 'Remember I told you about her? She is the parlour maid. Although she has had to take on more duties since we have come here. We do not need a full staff with only Mother and me, and no guests to entertain. Hetty is more of a maid-of-all-works at the moment.'

'But you have plenty of other servants too,' said Marnie, remembering the gaggle of maids and footmen on the beach when Lady de Clevedon had first come to bathe.

'Yes, I suppose we do,' said Noah. 'We have Clarissa, of course, Mother's lady's maid, and Sally the cook, and Mr Todd, or the Toad as I call him. He is Father's old butler. He oversees the servants here. It keeps him occupied in his old age. There are a couple of footmen too, and a stable boy. There may be one or two other maids, I do not know! I confess I rarely see them. They are like invisible mice that run around keeping everything in order.'

As they walked through into the heart of the kitchen, Marnie saw the wolfhound lying in front of the fire. He whined and came bounding over at the sound of Noah's voice. 'Sshush,' said Noah, stroking him under his muzzle. The hound growled low in his throat and edged towards Marnie. 'Stop that!' Noah ordered. 'Come, Prince. Come,' he said. He took Marnie's hand and held it under the hound's nose. 'See? It is only Marnie. You remember her from the beach, don't you? She is our friend.'

The hound's growl turned to a whine of pleasure as Marnie rubbed behind his ears.

'He is a wise dog,' said Noah. 'He remembers you well. Now . . . the kettle is still hot. Would you care for some tea? And a slice of Sally's seed cake?'

They sat together at the end of an enormous wooden table. Marnie sat stiffly, listening for the sound of footsteps or the groan of a door. She knew she shouldn't be there, a girl like her supping with a proper young gentleman! But somehow it felt right; like part of her had always belonged.

Noah poured her tea from a white china pot and served her a slice of the softest, sweetest cake she had ever eaten. They sat until the teapot was empty and Noah told her of his life in London. How his days were filled with visitors and outings to the theatre. How he studied under a private tutor, and of the dances that were held almost every week in the houses of his father's wealthy friends.

'You can't imagine how tedious it has been coming here,' Noah said. 'No friends, no amusements. Until I met you, of course. You have made my stay here so much more bearable.'

Marnie swallowed down a smile. She didn't want Noah to see how much his words pleased her. 'Will you have to go back to London, then?' She caught her breath as she waited for his answer.

'I will have to go back some time,' said Noah. 'I *want* to go back. But only when Mother is well again. And I cannot tell you when that will be.'

'I didn't know she was still sick,' said Marnie. 'It's a shame Ma can't give her another dipping. That would sort her out.'

'Doctor Russell advised against it,' said Noah. 'He said it was doing her more harm than good.'

'Pah!' said Marnie. 'And what does he know about it? I've never known anyone not benefit from the sea-cure!'

'That may be so,' said Noah. 'But your bathing machines are away now and Mother has been told to keep quiet and rest.'

Marnie was stung. How could any of them know the true

121

marvels of the sea? They knew nothing. Still, she was glad Lady de Clevedon was sick. She hoped it would be a long, long time before she returned to health. The longer she remained sick, the longer Noah would stay.

A clock somewhere in the manor chimed one. Noah yawned. 'It is late. I must let Prince out for his last turn around the grounds. We will walk you to the bottom of the road, shall we?'

Marnie was glad to get back to the cottage. Her head was bursting and she wanted to be alone to sort out her thoughts and to remember every detail of the manor and the hours she'd spent with Noah. It was cold inside the cottage kitchen, the air still damp with wet washing. She poked at the fire but there were no embers to coax to life. So she lay on her mattress, wrapped tight in her blanket, and imagined she was cosied up next to the kitchen fire at the manor, with Prince lying across her feet to keep her warm. She closed her eyes. Had she truly been drinking tea with Noah de Clevedon? Had she truly been inside Clevedon Manor? Inside the Great Hall? She hadn't been dreaming, had she? No. She could never have imagined all she'd seen and heard and tasted. It had been real. And it had been wonderful.

There was the sound of a door opening. Marnie lay still.

'You asleep, Marnie?' Eldon Cross whispered from across the room.

Marnie said nothing.

'I know you're awake, Marnie. I just heard you come in.'

Again, Marnie didn't stir, although her heart thumped painfully against her ribs.

'I just want to talk,' said Eldon. 'That's all. Sometimes I don't sleep at night either.'

There was silence for a moment. Then Marnie heard Eldon sniff and clear his throat. 'Where do you go at nights, Marnie Gunn? I wonder.'

He shuffled back to the bedchamber and closed the door.

Marnie didn't move. But anger flashed white in her head. How dare that man come to her like that! She shuddered. This was her space at night. He had no right to come near. It would be no good telling Ma or Smoaker, though. She couldn't chance Eldon telling them of her night excursions.

The problem wormed its way round and round her head and into her dreams of Noah and Clevedon Manor, so when she woke in the morning she couldn't be certain if Eldon Cross had come to her in the night or not.

29

The Journal of Noah de Clevedon

Clevedon. OCTOBER 1st 1868, *Thursday*

Father is home for two days. He is come to inspect the progress of the pier. The piles have all been sunk now and work is ahead of schedule. Everyone is praying for a mild winter so there is little disruption.

Mother brightened a good deal to see him. She dressed for dinner tonight and looked like a pale but beautiful angel. I wish Father would love her more. I wish he would stay and love her back to health again. But pressing business means he has to return to London tomorrow. Besides, he is an impatient man and would not make an ideal sick-bed companion.

At least I have Marnie to distract me. She is a light in a house of darkness. I hope it was not unwise of me to have brought her to the manor Sunday last. But I could not resist showing her this place. She is not used to such things and I wanted to show her something new, as she has shown me something new. It was heartwarming to see the look on her face. There is a part of me, I admit, that revelled in showing off. But still, I do hope that none of the servants saw us.

30

A Long, Sweeping Staircase

'Come,' said Noah to Marnie. 'Let me show you a game I played when I came here as a young boy.' He took her out through one of the doors in the manor kitchen and into a large hallway. He ran and placed a candle at the top of the long, sweeping staircase, then came down and put another on a table at the bottom. The candle flames formed dancing shadows on the green and gold papered walls, and lit up the faces of dour-faced gentlemen who gazed down out of dark oil paintings. Marnie was curious. What was he going to show her? She'd been as pleased as Punch when he'd invited her back to the manor again, after a strong gale had chased them off the beach earlier. They'd had tea, as before, sitting at the kitchen table. Prince had recognised her straight away and nuzzled his head into her lap. The hound could never have known how that one gesture had almost made her weep. And now this. Marnie's heart danced like the shadows on the wall.

'Follow me,' whispered Noah. 'But we must be as quiet

126

as mice.' He led the way up the stairs slowly, so that Marnie could keep up. She crept after him, marvelling at the soft green carpet that covered each stair and muffled the tap of her stick. The staircase climbed up and up in a gentle curve and then, just as Marnie's leg began to ache, the climb ended abruptly and she stood next to Noah on a wide landing that disappeared to the left and right into darkness. Noah put his finger to his lips. 'Watch me,' he whispered.

Noah suddenly lifted his leg and mounted the polished oak banister with ease. He smiled widely at Marnie. She noticed how one of his front teeth was slightly crooked. Then, before she could ask what he was doing, he was gone. Marnie gasped out loud as Noah swooped down the great curved banister. He stopped with a bump against the carved post at the bottom of the staircase and waved up at Marnie.

Marnie realised she'd been holding her breath and, as she looked down at Noah smiling up at her, a titter burst out of her. She clamped a hand over her mouth and peered to the left and right, down the dark corridors. There was no sound and no movement from anywhere. Noah ran back up the stairs. 'Now it is your turn,' he whispered.

'I can't do that!' spluttered Marnie. Was he mad? She looked down the staircase. It was a dreadfully long way to the bottom.

'What? The Maid of the Sea, the Queen of the Waves, cannot brave a simple staircase? I am disappointed in you, Marnie Gunn. I thought you had more fire in your belly.'

Marnie looked at him smirking at her and looked again at the banister winding down to the flickering flame on the hall table. Her legs trembled under her skirt, but she glanced back at Noah and set her shoulders straight. 'You're not right in the head,' she whispered. 'But go on. Help me up, then.' Noah bent down and before Marnie knew what was happening, he had gripped her twisted foot in his hand and hoisted her over the banister. Hot waves of shock rippled through her body and stung her face. It was as though Noah had just touched her in her most private of places. She was stunned, but held on to the stair-post tightly as she straddled the banister.

'Just go!' whispered Noah. 'Don't think about it. Just let go!'

Marnie's fingers ached. She couldn't hold tight any more. The stair-post began to slip from her grip. 'Noooo!' she hissed. But it was too late. The musty candle-air of the manor rushed past her ears as she flew down the banister. Her skirt and drawers were pushed to a bunched tangle between her legs and her eyes sprang astonished tears. Then, just as she was filled to the brim with the extraordinary sensation, it ended. She hit the bottom stair-post and the air was knocked out of her lungs in one loud shout. She tumbled to the floor, knocking the candle from the table.

Noah was by her side in an instant. 'Ssshhh,' he said, picking her up. 'You'll wake the whole household.' His voice had a streak of laughter in it. 'That was good, was it not?' he asked.

The flame from the candle that Marnie knocked to the floor drowned in a puddle of wax and the only light now came from the top of the stairway. Marnie was dazed. Everything had happened so quickly. From Noah touching her foot, to her landing on the hall floor – it had all been a whirl of feelings that Marnie hadn't had time to put in their proper place. 'It was . . . it was . . . ' Marnie couldn't catch her breath as she tried to steady herself and find her bearings in the darkness.

A door banged from somewhere in the manor and Marnie stiffened.

'Who's there?' a small voice echoed from the far side of the hall.

'It's Hetty!' whispered Noah, and he pulled Marnie into an alcove. They pressed themselves against the wall and watched as a candle flame flickered on the paintings opposite. Marnie bit on her tongue to keep a nervous snigger from escaping. It was good to be so close to Noah. She could feel his body rise and fall, and the warmth of him seeped through the cotton of her frock and touched her skin.

'Prince? Is that you?' Hetty's nervous voice came again. Her candle flame quivered on the wall and Marnie saw the shape of her appear from out of the darkness. It was the maid she'd seen at Mr Tyke's. Beside her, Noah's body shook with suppressed laughter. Hetty stood still with her head cocked to one side. Marnie heard her shallow breaths.

Suddenly a tickle caught in Marnie's throat. She tried to swallow it down, but it grew bigger and more irritating and although she pressed her hand to her mouth, a cough suddenly spluttered out from between her fingers.

Hetty jumped and as she whirled around to face the alcove, Noah stepped out of the shadows. 'Hetty,' he said. 'I am so sorry to have startled you.'

'Master Noah! Is everything all right? I heard a shout.'

'It was only me, Hetty. I tripped on something. I was just trying to see what it was.'

'But where is your candle, Master Noah? You can't see in the dark.'

'I dropped it. Look.' He took Hetty's candle and shone it on the floor to where Marnie had knocked the candle from the table. 'Here it is!'

Marnie stayed put, waiting for Noah to call her out of her hiding place and introduce her to the maid.

Noah lit his candle from Hetty's flame. 'Thank you. You may go to bed now. I will make sure everything is locked up.' Hetty bobbed a small curtsey and scuttled back down the hallway.

'You can come out now!' whispered Noah.

'I'll need me stick,' said Marnie. 'We left it at the top of the stairs.'

'Of course,' said Noah. 'I will fetch it.'

Marnie listened as the sound of his footsteps faded up the stairs. The bright thrill she had felt all evening turned dull now. It was all ruined somehow. When Noah came back with her stick, she snatched it from him. 'Why did you keep me hidden from Hetty?'

Noah looked at her in surprise. 'You know why,' he said. 'We cannot be seen together like this.'

'But she's only a maid,' said Marnie. 'What does it matter to her?'

'You cannot really be so innocent,' said Noah. 'Servants are the very worst of tittle-tattles.'

Marnie was silent.

'Hey!' said Noah. 'Why look so grave? Have you not enjoyed yourself?' He poked her in the ribs. 'Did you ever think you would sail down the banisters of Clevedon Manor?'

Marnie shook her head. A smile twitched at the corner of her mouth.

'Well, all is not lost, then,' said Noah. 'Come. I think it is high time we both went to our beds.'

Marnie crept into the kitchen at Ratcatcher's Row. She checked for a light under Eldon Cross's door. There was nothing. Good. Maybe she had imagined the other night after all. Without bothering to undress, she lay on her mattress and pulled the blanket over her head. She thought of Noah pressed against her in the alcove and she touched her arm where his warmth had been. She dared herself to remember the moment he'd held her twisted foot in his hand. Nobody had ever done that before. And Noah hadn't even flinched. Under the blanket, Marnie's face flushed hot and a warm softness spread through her, filling her belly and limbs. She fell into such a deep sleep that she didn't hear Eldon Cross tiptoe across the room. She didn't smell the beer on his breath as he leaned over her. She didn't feel his hand stroke her hair and she didn't hear him whisper, 'I mean to marry you, Marnie Gunn. You mark my words.'

31

The Journal of Noah de Clevedon

Clevedon. OCTOBER *5th 1868, Monday*

Hetty has been giving me strange looks all day. I cannot help but wonder if she saw something last night. I certainly hope not. I cannot have Mother bothered with rumour and nonsense. Maybe I should not bring Marnie to the manor any more. But that would be a shame, as I do so like the look of wonder that being here brings to her face. And surely I should be permitted to indulge in whatever innocent diversions I can find in this place? I will catch Hetty alone tomorrow, and have a quiet word with her.

Since Father's visit, Mother has continued to improve. She even took a small turn around the garden this afternoon. She clung to my arm tightly and the footmen followed with a chair, but she was brave beyond words and the chair went back into the manor unused. She is talking more and more of London and of how she misses the house and the company. I dare not hope that we may return soon!

In the meantime, I have written to Arnold and asked him to pass on my regards to Cissie Baird. After all, there is a chance now that we may be back in London for the Christmas season!

32

A Walk Along the Esplanade

October brought howling storms to Clevedon and brought work on the pier to a halt. Smoaker and Eldon Cross filled the kitchen with their pipe smoke and complaints. Talk was all of the pier and of a labourer who had been crushed to death by a falling girder. 'Bashed his head right in, it did,' said Smoaker. 'T'wasn't right having us out there in them winds. Glad they've seen sense now.'

Eldon Cross nodded his agreement.

'Mind you,' said Smoaker, 'there won't be no more wages till we're back on it. Bleedin' weather.'

Round and round the words went; in and out of Marnie's ears till she wanted to scream. She wanted the weather to calm too. But for different reasons. Noah wouldn't come to the beach in a storm and she couldn't turn up at the manor unannounced. All she could do was wait out the days and pray the coming Sunday would bring finer weather.

Eldon Cross was getting on her nerves as well. Every time

she turned around, he was staring at her. Smiling and staring, like he knew something she didn't. Ma didn't help matters. 'Be nice to Eldon,' she said. 'Here, look. Take him this pot of beer. And smile, Marnie! You're so much more pleasing to the eye when you smile.'

'I don't want to be nice to him!' Marnie hissed. 'He makes me skin itch!'

Ma pushed her face up close. 'Don't you think to be too choosy, my girl. He's a good catch for someone like you. Never thought I'd see the day when any man showed an interest. So you do as I say and be nice to him. You hear?'

Marnie set the beer on the table in front of Eldon Cross. 'Ta,' he said with a wink. 'That's very kind of you, Marnie.' He stroked his tatty beard. 'I should like to take you for a walk later. If this storm abates.' He looked at Smoaker, who at once nodded his head. 'That's agreed, then,' said Eldon. 'Soon as this storm blows itself out, eh, Marnie?'

Marnie turned away without saying a word. She was boiling inside. How could Ma and Smoaker encourage the man, when Marnie had made it quite clear he turned her cold? It was on the tip of her tongue to tell them about Noah. How good it would be to see the astonishment on their faces when she said, *'I've been bathing with the son of Sir John de Clevedon. I've taken tea at the manor. Noah de Clevedon is a friend of mine.'*

They'd never believe her, though. They thought she was fanciful as it was. *'Don't you be telling such lies, girl,'* Ma would say. *'Why would a gentleman like him wish to befriend the likes of you? You're daft in the head, you are!'* Marnie could just hear it.

It would take Noah himself to come knocking at the cottage

door to make them believe her. And that wasn't going to happen any time soon. Noah had his position to think of. Marnie knew that. But one day, maybe. One day something would happen. And then she'd shock 'em all.

So Marnie said nothing. Instead she went back to pressing the pile of shirts that were stacked at the other end of the kitchen table. She took a rag and picked up the flat iron that had been heating by the fire. She spat on it as Ma had taught her, and the hiss of her spittle told her it was good and hot. The iron weighed heavy as she smoothed the creases from a shirt sleeve, but Marnie's arm was strong and she savoured the pull and ache of her muscles.

She sensed Eldon Cross watching her from across the room and she banged down hard with the iron, wishing it was Eldon's smug face.

'Careful, girl!' shouted Ma. 'You'll be scorching that in a minute. We don't get paid for ruined linen, you know!'

By mid-afternoon the winds had died and although the skies were thick with hard grey clouds, the rain had stopped too. Eldon, who had poked his head out of the kitchen door at least a dozen times during the afternoon, got up from his chair yet again and, on account of one too many pots of beer, walked unsteadily to the door. He opened it and sniffed at the air.

'Ahhh,' he breathed. 'The scent of freshly turned earth. There's nothing quite like it after a storm, is there, Marnie? I think we could chance our walk now.'

Marnie winced at his words. 'Ta, Mr Cross. But I think maybe another time would be better. I've all this to finish yet.' Marnie nodded towards the shirts that were still to be pressed.

'Nonsense!' said Ma quickly. 'There's no hurry for these. You go on now, Marnie. Don't keep Eldon waiting.' Ma snatched the iron from Marnie's hand. 'Go on!'

'But Ma!' protested Marnie.

'I said go.' Ma nodded pointedly towards Eldon.

Marnie clenched her fists tight. It was only a walk, she told herself. No more than that. And it wouldn't be for long. At least she could escape the fug of the cottage and breathe in some sea air. She quickly knotted her shawl around her shoulders and took up her stick. The sea was best after a storm. Its surface rose and dipped like the chest of some great panting beast and the depths of it turned an angry inky black. Marnie imagined she could already smell the salty cleanness of freshly washed shingle.

She pushed past Eldon Cross, still hovering in the doorway, and made her way to the lane in front of Ratcatcher's Row. Eldon hurried after her, pushing his arms into the sleeves of his jacket. 'Didn't expect you to be able to walk so fast,' he said as he caught up with her.

Marnie ignored him and set her sights on the end of the lane, where it wound round to meet the esplanade. It was too wet to slide down the embankment, although it would have been amusing to see Eldon get the seat of his britches wet. 'Here, Marnie, take my arm,' he said. 'It'll be better than that old stick.'

'No ta,' said Marnie. 'I can manage well enough.'

She led the way down the lane, muddied by the rain, and on to the esplanade, with Eldon Cross following silently by her side. She was damned if she was going to talk to him. Let him follow behind like a lost dog if he wanted. She wasn't going to give him a thing.

There were several figures walking up and down the esplanade. A couple of village women nodded to Marnie and gave knowing glances towards Eldon. 'Afternoon,' he said, as though he'd known them all his life. Marnie didn't care an inch what they might think; she only prayed that Noah wasn't out and about. She would die of shame if he were to see her out walking with Eldon Cross.

She reached the railings that overlooked the beach and gripped the cold iron with her hand. The sea-wind blew in her face and she closed her eyes. For a moment she imagined she was on her own, that the sea and the beach were all hers. Just like it used to be. Then Eldon's voice came loud in her ear. 'Are you cold, Marnie? I could put my jacket over your shoulders if you would like?'

'I'm quite warm enough,' said Marnie stiffly, although the cold of the railings bit into her hand and she wished for deep pockets or a velvet and fur muff that she'd often seen the winter visitors carrying on their daily perambulations. She opened her eyes and saw that Eldon had turned to face the north end of the beach where the pier workings were lying in what looked to Marnie like of heaps of tangled iron.

'Look how light and elegant those legs are,' said Eldon. 'Who'd ever believe there was over three hundred tons of wrought iron in 'em. Had to screw the deepest piles into the limestone and mud, you know. A feat of engineering, that pier is. I hope you appreciate what you see being built in front of your very eyes, Marnie Gunn. It's going to be a thousand feet long by the time it's finished. Did you know that?'

Marnie didn't answer. She let him ramble on and he didn't seem to notice. She couldn't care less about the pier. Only that it would be finished soon so she could have her beach back; and the sea. She missed the bathing machines, she realised. She even missed Smoaker's hut.

'When *will* it be finished?' The question was out of her mouth before she could snatch it back. She hadn't wanted to encourage him in conversation.

Eldon turned to her and it seemed to Marnie his piggy eyes lit up in triumph. His chest broadened and he rocked back on his feet as if he were the fount of all knowledge. 'Ah. Won't be finished till Easter, Marnie. That is if all goes to plan and we don't have too bad a winter ahead of us. The tides can play havoc when they want to.'

Easter! That was months away. Marnie wondered how she would endure Eldon's attentions for that long. For surely he would leave when his work was done? She chanced a glance at him. He was smiling at her encouragingly. Waiting, it seemed, for her to say something more. His smile didn't make him any more pleasant to look at. The gesture had made his eyes disappear in a mass of crow's feet.

'I'd like to go back now,' said Marnie.

'Already?' said Eldon. 'But we've hardly walked a few yards.'

'Me leg is aching. I can't go any further,' Marnie lied.

'Well, that's a shame,' said Eldon. His smile dropped. 'But I'm sure we'll have plenty more opportunities for an evening stroll in the days to come.'

Marnie's heart sank.

'You must take my arm now,' said Eldon. 'Now that your leg is bothering you.'

'I can manage well enough, Mr Cross.' Marnie took a deep breath. 'I *prefer* to manage on me own.' She stole a last glance at the sea before she turned to go. '*Where are you when I really need you, Pa?*' she whispered. '*Don't be too far away.*'

'What did you say?' asked Eldon.

'Wasn't talking to you,' said Marnie and she walked off, leaving Eldon Cross standing there with his mouth open.

'Back so soon?' exclaimed Ma as Marnie walked back into the kitchen. Eldon Cross followed sullenly behind.

'Her leg was bothering her,' he said, gruffly.

Ma scowled. 'Oh, was it indeed? Well, you'd best get to finishing these then, my girl.' She threw a fresh pile of linen on the kitchen table.

Marnie couldn't help smiling as she picked up the iron. Ma couldn't realise that she'd rather press a mountain of washing than spend one minute more in the company of Eldon Cross.

Besides, the skies over the horizon had looked clear and promising. Tomorrow would be fine. She was sure of it. Smoaker and Eldon Cross would be back to work and in two more days it would be Sunday again. Then Noah would be waiting for her by their rock on the beach. The iron felt as light as a feather in her hand as it flew through the pile of shirts, collars and bed sheets.

33

The Journal of Noah de Clevedon

Clevedon. OCTOBER 18th 1868, Sunday

What grey and miserable weather we have had the last two weeks. Mother, Clarissa and I have stayed huddled around the fire in the library, our heads buried in our books. To see Mother with the energy to read again is a complete joy! Sally has furnished us with nourishing broths and hot toddies, so it has not been an altogether unpleasant experience. I am just happy that Mother is away from her bed. She is so improved that I believe Father will hardly recognise her when he sees her next.

I received word from Arnold again yesterday. He informed me that Cissie Baird flushed to the roots of her raven hair when he passed on my kindest regards! He implored me to come back to London for Christmas. 'My dear fellow,' he wrote. 'If I have to come and fetch you myself on horseback, I will have you back!' Ah! If only he knew how welcome that would be!

The skies seem more settled today. I noticed a patch of blue over the woods when I took Prince for a romp earlier. I think I may go to the beach tonight and see if Marnie is there. I am in need of entertainment, and who better to provide it than my spirited young friend? I have not seen her since 'the night of the banisters' and I confess I have missed her a little. I am convinced Hetty saw nothing that night. I questioned her the following day and she seemed only puzzled by my enquiries. Nevertheless, I shall endeavour to be more discreet if I am to bring Marnie to the manor again.

34

A Pot of Tea in the Kitchen

It was gone eleven o'clock on Sunday night before Marnie managed to escape from the cottage down to the beach. If Noah had come at all, she was certain to have missed him. She cursed Eldon Cross for loitering after supper and keeping Ma and Smoaker from their beds with his tales of working on the railways. The candles had burned to stumps by the time they bade each other goodnight. Marnie waited for the light under Eldon's door to be snuffed out and for the cottage to still before she dared to ease the kitchen door open as quietly as she could.

As she hurried along the esplanade Marnie spied a figure leaning over the railings. She slowed, not wanting to be seen by any villager or drunken worker still about at this time of night. But then the figure turned and she recognised the tilt of the hat and the neat set of shoulders. She knew at once it was Noah and she couldn't help but smile widely.

'I had given up on you coming,' he said, when Marnie reached him. 'I thought you had grown bored with our rendezvous.'

'*Never!*' said Marnie fiercely. 'I had some bother getting out, is all.'

'Well, I am glad you came, Marnie. I have missed you these past weeks.'

Marnie's eyes widened. 'I'm sure you have better things to do than miss me,' she said. But inside she was brimming over with smiles. If only Eldon Cross could see her now!

Noah laughed. 'You are a breath of fresh air, Marnie Gunn. You really are. Come.' He held his arm out to her and without hesitation she took it and he guided her down the stone steps and on to the beach.

The sea was flat and calm and the moon shone a gentle yellow on its surface. Noah took himself behind a rock to change into his flannel shirt and Marnie pulled off her boots and stripped to her shift. Then Noah held on to Marnie's hand and they walked into the sea together, sucking in their breaths. The water was hard and bitterly cold, but they sank into it without a murmur. They swam side by side, not speaking or making a splash. After a while Marnie felt the blood rush hot through her body.

She sighed. 'It's perfect, isn't it?' she whispered to Noah. He didn't answer. Maybe he hadn't heard her. But she was glad anyway. She felt they were caught in some strange magical world – just the two of them – and talking would have broken the spell.

Noah was the first to swim back to the shore, and although she could have stayed in the sea all night, Marnie followed him out. He looked a sight standing on the beach, dripping wet and shivering furiously in his flannel shirt. 'Hurry and get your dry clothes on,' she said. 'Then you can take me back to the manor for a warm.' She was sure she saw him pause for a moment and open his mouth as if to say something. But then he was gone, behind a rock to change. Marnie took off her wet shift and pulled her frock back on. By the time Noah came back, she had her shawl tied around her shoulders and her boots on. Noah came behind her and gathered her hair in his hands. He twisted it and squeezed the seawater from its length.

'There,' he said. Marnie's breath caught in her throat and her heart thumped hot and hard under her ribs.

They walked up the road to the manor in companionable silence. Marnie held on to Noah's arm and he matched his pace to hers. As they reached the entrance gates he bent his head to her and said, 'There will be no sliding down the banisters tonight, Marnie. I cannot risk waking Mother. She's been doing so well lately.'

'A pot of tea in the kitchen will suit me just fine,' said Marnie. She wondered why Noah seemed more nervous than usual. He ushered her around the side of the manor and in through the servants' entrance, his fingers to his lips the whole time. The kitchen fire was burning low and the whole room smelled of warm bread and sweet things. 'Sally has been baking today,' said Noah. 'I will see if I can find us one of her cakes in the pantry.'

'I'll make the tea, then,' Marnie called after him. There was an assortment of teapots on a shelf by the fire next to a stack of cups and saucers. The kettle was on the hearth. When Marnie lifted it she found it still heavy with water. She put it to boil, then looked about for the tea. A silver caddy was on the kitchen table. Marnie picked it up and opened the lid. She sniffed at the black perfumed tea inside. It smelled wonderful, a world away from the cheap sawdust they had at home. As she glanced around for a spoon, a door opened behind her. Thinking it was Noah back with the cake she said, 'I've found everything. Been making meself quite at home, I have.'

'I can see that!' said a voice.

Marnie whirled around. It was Hetty, glaring at her from across the room. 'Who the bleedin' hell are you?' she asked Marnie.

Before Marnie could answer, Noah came back into the kitchen carrying a plate of cake. He darted a warning look at Marnie as he walked past her towards the maid.

'Hetty!' he said. 'I am glad you haven't taken to your bed yet. Would you wrap a portion of cake for this young girl, please? She called at the side door just a moment since, begging for food. I have taken pity on her and granted her a warm by the fire and promised her something to eat.'

'Oh, sir. I see, sir,' said Hetty.

Marnie slowly put the tea caddy back on the table. What was happening? She suddenly felt like a thief caught red-handed. She looked to Noah. Surely he was playing games? He would burst out laughing in a moment and tell Hetty that everything was all right; Marnie was his friend from the village, he would tell her. He had invited her to the manor and she was welcome. But Noah didn't look at her. He turned his back and poked at the kitchen fire while Hetty cut a chunk of the cake and tore a piece of newsprint to wrap it in.

There was silence in the kitchen, save for the scrape of the poker and the crackle of the paper. Marnie wanted to laugh and cry all at the same time, but the stiff set of Noah's back told her somehow that she must keep quiet.

'Here.' Hetty thrust the parcel at Marnie.

'Much obliged,' murmured Marnie.

Noah turned from the fire and Marnie saw his face was flushed redder than it should have been with only a feeble flame in the grate. 'Thank you, Hetty,' said Noah. 'I will see the girl out. And Hetty?'

'Yes, sir?' said the maid.

'Please do not trouble yourself to mention this to anyone else. I do not wish Lady de Clevedon to be disturbed by the thought of beggars at our door.'

'Of course not, sir,' said Hetty. She curtseyed lightly, then, after flinging a look of contempt at Marnie, she left the kitchen.

Marnie stood frozen, though her head was bursting with rage.

Noah smiled at her tentatively. 'I am sorry for that, Marnie,' he said. 'But thank you for playing along with me.'

'A beggar?' Marnie spluttered. 'You had me down for a beggar?' She threw the parcel of cake across the kitchen floor.

Noah laughed nervously. 'Come now, Marnie. You know it was only a game. You are not truly angry with me, are you? You know I had no choice, don't you? Imagine the gossip and the scandal if our friendship were to be found out!' He went to her and placed his arm round her shoulder.

'But a beggar?' Marnie asked, her anger easing at the touch of him. 'Do I look like a beggar?' She stopped and glanced down at herself; at her stocking-less legs and her old frock,

147

still damp at the hem. She put her hand to her hair and felt it a tangle of wet strands.

'If you look like a beggar,' said Noah gently, 'then you are the most beautiful beggar I have ever seen.'

Marnie walked back to the village alone. Noah said it would be for the best. In case Hetty was looking out for her departure from a window somewhere. Marnie tried to stay mad with Noah. She knew she was hurting somewhere inside. She knew she should think the whole evening spoiled. But all she could hear were Noah's words. *You are the most beautiful beggar I have ever seen.*

35

The Journal of Noah de Clevedon

Clevedon. OCTOBER 25th 1868, Sunday (two o'clock in the afternoon)

I have the most marvellous news! We are very shortly to return to London! Mother has a bloom in her cheeks for all to see and has told me she feels her health almost fully recovered. She confided in me that it was the loss of a child that had sickened her so, but has asked me to say nothing to Father of the matter. 'He would only grieve to hear the news,' she said. 'And there is nothing to be done now.'

I confess I am surprisingly saddened at her revelation. I have always longed for a sibling and I had thought Mother past her child-bearing years. But rather she is still with us than lost to the dangers of childbirth. I will respect her request and say nothing to Father. 'You are such a comfort to me, Noah,' she said. I kissed her hair and told her she was the dearest mother of all and I was glad she was mine alone.

I will write to Arnold at once. He will inform the whole of London of our impending return, and I know Cissie Baird will be one of the first to hear the news!

I will go to Marnie tonight and tell her too. She will be glad for me, I am sure. I just hope she is not still cross about the events of Sunday last.

36

Maid of the Sea

Noah passed the bottle of wine to Marnie. 'Have a good swallow,' he said. 'It will warm our bellies before we brave the water.'

Marnie took the bottle and lifted it to her lips. Expecting the yeasty thinness of beer, Marnie spluttered when the thick, sweet wine filled her mouth.

'Steady!' said Noah. 'That is fine wine. Not rough vinegar.'

Marnie took another swallow and a trail of warmth seeped down her throat and into her belly. 'It's good,' she gasped. 'Can I have more?'

Noah laughed. 'Yes,' he said. 'But let me wet my lips first.'

They passed the wine between them and with every new mouthful Marnie felt her limbs grow softer and her head grow lighter. It was beautiful on the beach. The sea was calm and quiet and shimmered silver through a low mist. 'Have you forgiven me for Sunday last, little beggar girl?' Noah teased.

Marnie looked at him, leaning relaxed against a rock with

his hat by his side and his bare toes digging into the shingle. With the wine swirling around her senses, she could forgive him anything. 'I've worse things on me mind than your foolishness,' she said. 'But I forgive you in any case.'

'Well, thank you,' said Noah, and he lifted the wine bottle in a salute. 'Now, pray tell me what *worse things* you have on your mind?'

Words and pictures crowded into Marnie's head. The wine seemed to have loosened all the black thoughts and memories that had been tightly hidden away, like crabs wedged in the crevices of a rock: the misery of being a cripple, the drowning of Ambrose, the longing for her pa and the suffocating presence of Eldon Cross all scuttled out of their hidey-holes. If she could tell anyone anything, she knew she could tell Noah. And in the telling, maybe the thought or memory wouldn't be so bad.

'Come, Marnie,' Noah urged. 'Tell me what things a girl like you has on her mind.'

'An old and ugly suitor for one,' she said, and watched how Noah's eyes widened in surprise.

'A suitor, indeed! And is he so old and so ugly, Marnie?'

'He is,' Marnie said firmly. 'I can't bear the sight of him.'

'Can you not just tell him so?' said Noah. 'Or at least tell him you are unable to return his affections?'

'It's not so simple,' said Marnie. She thought of Ma's face, urging her to be nice to Eldon, of how she was made to sit next to him at supper now and of the nights she had woken to find him sitting silently in the kitchen watching her sleep. 'He's a lodger at our cottage,' she said. 'Me ma wants me to like him. She doesn't think I could do better. Being a cripple and all.'

'It is strange to hear you say that, Marnie,' said Noah. 'I never think of you in that way. To me, you are a mermaid on land. A maid of the sea!'

'If only others thought like that,' said Marnie quietly.

'Don't be so hard on yourself, Marnie. You have such spirit. I have never met anyone like you before. Come on, let us not be maudlin. Have some more wine.'

He was right, thought Marnie. Why let Eldon Cross spoil her precious time with Noah? She poured more wine in her mouth and swallowed. Her belly swirled warm and suddenly the black thoughts disappeared. She was just where she wanted to be, with the person she most wanted to be with and the sea was lying before them, inviting them in with its gentle hush. She stood up and steadied herself against the dizziness that rushed to her head. 'I've got an idea!' she said. 'Are you brave enough to do it?'

Noah stood up and bowed. 'Anything you say, my lady.'

'Let's bathe as the men do, then!'

'And how is that?' asked Noah.

'You know,' said Marnie. 'How they do at Byron's Bay. As naked as the day they was born!'

The smile fell from Noah's face. 'Marnie Gunn! In truth, I am shocked at your suggestion.'

'No, you're not,' said Marnie. 'You're just not brave enough!' She was giddy with the joy of it all. Noah had said she was spirited. Well, now she'd show him just how spirited she was.

'Come on!' urged Marnie. 'The quicker you're in, the better it is!'

Noah stood like a great dumpling, gawping at Marnie while

she pulled off her frock and underclothes. She didn't stop to think. It was Noah, after all. He'd touched her foot without flinching. There was nothing else to hide from him.

'Come on!' Marnie said again. 'If you're quick about it, you won't feel the cold.'

Then she saw the look on his face. How his cheeks were flushed pink and how he couldn't look her in the eye. It amused her to see him so ill at ease. She turned her back to him then, and shouted over her shoulder, 'I promise I won't look!'

Marnie heard him sigh and mutter something to himself. Then there were shuffling noises and the jangle of belt and braces. She turned around suddenly and Noah quickly put his hands to his manhood. Marnie looked at his unclothed limbs and chest and began to laugh.

'Why, Noah! Just look at you,' she teased. 'You're as white as the underbelly of a flatfish!'

Noah looked down at himself and then back up at Marnie. A smile twitched at the corner of his mouth. 'Well, look at you, Marnie Gunn,' he said slowly. 'You are as brown as a common farmhand!'

They stared at each other for a moment. Then Marnie turned and made for the sea. Noah came after her and they both yelped like puppies as the waves slapped against their naked skin. 'Shush,' said Marnie. She giggled and hiccoughed. 'We don't want to be waking the workers.' They swam in circles around each other and Marnie dived under the surface and pulled gently on Noah's legs. Then Noah held her hand and they let the waves wash over their heads. Everything that had ever troubled Marnie faded away into the sea mist: Ma,

Smoaker, Ambrose, Eldon Cross, the pier, her crippled leg and the whole of Clevedon. All that mattered now was the three of them. Her, Noah and the sea.

Even Pa was only a smudge on the horizon at that moment.

After they'd worn themselves out, Marnie and Noah stumbled back up the beach and dried themselves on their clothes. Marnie dressed quickly. Her shift stuck to her salty skin. Noah turned his back to her as he dressed.

A strange silence fell between them as they sat and finished the wine. The moon shone weakly through the mist as Marnie studied Noah's face. She noticed he had a small mole under his left eyebrow and the corners of his mouth were turned down slightly as he stared out into the blackness of the sea. She thought of his pale arms and legs, the few dark hairs on his chest and the small brown birthmark that she'd seen on his hip. She shivered. It was then, she was sure of it, that something inside her changed. Something shifted and fitted into place, like a key in a lock. It was then that she knew for certain that Noah was more than just a friend. He was her whole world, she realised. And he always would be.

37

The Journal of Noah de Clevedon

Clevedon. OCTOBER *25th 1868, Sunday (half past midnight)*

I cannot believe what I did tonight. It must have been the wine, I am sure of it. I have not behaved as a gentleman should, but I do not care. It was Marnie who encouraged me, let us not forget. Maybe all young women of her class behave in such a manner. Or maybe it is just her. I have always sensed she was different.

Whatever the case, I shall never forget the vision of her naked before my eyes. I never imagined a woman's body could be quite as lovely. The softness of her, the curve of her hips and the roundness and swell of her breasts struck me dumb for a moment. The colour of her skin took me by surprise too. I told her she was as brown as a common farmhand, but that was in jest. Her body was not the pearly white I have always imagined a woman hid under her petticoats and gowns, but the colour of milky tea. It was so utterly beautiful I had to turn my back so I did not embarrass myself.

I never thought I should learn about a woman in this way, but I am glad of it.

I did not tell Marnie of our imminent return to London. But I will tell her soon. There is time enough.

Now to my bed. I want to dream of Marnie and how her wet flesh shone as she emerged from the sea. I already feel a stirring in my underclothes. Is that so very wicked of me?

38

Beady Eyes

Ma wouldn't take no for an answer. 'You'll accept Mr Cross's invitation, my girl!' she hissed at Marnie as they stood in the backyard guiding a sopping wet sheet through the wringer. 'I don't know what's the matter with you. It's only a walk!'

Marnie pulled a face. 'He wants more than a walk, Ma. You know he does. And he's ugly. And old enough to be me pa. And . . . ' She paused. 'And he comes and looks at me in the night.'

'What do you mean, *he comes and looks at you in the night?*'

'Just what I said. I wake sometimes in the night and he's there sitting on a chair all quiet. And he's staring at me.'

Ma looked at her sharply. 'He hasn't touched you, has he?'

'No,' said Marnie. 'But I should scream me head off if he did.'

'Well, I reckon you're making a fuss over nothing. He doesn't mean any harm. He's just lost his heart to you, is all.' Ma carried the wrung-out sheet and draped it over the bare branches of a shrub. 'He's a good man, Marnie. You won't get any better. He's a good worker and earns a good living. You'll learn to like him in time. You mark my words.'

'But Ma . . . !'

'No. I won't hear any more of it, Marnie. You'll go for a walk with that man and you'll like it. You hear?' Ma picked up the empty wash tub and trudged back into the cottage. 'I'll tell him to come out and fetch you now.'

Marnie groaned angrily and kicked at the clean sheet. 'Bleedin' ugly toad!' she cursed. Well, she wasn't going to be nice to him. She just couldn't be. And nobody could make her, either. The cottage door opened and Eldon Cross came ambling out.

'Your ma says you're ready,' he said. 'Here. I've brought your shawl and stick for you.'

Marnie snatched them from him and moved to walk out of the gate. Eldon shifted fast in front of her and got to the gate first. He opened it and gestured for her to walk through. 'Ta,' said Marnie before she could stop herself. She grimaced. Why did he have to pretend to be such a gentleman, when he was nothing but a coarse old labourer? Even dressed in his Sunday best he could never compare to a real gentleman. He still had crumbs of bread stuck in his beard! And though Marnie hated to think of it, the sound of him coughing up his phlegm in the mornings came back to her. She shuddered. At least Eldon knew better than to offer her his arm now – though he walked much closer to her than she would have liked.

It was a good, dry, breezy afternoon and there were plenty of people about on the esplanade. Most of them were standing by the railings gawping at the half-built pier. It was a strange sight to be sure. All the legs were in place now; long, spindly

159

things that tiptoed far out to sea. Eldon began to drone on about spans, girders and braces and how the wooden decking was to be made from an African hardwood.

Marnie let him talk on and she thought of Noah instead; how his smooth face was so pale compared to the darkness of Eldon's roughened features. She thought of Noah's voice. It was soft and . . . silky, almost. She wanted to dive right into it. It was nothing like Eldon's harsh tones. He was still going on and his words were dull and hard and hurt her ears.

She looked at the people milling about and wondered if Noah was walking around the village with Prince. She wouldn't mind him seeing her with Eldon now. Not now that she'd told him of Eldon's unwanted attentions. They could laugh about it later, and if Noah saw Eldon, he would understand why it was so dreadful for her. Maybe she could persuade Noah to say something to Eldon to put him off . . . or . . . Suddenly Marnie had an idea. Noah could have his father put Eldon out of work! He could send him off the pier and away from Clevedon.

'Marnie? Are you listening to me?' Eldon's voice cut through her thoughts.

Marnie threw him a dismissive glance and began to walk faster, her limp becoming exaggerated as she widened the space between them.

Eldon caught up with her in two long strides. 'I was saying, Marnie. I should like to be the first to accompany you along the pier once it's opened. What do you say to that then?'

But Marnie had stopped and was looking down on to the beach – just along from the pier and the workers' huts – to where she and Noah had met last Sunday. She let herself remember the whiteness of his naked skin; how tender it had looked and how she'd itched to touch him. She thought of how peaceful it had been in the sea and how right it had felt. She smiled to herself and her cheeks glowed warm.

'Ha! I see you like the idea!' said Eldon, pressing his shoulder to her as he stood next to her at the railings.

Too late, Marnie realised he'd mistaken the meaning of her smile. 'No, Mr Cross,' she said. 'I was thinking of other things. And it's a long while till the pier opens. Anything could happen before then. It's best I don't make you any promises.'

'You're not making it easy for me, are you, Marnie Gunn? But you see, I like that about you. It makes me want you more.'

Marnie looked at him then, straight into his small, empty eyes. 'Well, I don't want *you* at all, Mr Cross.' She moved away from his shoulder and brushed at her own to get rid of the feel of him.

Eldon Cross laughed, revealing his tobacco-stained teeth. 'I know you don't mean that, Marnie. You'll grow to like me in time. I'm a kind man, you see. And, don't forget, I'm keeping your little secret safe.'

Marnie glared at him.

'What would your ma say if she knew you were sneaking around at night? You can take me with you next time, eh? Show me what it is you get up to.'

Marnie flinched. 'I only go out for air,' she said slowly. 'When I can't sleep, the night air helps. That's all.'

'Maybe that's so, maybe it's not,' said Eldon. 'But promise to be kinder to me and I promise not to let on to anyone.'

Marnie took a deep breath. It was all she could do not to

smash her stick across his head. 'I'll do me best, Mr Cross,' she said tightly.

'Good! Then everything's tickety boo, in't it? Come on, I 'spect your ma's got supper ready by now.' He held out his arm and Marnie had no choice this time but to take it.

All the way back to the cottage Marnie struggled to keep her temper in check. She clamped her mouth shut and ground her teeth. The slimy, shifty worm, she thought. Wait till she told Noah. He'd have to get his father to do something now. Get Eldon kicked off the pier and away from Clevedon for good.

Marnie couldn't settle to anything. Her feet were fidgety and she'd already dropped a pile of supper plates to the floor and set Ma off on a scolding. She knew Eldon Cross was watching her closely as she tried to sew a tear in a shirt that Ma had set her to do. The stitches were clumsy and uneven and she spotted the shirt with blood from her pricked finger. She had to get out and meet Noah tonight. But how she was going to dodge Eldon's beady eyes and wary ears she didn't know.

The evening dragged on. Smoaker and Eldon's pipe smoke hung low under the kitchen beams. Ma dropped to sleeping in her chair and Smoaker and Eldon sat quietly – seemingly all out of pier talk – sipping pots of beer. The fire spat into the silence and Marnie let her sewing slip into her lap as she listened out for the church bells. Soon there came ten chimes and Smoaker drained his beer and yawned loudly. Ma stirred in her chair. She rubbed her eyes and grunted as she went to stand. 'Oh, my bones,' she grumbled. 'Smoaker. Get me up.' Smoaker took her by the arm and pulled the weight of her from the chair. He staggered backwards as Ma found her feet. 'Bleedin' hell, woman, we'd best tell the engineers to strengthen the braces on the pier if you're ever to walk on it!'

Ma slapped him playfully on the arm. 'Keep you warm enough at nights, don't I? Don't hear no complaints then.' They both laughed. 'You'll be to your bed now I expect, will you Eldon?' Ma said.

Eldon nodded. 'I will, I will. Just finish this bowl of baccy and I'll be away.' He winked at Marnie and she quickly bent her head as if she hadn't seen.

'Right. Snuff the candles out then, Marnie, and I bid you both goodnight,' said Ma. 'Come on, Smoaker. Help me up these stairs.' They left the room, teasing each other as they went. The kitchen fell silent again and Marnie tensed. She folded her sewing and put the needle and thread back in its tin. What was Eldon going to do? It was only a short while before she had to meet Noah. How was she going to get out this time?

'Fetch me another beer, will you, Marnie,' said Eldon easily. He pushed his chair back and stuck his booted feet upon the kitchen table.

Marnie glared at him.

'Remember. You promised to be nice to me,' he said.

'But I'd like to go to me bed too, Mr Cross,' said Marnie. Desperation crept through her and her voice quivered with it.

'Yes. Yes,' said Eldon. 'In a while. I won't keep you up too long. Don't you fret. Just fetch me a beer and sit with me a moment.'

Marnie limped slowly to the larder for the jug of beer. Time was passing and she was afraid she would never get out tonight.

Or maybe any other night now. Not if Eldon had his way. She picked up the jug and gathered some thick spit in her mouth. The whole lot went into the jug and she stirred it round into the golden liquid with her finger. Back in the kitchen, she filled Eldon's pot and watched with satisfaction as he poured a glug down his scrawny throat.

'You know your ma and pa trust me with you, don't you, Marnie? Well, I say your pa, but we both know he in't really.' He winked at her again and shifted his feet on the table. 'Be a good girl and undo me boots for me, would you?' He took another swallow of beer.

Marnie put the jug on the table and began to pick loose the knotted lace on one of his boots.

'Yes. I know Smoaker in't your pa. But I know your ma likes to think she's a decent woman. That's the truth, in't it? But they don't need to pretend they're all above board for my sake! It don't matter to me, does it? They've been good to me, your ma and Smoaker. I'm not going to hold a thing like that against them, am I? He paused and watched as Marnie pulled the laces of his boot open. 'Who was your pa anyway, Marnie? You ever ask your ma that?' He snorted dirtily, as though he had just said the funniest thing.

Marnie clenched her teeth and turned to his other boot. How dare he snigger like that; as though her pa was someone to be ashamed of. He wouldn't have his big, hoofin' feet on the table if her pa was here, that was for sure.

'Anyway,' Eldon continued, 'you wasn't planning on going out tonight, was you? Because I'll be listening out, you know.' He laughed to himself. 'I think I should like to settle in Clevedon,

Marnie. There's good folk around here and I'd find plenty of work with my skills. I can turn me hands to anything, you know.' He drained his pot and took a wet suck on his pipe. 'Yes, I think I should like it here.'

Marnie finished loosening his laces and went to sit back down. In the distance, the church bells chimed half past ten. Her thoughts raced. She would have to go soon if she was to meet Noah. And she *had* to meet him tonight and plead with him to do something about Eldon.

'Just a little kiss, Marnie.' Eldon was slurring his words. 'A goodnight peck on the cheek is all I ask.'

'I . . . I have to use the privy first,' Marnie stuttered. She casually picked up her stick from where it was resting by the side of the fire. She would just have to go. Straight now. She would have to try and get to the beach before Eldon realised she'd gone. She limped to the door as Eldon kicked his boots off.

'Don't be long now,' he called after her. 'I'll be waiting for me kiss.'

Marnie hurried as fast as she could out of the gate and along the lane. She slid down the grass embankment, not caring about the mud that striped her skirt and the backs of her legs. She reached the bottom too quickly and fell to her knees. As she stood up she felt a sting and the warm trickle of blood down her leg. *Move*, she told herself. Her ears strained for a sound of Eldon running along the lane to catch her. But all she could hear was the sea whispering to her. *Hurry, hurry, hurry.* She stumbled again and cried out in pain as her face struck the hard surface of the esplanade. Her stick skittered out of reach, so she crawled the few yards to get it and hauled herself back to standing. It wasn't far now. She could see the beach steps just ahead. If she could get off the esplanade and out of sight, she could hide behind a rock and wait for Noah. As she staggered down the steps she heard her name being called in the distance. It was him. It was Eldon! She skidded the rest of the way down the steps, but then she was there, on the beach ,and she quickly squeezed herself against the nearest rock, her heart banging and her breath ragged. She heard him running along the esplanade above and he called her name again, but the wind caught the sound and carried it out to the horizon where it was lost in the darkness.

She held her breath and pressed herself further behind the rock. She listened closely, and to her horror she heard the sound of someone coming down the steps; even, deliberate footsteps and then the noise of boots on shingle. The sound moved closer. Marnie held her breath, not daring to move an inch. A shadow moved in front of her. Marnie stared.

She saw at once it was Noah and she groaned out loud in relief. He turned towards the sound. 'Marnie?' he whispered. 'Is that you?'

Marnie stumbled out from behind the rock and fell into Noah's arms. 'Did you see him up there?' she gasped. 'Did you see him?'

Noah held her to him. 'See who?' he asked. 'Whatever is the matter?'

'Eldon Cross!' said Marnie. 'The man I told you about. He's followed me. He came after me. He won't leave me be.' She clung to Noah's arm.

'I saw no one,' said Noah. 'The place is empty. There is no one about, Marnie, only you and I.' He pulled her from him gently. 'Look at your face,' he said. 'What have you done? Did *he* do this to you?

Marnie shook her head. 'I fell,' she said. 'I took a tumble trying to get here to you.'

'Hush,' said Noah. 'Look.' He took a handkerchief from his pocket and carefully wiped at Marnie's cheek. 'It is only a graze,' he said. 'Does it hurt?'

'No,' said Marnie. 'Me knee is worse.' She leaned her back against the rock and lifted her skirt. 'Can you see?'

Noah hesitated before bending down. 'I cannot see very well,' he said, 'but I think you have cut it. There is a fair amount of blood on your leg. Wait here.' He headed towards the sea and Marnie watched the shape of him and the purposefulness of his walk.

She was safe now, Marnie realised. Noah was here and he would take care of her. And he would know how to deal with Eldon too. Marnie smiled, imagining how foolish Eldon must be feeling to have been so outwitted.

Noah came back with a wet handkerchief. 'It will sting,' he warned. 'But the saltwater will do it good.' He wiped at the gash on her knee and Marnie sucked in her breath as the salt mixed with her blood. Then Noah tied the handkerchief around the wound. 'That should do until you get home. Then you must get your mother to look at it. She will know better than I what to do, that is certain!'

'Ta for looking after me,' said Marnie.

'It is my pleasure,' said Noah. 'But you must tell me what

167

you mean to do about this Eldon Cross character. Surely your mother and Smoaker will help. They cannot wish you to be chased around the village by a mad man!'

'They won't care,' said Marnie miserably. 'They don't know I sneak out at night and they'll only think that Eldon is looking out for me. They'll most likely thank him for his trouble. They think he's me only chance of being wedded off, you see. Who else would want someone like me?'

'Don't say that, Marnie. There will be many men who will want to marry you. I promise. You are beautiful and brave and . . . and –' He stopped.

Marnie's heart tapped hard against her ribs. She could scarcely believe what she was hearing. If her knee wasn't throbbing so, she would have sworn she was dreaming.

'There must be something you can do,' Noah was saying.

'About what?' said Marnie. She wished the moon was brighter and she could look first into his grey eye and then into his blue eye.

'About Eldon Cross.' Noah ran a hand through his hair and kicked at the shingle.

'Oh,' said Marnie. She touched Noah on his arm. 'I was thinking you could speak to your father about him.'

Noah frowned. 'Why? What could he do?'

'He's having the pier built, isn't he? So he has a say who works on it?'

'I have no idea. He has invested a good deal of money in it. But I cannot say he is in charge of the workers.'

'Get him to put Eldon Cross off the pier. To put him out of work so he leaves here. Please, Noah! He'll do that for you, won't he?' Marnie tightened her grip on his arm.

Noah took her wrist and lifted her hand away. 'I don't know how I would do that, Marnie. How would I explain my reasons?'

'Tell him the truth. Tell him how he's been bothering me and you want it stopping.'

'But he doesn't know about you, Marnie. No one does. You know that.' Noah sighed. 'And besides, he is in London and won't be coming to Clevedon for some time.' He took her hand. 'Oh, Marnie,' he said gently. 'What am I going to do with you?'

Marnie didn't know how to answer him. He was looking at her so solemnly. She held on to his hand. It was warm and soft and he let her lace her fingers through his. She stared at his face. It was so perfect. So clean and bright and honest. She was bursting inside with a feeling she couldn't name. She'd never felt anything like it before, but somehow she knew it was the most important feeling in the world. It made everything else seem like nothing. Eldon Cross didn't matter, nor did Ma or Smoaker or Pa. Even the sea, waiting calmly behind, seemed to have lost its magic for now.

Noah came closer and Marnie felt his breath on her cheek, like a warm whisper. 'Oh, Marnie,' he murmured. He pulled her hand and suddenly she was against him, her breast against his. 'Do you mind if I hold you?' he asked. His voice sounded strange, almost nervous.

Marnie shook her head. 'I don't mind,' she whispered. He unwound his fingers from hers and slowly slid his hands around her waist. Marnie turned her head to one side and rested her cheek against his chest. The linen of his shirt was smooth and smelt of fresh sweat. A button from his jacket dug into her face, just below her eye. She didn't care. It was all she could ever have hoped for. Being held safe like this in someone's arms.

Noah pulled her closer. Marnie felt the firmness of his hands through the worn cotton of her frock and shift.

'Are you warm enough?' Noah whispered.

Marnie nodded against his chest. She didn't know what to do with her hands. They were dangling by her side, one still holding her stick. She closed her eyes and let the stick fall from her hand. Then as carefully as she could, she brought her arms around Noah and rested her hands on his back. The fabric of his jacket was stiff and thick and she wanted to press harder and feel the shape of him.

They stayed still and silent for a moment. Marnie listened to the fizzle of waves on shingle and prayed that time would stop.

Noah shifted his feet. 'Marnie?'

She took her head from his chest and looked up at him. He leaned down and his face became a blur as it came closer. Marnie tilted her head, not knowing quite what to do. Then Noah's breath was hot in her ear and his hands moved from her waist and pressed the back of her neck. 'Marnie,' he said again. 'I can't stop thinking about how beautiful you looked the other night.'

Marnie's throat tightened. She pressed her hands into Noah's back and he groaned into her neck. Another moment passed. Then Noah moved his head and gently pushed her away. 'Shall we go in the water?' he said in a low voice.

'You mean like . . . like before?' said Marnie.

'Yes. Like before.'

It was a dream, surely. The best dream she'd ever had. Marnie didn't want to talk any more. She didn't want to break the spell.

She bent down to loosen her laces and saw Noah was doing the same to his. She pushed off her boots and pulled her frock over her head. Noah had his jacket off and was unfastening his britches. Everything was happening so slowly. It was as though the world was holding its breath.

Marnie turned to face the sea then slid her drawers off and finally her shift. The night air tingled on her skin as it touched every part of her naked body. Then Noah was beside her and he took her hand and walked with her to the water's edge. They didn't speak or even look at each other. They simply inched their way into the waiting sea.

As the waves washed over them, Noah wrapped his arms around Marnie and brought her to him. She could feel the heat of him through the cold of the water and she let him steady her against the motion of the tide. There was an ache inside of her which she knew without doubt was for Noah. She knew she would gladly stay a cripple for ever if he would be with her like this for always.

Marnie pressed herself against Noah and felt her skin stick to his. Noah pushed his face into her hair and she felt his breath hot and hard against her neck. His hands slid down her back and over her behind. He squeezed at her flesh and she let her hands wander over his back and felt the satin of his white skin and the shape of his muscles.

Then Noah was carrying her back out of the water and he was panting like a dog. He lay her on the shingle and small sharp pebbles bit into her back and made her cry out. Then the weight of him was on her and the pain of the shingle numbed as another pain, much sharper and deeper, broke inside of her. 'Marnie. Oh, Marnie.' Noah was saying her name over and over again and the waves were lapping over their legs.

Don't let me wake, thought Marnie. Don't let me wake now and it all be a dream.

She stared up at the moon and it stared back at her for so long that she thought it couldn't be a dream. And her knee was still stinging, and the graze on her face. Then, when Noah stood up and helped her to her feet and brushed the shingle from her back and said he was sorry if it had hurt her, he was still there, as solid as anything. He didn't disappear and fade away into the night. She knew then, without doubt, that it was all real and true. The truest moment of her life.

Later, after they'd dressed and laced their boots back up, Noah said he was sorry again.

'What are you sorry for?' asked Marnie.

'I just am,' said Noah. 'I hope you'll forgive me.'

'There's nothing to forgive,' said Marnie. She wanted him to hold her again, but he seemed in a hurry.

'I must get back to the manor now,' he said. 'Will you go home now too?'

'Soon,' said Marnie. 'Will you come here again next Sunday?'

Noah smiled quickly and touched her shoulder. 'I will try,' he said. He picked up her stick and handed it to her. 'Get home safely,' he said. Then he hurried up the beach steps and was gone.

Marnie sat on the shingle with her knees tucked under her chin. She stroked the handkerchief that Noah had tied around her leg and watched the sky until a pale pink streak appeared on the horizon and her hair had dried in stiff clumps. 'He loves me, doesn't he, Pa?' she said. 'What we just did. It means Noah loves me.' She could still feel the ache of him between her legs. 'Fancy that, Pa,' she said. 'A true gentlemen he is and all.'

It was going to be a long wait till next Sunday. Marnie wasn't sure how she'd get through the days. Maybe she'd call on Noah at the manor if she got the chance. He'd be glad to see her and it would show him how much she cared. Marnie pinched her arm hard. She still couldn't quite believe it.

39

A Lying Little Tart

The sky began to lighten and Marnie yawned. She knew she should make her way back to the cottage now. She heaved herself to standing, her knee stiff and sore now. Then suddenly she remembered Eldon Cross. A deep frown creased her face. As she walked slowly back across the beach and up the steps, she thought hard. There had to be a way of dealing with him. All the way back along the esplanade she thought and thought. By the time she got back to Ratcatcher's Row, she knew exactly what to do.

Marnie opened the cottage door and let the latch clunk loudly back into place. Through the first gauzy light of morning, she saw Eldon Cross start awake in the chair where he was sitting, waiting for her. She walked over and stood in front of him, letting her stick fall to the floor with a clatter.

'Marnie?' he growled sleepily.

Suddenly, Marnie threw herself to the floor. 'Ma!' she screamed. 'Ma! Get him off me!' Eldon Cross jumped from his chair. 'What are you doing?' he shouted. 'Stop it!'

'Ma! Ma! Ma!' Marnie screamed until her throat hurt.

There was a bang from above, then the thud of hurried footsteps coming down the stairs. The door crashed open and Smoaker flew into the kitchen, his shirt tails flapping round his knees. 'I done nothing, Smoaker! I done nothing!' yelled Eldon Cross, dancing around Marnie as she lay, whimpering now, on the floor. There were more thuds and Ma appeared in the doorway clutching a shawl to her throat.

'Whatever's the matter? Marnie? Smoaker? What the Devil's going on?'

'He tried to touch me, Ma!' Marnie screeched. 'He . . . he hit me and tried to touch me!'

'I never!' shouted Eldon Cross. 'I didn't go near her, Smoaker. I swear I didn't go near her! You lying little cow!'

Ma bent over Marnie and tried to lift her from the floor. 'Come on and get up from there now. And hush that noise.' Marnie turned her head to make sure Ma got a good look at the graze she'd got on her cheek from earlier. It was hard not to laugh seeing the looks on their faces.

Ma gasped. 'Smoaker! He's bashed her face. Look. See?' She twisted Marnie's head so Smoaker could see her cheek.

'Wasn't me!' bleated Eldon Cross. 'I been here all the time. She went out, she did. She went out!'

But it was too late. Smoaker was across the room and his fat fist crunched into Eldon Cross's face. Ma pulled Marnie out of the way as Eldon crashed to the floor. The room went still for a moment as Smoaker hovered, fists clenched, and Eldon lay unmoving. Marnie's heart was bubbling fast, like a

175

pan of milk coming to the boil; a few plain words and she'd made all this happen!

Then Eldon groaned and lifted his head from the floor. Blood, glistening and thick as bramble jelly, seeped from his nostrils. 'You get out of here now,' Smoaker demanded. 'Fetch your things and clear off!'

Eldon put his fingers to his nose and smeared the stickiness across his face as he felt for damage. 'She's a lying little tart, Smoaker. I never went near her.' He groaned as he stood up. 'You ask her where she goes at night. See what she says then.' He turned his head and stared down at Marnie. 'Why would I lower meself to touch a cripple? A whoring cripple at that.'

Ma sat heavily in her chair and Marnie crawled to her and pushed her face into the lap of Ma's worn cotton nightgown. 'Don't let him touch me again, Ma,' she said, making her voice tremble. 'He scares me, Ma. He scares me.'

Ma put a hesitant hand on her shoulder. 'You leave us now, Mr Cross,' she said. 'Don't go saying any more. Just go.'

Eldon Cross lurched towards the bedchamber. 'Don't bleedin' worry. I'm off. But don't think you've heard the last of this.'

Marnie kept her head buried in Ma's lap and listened to Eldon's banging and crashing in the bedchamber. Nep padded into the kitchen, mewling loudly. But no one else moved or said a word. Pushed into Ma's nightgown, Marnie's face grew hot and her cheek began to sting. The musty scent of Ma's sweat filled her head and for a moment Marnie was five years old again, with no idea of what the world had in store for her. She wished she could fall asleep and not wake again till it was all over.

Then she heard Eldon's voice again, muffled through the depths of Ma's lap. 'I'll have you off the pier for this, Smoaker. See if I don't. And as for her . . . she needs locking in the madhouse!' The kitchen door rattled on its hinges as Eldon slammed out.

Marnie could hardly believe it. She smiled into Ma's nightgown.

'Right, my girl.' Ma shifted her legs. 'You'd better get up and explain yourself.'

Marnie sat up slowly and put her hand to her cheek. 'He hit me, Ma, I told you.' Marnie kept her voice small. 'He . . . he tried to kiss me. And . . . and other things. I didn't want to do them, Ma. I told you I don't like him. I told you!'

Ma got up from her chair and adjusted her shawl. A thin wheeze escaped from her chest on every out breath. She walked over to Smoaker and stood next to him with her arms crossed under her bosom. Smoaker rubbed at his knuckles and scowled at Marnie. 'There's no truth in what he said, is there? That you been going out at nights?'

Marnie shook her head.

'You haven't been going down to them workers' huts, have you?' Smoaker took a deep breath. 'Whoring yourself?'

'No! No! I swear!' Marnie squeezed a tear from her eye.

'Well, there's plenty round here that would,' said Smoaker, 'and a few that does.'

'But not me!' said Marnie. 'How could you think that of me?'

In the sickly half-light of early morning, Marnie saw Smoaker's face darken under his grey whiskers. There was a long silence.

'No point in going back to bed,' he said eventually. 'How about some tea?' He took his pipe from the mantelpiece and sat in his chair.

'I thought he was such a decent man,' said Ma. 'Can't understand why he'd do such a thing.' She stomped to the fireplace and shoved the poker angrily into the dead ashes. 'We've lost the rent too now,' she grumbled. 'That's the worst of it.'

'I'll set the fire, shall I?' asked Marnie tentatively.

As she pottered around, putting her bedding away, fetching kindling and filling the kettle, Marnie tried not to smile. She wanted to rush straight out, up to the manor and tell Noah what she'd done. It'd been the simplest of things. And she'd done it for him. After what had just happened on the beach, she couldn't have another man paying her attentions. She'd had to get rid of Eldon straight away. And now Noah wouldn't have to ask his father for help. He hadn't seemed too keen to do that anyway. Sir John de Clevedon was a busy man, after all.

It was a good thing that she'd done. Goodness knows Eldon had been ready to jump on her to claim a kiss. And that wasn't right.

She was Noah's for good now. And that was that.

40

The Journal of Noah de Clevedon

Clevedon. NOVEMBER 1st 1868, Sunday (one o'clock in the morning)

I am no longer an innocent. I don't know whether to feel ashamed of myself or exhilarated. Arnold would laugh at me if he knew how confused I am. 'Come, man,' he would say. 'You have to be broken in sometime.'

It was not a perfect set of circumstances, I will admit. A pebbled beach is not the most comfortable of places. But Marnie was so willing and so encouraging. She lit such a fire inside of me, I'm afraid I was perhaps too hurried with her. I have to say, though, I would be surprised if she was as new to it all as me.

But it is done now, and finally I am a real man. And at least now I will have some experience to offer on my wedding night. Arnold has always said that it is best the first time is with a harlot or a girl from the lower classes.

I feel guilty that I did not tell Marnie of our impending departure, but last night we had other things on our minds. I will go to her one last time and let her know. She will be happy for me, I am sure.

I cannot believe I will be seeing Arnold soon. It is only a matter of days now before we travel back to London. And Cissie Baird. How good it will be to see her again.

41

The Last Kiss

Marnie put her hand to her belly. It was a week now since Noah had shown his love for her. Marnie knew that what they'd done was how babies were made and she was certain they had made one that night. She could feel it in her blood. Every day she'd been desperate to go up to the manor to see Noah. She wanted him to know how happy she was, and to tell him that if a baby was coming they'd best get married as soon as possible.

But after Eldon Cross had left, Ma had kept her so busy there hadn't been a chance. All week she'd worked Marnie's fingers to the bone, like she was punishing her for something she wouldn't say. Marnie had scrubbed and pummelled and pressed a mountain of linen. She'd fetched countless buckets of water from the pump and she'd cleaned and aired Eldon's bedchamber to rid it of his sour smell. She was back in there at nights now, with Ma's brooding bulk beside her.

Ma wouldn't shut up about Eldon. All week she'd been going

on. 'You lost out there, my girl,' she said. 'We can't afford to keep you for ever. You'd have done all right with Eldon. He'd have kept you well enough. Who else is going to want you?'

Marnie had kept quiet all week. She wanted to give Noah a chance to tell his father about her. She wanted to wait for Noah to come to the cottage for her. She wanted to see Ma and Smoaker's faces when they found out her suitor was the son of Sir John de Clevedon, no less. It would be a sight worth waiting for.

But Ma wouldn't let up. At supper that night, she was at it again. 'If only you'd been nicer to Eldon. If you hadn't led him on. A man can only be teased so far, you know. You'll regret this, my girl, you mark my words. When no one else wants you and you end up an old maid, you'll wish to God you'd been nicer to that poor man.'

Marnie couldn't hold it in any longer. The secret bubbled up inside her and came spitting out along with the bacon broth she was trying to swallow. 'Shut up, Ma!' she shouted.

Ma's spoon clattered to the table.

'Someone else does want me!' Marnie wiped the broth from her chin with the back of her hand.

Ma's mouth dropped open. 'What do you mean, *someone else wants you?*'

'Noah de Clevedon,' Marnie said carefully. 'Noah de Clevedon's in love with me and is sure to be asking me to marry him soon.'

Ma stared at her for a moment. She looked across the table at Smoaker and raised her eyebrows. 'Hear that, Smoaker? Our Marnie's got herself a gentleman suitor.'

'Oh aye,' said Smoaker. 'I heard well enough.'

'Noah de Clevedon you say, eh? Well, I beg your pardon, my lady. You have done all right for yourself then.'

'You'd best go and buy yourself a new bonnet,' said Smoaker. 'If we've a wedding to go to.'

Marnie looked at Smoaker, then at Ma. They were smirking and winking at each other.

'It's true,' she shouted. 'Me and Noah love each other!'

A laugh burst out of Ma's mouth and Smoaker smiled broadly.

'You don't believe me, do you?' said Marnie. 'Why don't you believe me?'

But Ma only laughed louder. 'I always thought you were barmy, my girl, and you've gone and proved it now. Oh ,Smoaker,' she gasped between laughs. 'She's going to end up in the madhouse for sure!'

Marnie pushed herself to standing. 'Don't laugh at me,' she said. She was angry now. Her ears were pounding. 'It's all true. And soon you'll know it. You won't be laughing when I'm living up at the manor and you're still scratching around down here!'

Ma wiped tears from her eyes. She took a deep breath. 'Now, my girl,' she said. 'You've got to stop saying such things. It'll get you into trouble if you're not careful. People round here already think you're not right in the head. Why can't you just act ordinary, like the rest of us?'

Marnie shoved her chair back and walked clumsily to the fireplace. She grabbed her stick and made for the door. 'I'll show you,' she said as she left the cottage. 'Just you wait. You won't be laughing at me for long.'

***

Marnie was out of breath by the time she reached the esplanade. 'Why won't they believe me, Pa?' she kept asking. '*You* know it's true, don't you?' She ignored the stares of passers-by and the taunts of a straggle of children who ran after her shouting,

'Marnie Gunn, Marnie Gunn
Where's her brain?
She hasn't one!'

Then Mistress Miles walked by and touched Marnie on the arm and asked, 'Are you all right?'

'I'm fine,' spat Marnie. 'Just leave me alone, you old cow!'

Mistress Miles's hand fluttered to her mouth and she gave a little squeak before hurrying off.

The church bells chimed six. It would be hours yet before Noah came to the beach. But Marnie didn't care. She would wait as long as she had to. At least it was dusk now and the village was emptying.

No one bothered Marnie as she huddled against the railings, watching the workers on the beach put their tools away and march up the slipway to their lodgings. She watched as those left on the beach lit lamps and set small fires to burn outside their huts. The smells of charred wood and fish skin blistered in flames drifted up to her and made her belly growl.

The sky darkened to charcoal and the movements on the beach slowed until all was still except for the shifting embers of dying fires and the flickering of the lamp in the night watchman's hut.

Marnie stretched her arms and pulled herself to standing. Her whole body ached, but more for Noah than it did from

184

the pain of her leg, which was stiff and sore from sitting for so long. It must be soon now. She'd counted the church bells as they'd struck seven, eight, nine and then ten times. She walked awkwardly. A few steps along the esplanade and a few steps back, to get the blood flowing in her legs. She rubbed at her arms and pinched her cheeks and stared as far as she could see in the darkness towards the road up to the manor.

Marnie had no doubt that Noah would come. She just had to wait, that was all.

His face was a splash of white in the distance when she first saw him. She watched as he came closer and the outline of him became clearer. Her anger at Ma and Smoaker melted away and she wished she could run to Noah. She wanted to fly the distance between them and feel the realness and warmth of him.

He wasn't hurrying, though. He had his hands in his pockets and he was strolling for all the world like it was a sunny afternoon. Marnie wanted to shout his name out loud; to make sure he'd seen her waiting there for him. But she bit her tongue and tapped her foot impatiently on the ground.

As he neared her, she raised her hand and waved at him. Her heart was beating so fast she felt bruised with the pain of it. 'Hello, Marnie,' he said.

'Noah,' she breathed. She felt suddenly shy. The memory of what they'd done the week before pounded low down in her belly and burned in her private place.

'Are you well?' he asked her.

Marnie nodded.

'Good,' he said. He looked around, then yawned into the back of his hand.

'Are . . . are you well?' Marnie asked.

'Very well,' said Noah. 'Yes, thank you.'

He hadn't looked at her properly yet. And he seemed ill at ease somehow. Perhaps he would be better on the beach, where there were no eyes to spy them.

'Shall we go for a swim?' Marnie asked brightly.

'No . . . no,' said Noah. 'I . . . I did not mean to swim tonight. I came to tell you some news.'

Marnie waited, her heart fat with expectation. Had he told his father about her? Was it good news?

Noah hesitated. He reached out for Marnie's hand and when he took it she was so thankful she gasped.

'Mother and I are going back to London,' said Noah. 'That is what I came to tell you.'

Noah's fingers squeezed kindly around her hand. They were so cold. She wanted to lift them to her mouth and warm them with her breath. 'Did you hear me, Marnie?' he said.

Marnie had heard, but it was as though everything had stopped: her heart, her breath, the winds, the tide. It all stood still and waiting, like frightened deer in a forest. Then in a rush, a wave broke on the shingle and Marnie caught her breath. 'To . . . to London?' she whispered.

'Yes,' said Noah. 'We leave on Tuesday.'

'For ever?' The word slid slowly and timidly out of Marnie's mouth.

'No. Not for ever,' Noah said. 'We will be back at Easter for the opening of the pier.'

'Easter?' Marnie's voice cracked. 'That's for ever.'

'Your fingernails,' said Noah. 'They are digging into my hand.'

Marnie pulled her hand away and let her arms drop to her side. 'Sorry,' she whispered. An ache was growing behind her eyes, a tide of tears threatening to spill. She couldn't look at Noah or speak.

There was a long silence. Another wave broke lazily on the shingle. 'I have to go,' said Noah. 'I have to get back to the manor now.' Still Marnie couldn't look at him. She swallowed the hard lump in her throat.

'What about me?' she managed to say as she stared down at her sand-scuffed boots.

'You?' said Noah. 'You will be fine, Marnie. Listen. We are still friends, aren't we?'

Marnie nodded. They were more than friends, weren't they?

'You will come back?'

'I told you,' said Noah, his voice growing lighter. 'I will be back at Easter. It is not so far away. Then we can celebrate the new pier! I will meet you here on the beach, the first night I am back!'

Marnie rubbed at her nose with the back of her hand. Still she couldn't look at him. Her jaw and eyes throbbed with the effort of keeping her tears at bay. Suddenly Noah leaned towards her and cupped the side of her face in his hand. Marnie blinked hard. Then she felt something soft and warm on her clamped lips. It was light and fleeting and as quickly as it had come, it was gone. Marnie put her fingers to her lips.

'Goodbye, Marnie Gunn,' said Noah. 'Don't forget to wait for me on the beach.'

Then he was gone. Before she'd even had a chance to tell him there might be a baby in her belly. He was away, across the shingle and back up the beach steps to the esplanade. Marnie stood with her fingers still pressed to her lips. She thought if she moved her hand, the kiss would disappear and she'd have nothing at all left of him.

She walked awkwardly and stiffly towards the sea, her fingers still pressed to her mouth. Her chest hurt. A deep pain twisted around and pulled at her heart. When she reached the water's edge she let the incoming waves slosh over her boots as she stared far out to where the stars dropped from the sky. Her fingers fell from her mouth. 'I wish you was here, Pa,' she whispered. 'I need you to tell me what to do.'

She put her stick down on the shingle and slowly undressed. First her boots, then her frock, then her shift and lastly her drawers. She dropped the clothes next to her stick and walked without thought into the sea. When she'd gone far enough out, she lifted her feet and began to swim. It was only then that she let the tears come. Hot, painful tears that burned her eyes and made her wail like a stricken cat. She plunged her head under the water and let the salt of her tears mingle with the salt of the sea, until she couldn't tell which was which.

42

The Journal of Noah de Clevedon

Clevedon. NOVEMBER 9th 1868, Monday

Today was our final day in Clevedon. The weather was crisp and clear with the last golden leaves of the season still clinging to their branches. Mother fancied taking the air, so we took the carriage down to the village (the footmen following behind with Mother's Bath chair). Clarissa and I took turns in pushing Mother along the esplanade. It is the first time Mother has seen the pier works, so we stood awhile and watched the swarm of workers go about their business. The harsh ring of iron on iron and the constant hiss of the steam-crane soon gave Mother one of her heads, but not before she had fully admired the magnificent spectacle.

I was glad not to come across Marnie during the outing. It was awkward last night on the beach. When I told her of our impending departure she seemed quite distressed. I do hope she hasn't developed feelings for me, poor girl. Maybe I have been unkind and foolish in encouraging our friendship to such a degree.

But she seemed as willing as I, and surely she knows that a friendship between someone of her class and someone of mine can only ever be fleeting? Still, I feel quite wistful for our time together. I will never know another like her, I am certain.

But what is done is done. I was as gentle as I could be. I can only wish her well and remember her fondly. She will have forgotten all about me by Easter, I am sure.

But to now. My trunk is packed. One more night in this bed, then to London tomorrow. I am giddy with excitement.

43

The Handkerchief

Tuesday morning dawned grey and cold. Marnie lay in bed with Ma snoring noisily beside her. There was only one thought in her head. Noah was leaving today.

Marnie was numb with the shock of it. All day yesterday Ma had kept asking, 'You ailing, girl?'

'What do you care?' Marnie had replied as she folded newly pressed shirts into piles on the kitchen table.

'Suit yourself,' said Ma. 'But don't think I haven't noticed you haven't been right since Eldon left. You're pining, if you ask me.'

Marnie ignored her. There was no point in telling her otherwise. Ma could believe what she wanted.

All night Marnie had lain awake. Going over and over in her head the last minutes with Noah. He'd kissed her, at least. She held on to that, closing her eyes and reliving the touch of his lips on hers. She hadn't slept a wink. But she knew what to do now. She was going to the manor to see him before he left for London. She had to tell him about the baby. And she had to tell him how much she loved him.

Ma barely stirred. But Marnie wouldn't have cared if she had. Nothing was going to stop her seeing Noah.

Outside, the early-morning sky hung low and damp. The workers on the beach were already up. Smoke and steam mingled with the sea mist and the clanking of tools echoed across the esplanade. Marnie passed by it all, her eyes fixed on the road up to the manor. She felt strong that morning, and she pushed herself along on her stick with ease. All the way up the road she pictured Noah's face; the shock, the surprise and hopefully the pleasure when she told him she thought she was with child. 'And don't you forget, Pa,' she said. 'You'll be a grandpa too!'

Up ahead there was a distant rumble. Then the unmistakeable sound of hooves on stone and the creaking of leather on wood. Marnie heard the horses snorting before they rounded the corner. Then with a rush of dust and air and heat she was thrown into the hedge as four black horses and a carriage thundered past.

By the time she'd pulled herself back to standing, the carriage was a smudge of gold in the distance. 'No!' she screamed. 'Noah! Noah!' She shouted his name over and over. Was it too late? Had she missed him?

It couldn't be.

Not caring about the mud on her frock and the pieces of twig and dried leaves in her hair, Marnie hurried on up to the manor. By the time she reached the long driveway, her face was sticky with sweat and her lungs ached. She leaned against the iron gates and tried to catch her breath. She closed her eyes and let the hammering of her heart slow to a steady beat.

'You're the girl from the village, aren't you?' The voice came from behind. Marnie opened her eyes and turned her head to see the maid, Hetty, walking towards her with her basket over her arm. 'You've been begging here before. I remember you from the kitchen. With Master Noah.' She looked Marnie up and down, challenging her with her eyes.

'I wasn't begging,' said Marnie. 'Me and Noah . . . we're . . . me and Noah are friends.'

Hetty snorted. 'I've heard about you,' she said. 'They say down in the village you're a bit queer in the head. Always talking to yourself. You let a boy drown too, didn't you?'

'That's what they think,' said Marnie. 'But I don't care what anyone thinks.'

'So did you?' asked Hetty, her eyes growing wide. 'Did you drown him?'

'No,' said Marnie. 'But you can think what you like too.'

Hetty stiffened and set her shoulders. 'Well, you'd best get away from here anyhow. You're trespassing, you know.'

'I'm not trespassing. I'm visiting,' said Marnie. 'I've come to see Noah.'

'Thought you said you were friends with him?' Hetty cocked her head, a glint in her eye.

'We are,' said Marnie.

'Not very good friends, if you ask me. If he didn't tell you he was going to London.'

'He did tell me. I know he's going to London with Lady de Clevedon. And I know they're coming back at Easter. I just hoped . . . I just hoped to catch him before he left.'

Hetty raised her eyebrows in surprise. 'Well, everyone knows *that*,' she said. 'Doesn't mean you're *friends*. And in any case, you're too late.'

Marnie groaned and closed her eyes again. A crushing disappointment made her sink to the ground. What was she going to do now?

'You can't stay there,' said Hetty. 'What's the matter with you? Get up! Mr Todd'll have your guts for garters.'

It was so unfair. Marnie thumped her fists on the ground. If only she'd come a bit earlier. Just five more minutes and she would have been in time. Now Noah would be in London for all those months without knowing how much she loved him and without knowing about the baby inside her.

'Get up!' Hetty was saying. 'I'm going to fetch Mr Todd if you don't get up now!'

Marnie looked up at her. 'Mr Todd? The butler? He's an old man, isn't he? Noah told me all about him. Calls him the Toad, doesn't he? Fetch him if you like.'

Shock flickered across Hetty's face. 'How . . . how do you know all that?'

'I told you,' Marnie said, pushing herself to standing. 'Me and Noah are friends. *More* than friends.'

Hetty's mouth gaped, like a fish on a slab.

Marnie looked at her hard. 'I'm telling the truth, you know. But you can believe what you like.' She turned and limped slowly out of the gateway.

'Don't come back,' Hetty shouted after her. There's a few of us staying on here till Easter, to keep the place going. So don't think you can sneak back!'

Marnie didn't answer. She was picturing Noah on the road, swaying from side to side in the carriage. Being pulled through the day and night by flagging horses. She had no idea how long it took to get to London. When he got there would he sit down to dinner with Sir John de Clevedon and his fancy friends? Would he go to the theatre, perhaps?

Would he be thinking of her? Would he be missing her? Would his heart be hurting as much as hers was now?

Later that evening, with the day's work done, Marnie lay on her bed and let the stillness of the hour settle around her. She listened out for the rhythmic whisper of the sea. The sound that had kept her safe her whole life, the sound she had always drifted to sleep to. But tonight sleep wouldn't come.

A murmur of voices drifted down from the upstairs bedchamber. Marnie listened half-heartedly, not caring what was being said. The voices rumbled on and Marnie let the sound lull her to another place; to a summer day when the waves were rolling gently on to the beach and she and Noah were sitting on the shingle watching a green fishing boat catch the breeze in its white sails. 'There's me pa,' said Marnie excitedly, pointing at the yellow-bearded fisherman who was waving at them from the boat. Noah took her hand and squeezed it tight. Seagulls were wheeling overhead, shouting and screeching in delight.

Then the shouts from upstairs grew louder and Smoaker's voice came strong and clear and pushed the images from Marnie's head.

'I've been shamed!' he shouted. 'I'm a laughing stock on

that pier. Word is we're running a whorehouse here!'

'Well, I hope you put them straight!' Ma's shrill voice pierced through the thin ceiling. 'She wouldn't know what to do with a man if a knife was put to her throat!'

'That man has set tongues wagging,' bawled Smoaker. 'I'm telling you. And the girl is naught but trouble! I've had enough of it. I'm warning you, you'd best see to it that you keep a close eye on her from now on!'

Ma mumbled something back that Marnie couldn't quite catch. A door slammed and Marnie heard the unmistakeable thudding of Ma coming down the stairs. 'Shift over,' she ordered as she strode into the bedchamber. Marnie slid over to the other side of the bed, leaving behind the warm spot she had made. Ma climbed in, grumbling and fidgeting until she'd got herself comfy.

'What's going on?' Marnie whispered.

'You might well ask,' said Ma. 'We've lost Eldon and his money and now he's spreading gossip. Smoaker's off his head with fury and you . . . ? Well, you've gone and got yourself a whole new livelihood as a whore. So it seems!' Ma huffed and turned on her side with her back to Marnie.

'You know it's not true, don't you, Ma?' protested Marnie.

Ma had taken most of the blanket with her and when she shrugged her reply, the last corner slipped off Marnie's legs. 'Don't stop Smoaker from having to deal with all the talk though, does it?' she said.

'But I've done nothing wrong!'

'Maybe so,' said Ma. 'But it don't make life any easier for us. You do nothing but bring trouble to our door, Marnie Gunn.'

'But Ma . . . !'

'But nothing!' snapped Ma. 'Go to sleep.'

Marnie opened her mouth to speak. Then shut it again. What was the point? She didn't care what they all thought. She was glad Eldon had gone. He could get washed off the pier and drowned out to sea for all she cared. She only wanted to get through the next months as swiftly as possible. She would keep busy: washing soiled linen till her hands were raw, she would press it smooth till the muscles in her arms ached and she would keep quiet. She would go about her work without a fuss and the rest of the world could do as it liked. She pulled at the blanket and secured the edge of it from Ma's fast-fading grip. Ma's breathing rattled its way into sleep and Marnie lay still, waiting for the heat of Ma's bulk to creep its way over to her side of the bed.

The following morning, on her way to the water pump, Marnie stopped in the backyard and moved the old firebrick that hid her lost treasures. She picked them up, one by one, and turned them over in her hand: a scrap of scarlet ribbon, a broken comb, a mother-of-pearl button and a torn lace handkerchief. They were useless things really. Lost things and no good to anyone any more. Marnie gathered them all in her hands and in one swift movement she flung them over the back wall into the scrub and tangle of grass and weeds. She didn't need them now. She had something to replace them with. Something much better. From the pocket of her frock she took out the handkerchief that Noah had tied around her knee. She'd washed the blood off, after dabbing at it first with milk, then she'd pressed it carefully, folded it and hidden it in her pocket. She looked at it now, and spread it out across her hand. It was made of the finest cotton and Noah's initials were embroidered in one corner. She brought it to her mouth and kissed the letters gently before hiding it away under the brick.

She could wait for him. She knew that now. She had no choice. But at least she had a piece of him. With the handkerchief and the baby in her belly, she had real treasures to look after now.

44

A Bone Hairbrush

Marnie was used to her monthly courses. They had been coming since she was thirteen. So she wasn't surprised at first when, a week after Noah's departure, she started to bleed. She tore up some rags as usual, to pad herself with, and began to sort through the pile of dirty linen Ma had dumped on the kitchen table.

Marnie was thinking of Noah, as she did every minute of every day. She was thinking of the odd colours of his eyes, the pale mole under his eyebrow, the set of his shoulders, the white of his skin, the birthmark on his hip and the clean, soft brown of his hair. But try as she might she couldn't picture the whole of him at once. She envied those lovers, the gentry mostly, who kept miniature portraits of their loved ones in silver lockets around their necks.

Her lower belly ached, as it always did on the first day of her courses. She rubbed at it with her hand. Then a terrible thought struck her and she let the shirt she was holding drop on to the kitchen floor. What if her bleeding meant there wasn't a baby? What if this was the baby's blood now, creeping out of her so slowly? She wasn't sure how it all worked and there was no one she could ask.

'Marnie!' Ma yelled at her. 'Stop daydreaming, girl, and get on with sorting that washing.'

Marnie looked across at Ma, huffing and puffing over the dolly-tub. She couldn't ask her, that was for sure. Ma would think she was imagining being with child and would have her in the madhouse for certain.

She would just wait, Marnie decided. She was getting good at that. Soon her belly would start growing and the truth of it would be there for all the world to see.

When Ma had finished with her for the day, Marnie wandered up the road to the manor and stood outside the iron gates. It made her feel closer to Noah somehow and made her feel special to know she'd been inside, that she'd been *invited* inside the grandest house for miles around. If truth be told, she was also checking that Noah hadn't unexpectedly returned. But the upstairs windows were shuttered, the driveway was thick with unswept leaves and, though the maid Hetty had said a few servants would be staying on at the manor, the whole place had a look of sleep about it. Marnie wanted to knock at the door and ask for Hetty. What if she had news of Noah? Even if not, she was someone Marnie could talk to about him. She knew Noah's habits; she cleaned his bedchamber, served his meals, even washed his soiled linen. Being close to Hetty would be a way of keeping close to Noah.

Marnie walked up the driveway, expecting any minute for someone to appear and warn her off. But except for the crunch of leaves under her feet and the dull tap of her stick, there was silence. She walked by the Grand door and a shiver ran through her. Once Noah was back and she told him about the baby, he'd be sure to marry her as soon as possible. Then she'd belong *here*. She'd use the Grand door like a proper lady and everyone down in the village would treat her like she deserved to be treated. There's be no more taunts, no more whispers, no more running away from her. She'd be proud then to walk through the village any time she liked. And Pa would be sure to come back too. He would never want to miss her wedding.

There was still not a soul to be seen as Marnie walked around the side of the manor to the servants' door. If she didn't know better she would swear the whole place was empty. But as she reached the door, she saw it was half open. She stopped. Should she knock? Would Hetty be kind to her? Or would she throw her off the grounds like she'd threatened to do the last time?

The open door was tempting. Marnie pushed at it gently and it swung full open without a squeak. She recognised the passageway inside. The screens passage, Noah had called it. It was as dark inside as it had been the first night Noah had brought her here. Only the light from the open door crept across the threshold. Marnie stepped inside. She listened carefully. There were voices, she was sure of it. But they sounded a long way off. She inched forwards.

She walked past doors on both sides of the passage. There was the one to the Great Hall, she was sure of it. And there was the door to the kitchen. The voices sounded louder now.

If it was Hetty and some of the other servants, they were there in the kitchen. No doubt enjoying the freedom while their masters were away. Marnie walked quickly by. Hetty could wait. She had something else in mind now.

When she reached the end of the passage, there was another door. She carefully opened it and peeped inside. It was the hallway, with the great sweeping staircase that she and Noah had slid down. Marnie smiled at the memory. It was quiet and hushed with only the sound of her shallow breaths moving the air around her. Marnie began to climb the stairs, remembering the softness of the carpet as her stick sank into each step. Up she went, marvelling again at the richness of the paper on the walls and the faces of Noah's relatives peering out at her from their heavy frames. It was hard to believe they would soon be her people too. Maybe one day a painting of her would be on these walls. Smiling down for all the world to see.

Marnie reached the landing and stood awhile to ease the ache in her leg and to listen for any sign of movement. There was nothing. Her body relaxed. She felt safe up here, with the servants away far below. She just had to find Noah's bedchamber now.

There were doors stretching away down the corridor on either side of the staircase. Marnie wasn't sure which way to try first. Left or right? Left or right? After a moment's hesitation, she let her good leg lead the way and turned to her left. The first door whined as she opened it, the sound loud in the still of the corridor. Marnie held her breath. She let it out again. No one had heard. She stepped inside the room and narrowed her eyes to see through the gloom. Large shapes were covered by sheets and there was the heavy scent of roses in the air. Marnie

202

knew at once it couldn't be Noah's room. It didn't smell like him. But just to be sure, she moved across the room to where a heavy pair of curtains were drawn tight over the windows. She stepped behind them and saw at once that this room looked out over the back of the manor. Over a sweeping lawn and flower beds and a wooded copse at the top. With a sigh she realised she'd chosen the wrong direction down the corridor.

With a growing sense of boldness, Marnie stepped back outside the room and turned to her right. *'Which room? Which room?'* she murmured to herself. She let her fingers play over the ancient wooden handles of the first two doors. Then, knowing that Noah's bedchamber window was in the centre of the top floor, she chose the third handle to eventually turn. There was no scent of roses in this room, just a pleasant muskiness of old ashes and candlewax. She went straight to the window, just to be sure. As she pulled aside the curtain, she knew with a leap of her heart that she had chosen correctly this time. She was looking out high over the village, at the rooftops, chimneys, tiny winding lanes and the mess of the pier works. And there, behind it all, spread out before her, was the ocean. She had never seen so much of it before; she had never realised how enormous it was. Or how very beautiful.

Noah had been right. He had the best view of the whole manor. Marnie felt a stab of envy. How lucky he was to wake to this every morning. Why would he wish to go back to London when he had this glorious sight to look upon every day? It was like the best painting Marnie could ever imagine. Perhaps though, she dared to think, once they were married they could keep this room and she too could look out upon all of this every morning and every night.

She turned from the window and looked at the dust sheets draped across the furniture. She went to the bed first and pulled back the heavy sheet that covered it. Her nose itched at the cloud of dust that rose in the air. Underneath, the bed was still made up. Marnie wondered if the bedding had been washed since Noah last slept there. She lifted the covers, then, resting her stick against the bedstead, climbed on to the mattress and lay down. It was so soft and the pillows were so high and so white. She turned and pressed her face into the smooth linen. Could she still smell him there? She sniffed deeply and was sure that in the depths of the pillow there was a trace of his sweat and saltiness. She lay still. Being there, so close to him, was almost as good as having his arms around her.

She lay there for a while, savouring the quiet, the scents and the luxury of it all. Her eyes closed and she drifted. She was safe and warm. She was where she belonged.

With a start, Marnie opened her eyes. The pillow was damp on her cheek and her neck a little stiff. How long had she been there? With a yawn, she quickly climbed out of the bed, straightened the covers and replaced the dust sheet. It seemed gloomier in the room now, the light a silver grey. She took up her stick and readied herself to leave. But as she walked by another sheeted object, she couldn't help but take a peek. It was a washstand, and lying by the jug and bowl was a hairbrush. Noah's hairbrush. Marnie picked it up. It was heavy, made of fine bone and stiff bristles. Marnie held it in her hand as Noah might have held it in his. Then she saw that tangled around the bristles there were pale brown hairs; a small handful at least. She pulled at them and eased them away. They were soft and clean. She wrapped the hairs around her fingers to make a small bundle, and tucked it safe in her pocket. She sighed with satisfaction.

It was harder to climb down the stairs than it had been going up. Marnie had to lean all her weight on her stick and take care not to slip. But she arrived in the hallway safely and took a moment to listen out for the servants. She hoped she hadn't slept for too long and that they were all still in the kitchen. As she walked back down the screens passage there was not a sound to be heard. The hairs rose on the back of Marnie's neck, but she could see the door to the outside now. It would only be a moment more and she would be away.

The door was still ajar and Marnie pushed it open with relief. She'd done it. She wanted to whoop with the joy of it, but she knew to save that for when she was out of the gates and back on the road. She stepped outside. It was later than she thought and the evening air was frosty.

'You again!' came the voice. Marnie turned to see Hetty striding towards her, carrying a bucket that was sloshing out water in agitation. 'What are you doing in there? I'll call the constable on you. You been in there nicking stuff?'

'No . . . no,' said Marnie, thinking of the bundle of hair in her pocket. 'Of course not. I'm . . . I'm sorry. I was just looking for you, that's all.'

'You've no right to be going in there unannounced. I've told you before, you're trespassing. Mr Todd! Mr Todd!' she shouted.

'No . . . please,' Marnie pleaded. 'I haven't done anything

wrong. I was just looking for you, honest. I was only in there a minute. I called, but no one answered.'

Hetty put the bucket down and put her hands on her hips. 'Why on earth would you be looking for me?'

'To see if you had any news of Noah.'

Hetty began to laugh. 'You really have got a problem, ain't you? Even if I had news of Master Noah, why would I go telling you it?'

'I told you,' said Marnie. 'We're friends. *More* than friends.' She took a deep breath. 'I'm expecting his child, I am.'

Hetty spluttered. 'Aw gawd.' She laughed again. 'You really are mad, in't you? Go on, just go. I won't call Mr Todd again. Not this time. But only cos I feel sorry for you.' She picked up her bucket. 'Go on,' she said merrily. 'Get out of here. And don't come back again.'

Marnie turned to go. She wanted to hit the girl. Wipe the smile off her face. Make her believe that she wasn't mad. But she couldn't chance Noah hearing of it. She never wanted him to think bad of her. She would bide her time, as she always did, and soon, when Noah returned, everyone would know the truth.

As she walked down the drive, Marnie heard Hetty laughing to herself. 'Wait till I tell the rest of 'em about this. What a lark!'

Marnie walked back down to the village with a heavier tread than she'd set out with. 'They'll all learn, won't they, Pa?' she muttered. 'They'll see I was right and they were wrong. I can't wait for that day, Pa. I'll rub their noses in it, I will.'

On her way back along the esplanade, she looked wistfully over the pier works and out to sea. She promised herself she wouldn't step a foot on the beach or dip a toe in the water until Noah came back. She was afraid the sea might never forgive her for her neglect, but a strange superstition had formed in her mind; if she went to the sea without Noah, then Noah might *never* come back. So she contented herself with catching the sea spray in her face and prayed that Easter would come quick.

45

The Journal of Noah de Clevedon

London. DECEMBER 24th 1868, Thursday

What a wonderful evening! In truth I cannot remember a better one in all my life. Not only have I turned eighteen, but I was favoured with the hand of Cissie Baird in several dances.

I thought I looked rather dapper in my new dress-coat and white vest (if I say so myself). Mother insisted I also had new patent leather boots and white kid gloves for the occasion of the Bairds' Christmas ball.

I took a carriage there with Arnold and Henry. Arnold brought a hip flask of brandy and proceeded to pass it around so as to warm ourselves for the evening ahead. He needn't have bothered as the refreshment room was awash with seasonal Bishop's punch!

A magnificent Christmas tree decked in all manner of geegaws greeted us upon our arrival in the Bairds' grand hall. Chandeliers dripping with candles and crystals lit our way into the ballroom where the prettiest girls in London, dressed in tulle, fine muslin and lace, sat with their chaperones, awaiting us gentlemen.

I led Cissie in the Grand March and the first waltz of the evening. Cissie was in great demand, but I made sure to gain her promise for several dances before her card was full. We danced the last waltz of the evening together and her head rested on my shoulder for the briefest of moments. She smelled divine; like rose petals and honey. I think I may be in love. In any case I bored Henry and Arnold senseless with my endless talk of her boundless virtues!

It is Christmas morning now and the sky is already growing pale. I must snatch a few hours' sleep and dream the sweetest of dreams (of Cissie's black hair and pearly skin) before the festivities begin all over again.

1869

46

A Lick and a Spit

November passed by, then December fell cold and harsh and January harsher still. Marnie's courses came again and then again. She wondered what it could mean. Her belly seemed as flat as ever. But perhaps it was too soon to show yet? She tried not to think the worst. There must be a baby inside her. There must. Sometimes it all seemed like a dream, that night on the beach with Noah. She thought through every moment, over and over again. The touch of his wet skin on hers, the heat of him inside her, the marks of sharp pebbles on her back that had stayed for days. How could she have imagined something like that? She was certain it had happened. But if only her belly would show some signs, it would make the waiting for Noah so much easier to bear.

Every evening, after she'd done her business in the privy, Marnie would check on her treasures under the firebrick. She would hold Noah's handkerchief gently in her hand, then she would unfold it to reveal the knot of his hair inside. They were the most precious things she had and she couldn't sleep until she knew they were safe.

Every night she questioned Smoaker on the progress of the pier. 'Will it be finished on time?' she asked anxiously. Had the decking all been laid? How long till the tollhouse was finished? Had the February storms put them behind too much?

'Anyone would think you had shares in that pier,' he joked.

Twice Marnie saw Hetty in the village taking her basket into Mr Tyke's. The girl had smirked and stared pointedly at her belly. Marnie had thrust her stomach out and glared back at her. But just seeing Hetty kept Marnie's hopes alive. As long as Hetty was still at the manor, keeping it ticking over, then Noah would surely be back.

Towards the end of February, Marnie began to bleed again and still her belly was as flat as the bottom of a frying pan. Smoaker came back from work one evening and announced that Eldon Cross had been given his marching orders. 'Been caught pocketing company property,' was all Smoaker would say. 'He's been chucked in Bridewell jail and'll be up before the magistrate next week.'

Ma kept tight-lipped. She wouldn't look Marnie in the eye and Marnie knew it was because she couldn't bring herself to say sorry. Marnie should have felt good that Eldon was banged up in jail, but somehow it didn't matter to her any more. She knew now after three times of bleeding that something was very wrong. Either the baby had died and was leaving her body, or else it had never been there in the first place. She felt empty and cheated, and worse, she had nothing more than herself now to offer to Noah. 'He will still want me, Pa, won't he?' she asked desperately.

'Who'll want who? What are you jabbering on about now, Marnie?' Ma gave her an exasperated look from across the kitchen.

Marnie was puzzled. How did Ma know what she was thinking? Had she spoken her thoughts out loud? 'Nothing, Ma,' she said. 'Nothing.'

She put her hand to her stomach and a slick of fear slid over her body. She was suddenly cold and her belly churned over so fast that a mouthful of burning vomit stung the back of her throat. She swallowed hard. She had to be strong now. Noah would be coming back soon. She couldn't allow herself to think bad thoughts. Baby or no baby, she and Noah were meant to be together.

As February drifted into March and the evenings got lighter, Smoaker took Marnie with him up to the big barn at Eccles Farm. With a ladder, a bucket of suds and a hard brush, Marnie scrubbed the grime and dust off the bathing machines while Smoaker followed behind with a paintbrush. 'A lick and a spit and they'll be good as new,' he said. Marnie swept the dust from the insides too, and the old grains of sand from last summer. It seemed like a lifetime had passed since she'd last stepped inside the machines' fusty bellies. She'd turned fifteen in that time, she realised, although the occasion had gone unmarked.

Finally there came a morning when Marnie woke to the sun pouring through the shutters and she knew Noah was at last on his way. It was Easter Saturday and Marnie would have skipped out of bed if she could.

Down in the village, the gloom of the last months seemed to have disappeared into the clear March skies and everywhere villagers were smiling, laughing and greeting each other merrily on the lanes. Marnie had never had so any pleasantries thrown her way. The beach had been cleared of machinery and only a few navvies remained, frantically hammering and knocking the finishing pieces of the pier into place. Smoaker had rebuilt his hut on the beach, and freshly painted signs now declared, 'Nash's Bathing Machines Reopening for Business Soon!'

The whole of Clevedon was alive with a bright sunshine excitement. Shopkeepers polished their windows to a peppermint gleam, the esplanade was swept clean of its winter debris, and tubs spilling over with spring flowers – crocuses, pansies and daffodils, like bags of confectionery delights – appeared as if by magic around the village. On the approaches to the pier, full-grown trees sprang up; a huge arch of evergreens was erected at the pier entrance and everywhere across the village flags and streamers fluttered in the good-natured breeze.

Even Ma and Smoaker were caught up in the mood and took their midday beers out on to the lane to watch the goings-on. Marnie walked to the top of the embankment and looked down on to the esplanade. She had never seen so many people. It was as though every cottage and house in Clevedon had shaken out its inhabitants and rolled them in clusters to the seafront to gawp at the iron monster that had risen from the depths of the sea. Noah was out there somewhere, thought Marnie. He could be in a carriage right now, rolling and swaying as the horses kicked up dust on their way to Clevedon. Or he could already be at the manor, standing at his bedchamber window peering through a new spyglass at the esplanade and beach, searching for a glimpse of her. Or maybe he was down there on the esplanade already, a speck of blue amongst the crowds. Although the day was warm, Marnie shivered. She could hardly bear it. She had waited so long. She had been quiet and patient and had kept her heart wrapped up tight and safe for Noah. But now the time was nearly here and every new moment she had to wait took longer than the one before. She was dizzy and breathless with longing.

By late afternoon the village had quietened down and Smoaker said it was time to move the bathing machines back on to the beach. Marnie walked with him to Eccles Farm and helped him harness up the largest of the horses. It had grown thin and grey over the winter months. Marnie led the creature to the barn and Smoaker hitched it to the first of the bathing machines. As they trundled down the lanes towards the pier, Marnie sat on the back steps of the machine listening as passers-by shouted greetings to Smoaker. 'Glad to see you back in business!' ''Bout time, Smoaker!'

Nine times they made the journey from Eccles Farm to the beach, and as the day began to dim the newly painted bathing machines were lined up neatly along the base of the tollhouse, their grey roofs darkened to a dusky blue by the pier's great shadow.

Ma had taken to her bed by the time Marnie and Smoaker got back to the cottage. 'Something not quite right with her,' said Smoaker. 'Not sure she'll be up to much dipping. 'Bout time you pulled your weight more, I reckon.'

'You mean do the dipping meself?' asked Marnie.

'It's what your ma always meant for you. Sooner or later. Just come a tad sooner, that's all. Think you're up to it?'

'Oh, I can do it, Smoaker,' said Marnie. She held her head high. 'Don't you worry. I'll be the best dipper you've ever seen!' Marnie wished she could dance. She wanted to grab Smoaker by the hands and spin round the kitchen with him. She was going to be a dipper! At long last she could go back in the sea and do all day what she loved to most. 'I'll be the very best, Smoaker,' she said again. 'The very best.'

Marnie couldn't remember a day when she'd ever felt happier. It was almost too much to think of at once. Noah was close by, she could feel it in her bones. And in a short while they'd be together again and she'd be so proud to tell him her news. She *would* be the best dipper ever. And now Clevedon had the most beautiful pier in the whole of England, maybe Queen Victoria herself really would pay a visit; on a hot day in June perhaps. She'd be sure to hear the name of Marnie Gunn and she'd be sure to ask for her special.

47

The Journal of Noah de Clevedon

Clevedon. MARCH 28th 1869, Sunday

We are back in Clevedon, having arrived last night, and the manor is bustling with busy-ness and noise! It is a far cry from the last time I was here. Then, it was only Mother and I and a handful of servants. Now there is a large party of us, and dozens of servants. Every room has a blazing fire and is full of chatter and amusements. Father is here with his dear friends Lord Baird and Sir William Elton (chairman of the pier committee) and their families – so of course Cissie is here too. Arnold has come – after some persuading on my part, and we are set, I am sure, for a splendid time!

Mother is now entertaining the women and I have just returned from showing Arnold the estate – with Prince in tow, naturally.

We attended church this morning and took over near half the pews with our pious party. I am sure the poor Reverend Strawbridge has never seen his collection tin so full!

Tomorrow is the opening of the Grand Pier and once the speeches are done with, we are set to return to the manor for a celebration dinner and dance with a few select locals. I am sure it will amuse Cissie. I so want her to enjoy herself.

I sat behind her at church this morning and I am afraid I did not hear a word of the sermon, so caught up was I in studying the small, pale hollow at the back of her neck. One day I will kiss that very spot. One day soon, when Cissie is mine.

48

Banners and Flags

Easter Monday dawned fair and breezy. A smattering of overnight rain had left a sweet scent in the air and glinting raindrops on tubs of flowers and waving flags and on rooftops and railings. Marnie thought the village looked for all the world as though it had been sprinkled with icing sugar in readiness for the grand occasion. She dressed carefully in her least shabby frock. It was short in the sleeves and tight around her bodice, but it was tidy and clean and, with her hair pinned neatly out of the way, Marnie was sure she looked respectable.

She wanted to look her very best for Noah.

Smoaker had oiled the grey tufts of his hair flat behind his ears and buttoned up a fancy wool waistcoat over his belly. Even Ma was up for some primping. She brushed the hem of her skirts clean and tied a starched white apron around her waist.

They headed to the pier early. Marnie's eyes darted everywhere. Would Noah be here yet? Where would he be standing? The village was filling up quickly with visitors from Bristol and around, who had travelled into Clevedon on specially arranged excursion trains. 'They reckon a couple of thousand are going to turn up,' Smoaker pronounced.

Ma was anxious to secure a good position. 'Might as well see what all the fuss is about,' she said as she elbowed her way through the thickening knots of jubilant spectators. Marnie couldn't help but be caught up in the giddy atmosphere. Children were running hither and thither between the legs of top-hatted gentlemen and behind the swaying bustles of tightly laced ladies. Every style and colour of frivolous hat and bonnet was on display. It looked to Marnie like a sea of flowers and ribbons bobbing towards the pier. Some families had brought picnics and were spreading out rugs on the grassy embankment and down on the beach. There were onlookers gathering high up on the nearby cliff tops, and everywhere banners and flags danced like lunatics.

Pressed up tight to Ma's side, Marnie was close enough to the pier entrance to see that a small platform had been erected and a large banner stretched above it read, 'Success to the Pier'. She stood on her tiptoes and looked around at the confusion of faces. Noah was here somewhere. If only she could catch sight of him and calm her hammering heart. Suddenly, over the noise of the crowd came the boom and thump of music. Gradually, voices drifted into silence and everyone, as if instructed, moved to either side of the esplanade. The punch of drums and the tinny spank of cymbals filled the air as a band dressed in scarlet uniforms marched through the parted crowd. Marnie's heart beat fast to the rhythm of the drums. *He must be here soon. He must be here soon.* The band halted in front of the pier and after a moment's pause began to sing. *God save our gracious Queen, long live our noble Queen.* The anthem was taken up by the crowd and soon Marnie found herself singing words she hardly knew. She sang loud and long and was filled with a strange but wonderful feeling. Only when the singing finally stopped and the crowd began to cheer did Marnie realise what was making her feel so good. For once in her life she felt like she belonged. She was part of it all; the same as everyone else. And best of all, she knew Noah was nearby. She squeezed Ma's arm, not wanting the moment to ever end.

Then, three dapperly dressed gentlemen stepped out of the throng and mounted the wooden platform. 'There he is. Sir John de Clevedon,' said Ma.

'Which one?' asked Marnie.

'Him there. The one in the striped waistcoat,' Ma answered.

Marnie craned her neck for a closer look. So that was him. That was Noah's father. Marnie stared at the tall, pleasant-looking man who was smiling at the crowd and clearing his throat ready to speak. He certainly had the neat and costly appearance of a proper gentleman. Everything about him looked spanking new and plush; from his suit of plain dark cloth and his immaculate silk hat to the shiny black toes of his shoes, which peeped out from under the flick of his trouser hems. A thick gold watch chain hung from his coat pocket and his black tie was pinned loosely at his neck with a red jewel. Marnie searched his face for any reminder of Noah. He was certainly handsome, this Sir John; his dark, close-cropped beard looked soft and his skin had the healthy glow of the wealthy. With a jolt, Marnie noticed his eyes; one blue, one grey.

'Ladies and gentlemen.' He began to speak in a clear, confident voice. But Marnie heard no more than that. Standing behind Sir John, nestled inside a small group of people, was a beautiful fair-haired woman dressed in flimsy white lace. Marnie recognised her at once as Lady de Clevedon. And standing next to her, with his face half hidden by the plumes of white feathers that sprouted from his mother's bonnet, was Noah.

Marnie took a sharp intake of breath and her fingers squeezed tight on Ma's arm. 'Ow!' Ma nudged her and frowned.

'Sorry,' Marnie whispered. Her mouth was dry and her throat hurt. She tried to swallow, but couldn't. She gazed at Noah and her eyes watered with the effort of not blinking. He was smiling softly at his father's back, and then he bent his head and said something to his mother. Lady de Clevedon stretched out a white-gloved hand and placed it on Noah's arm.

Please! Look over here! Marnie willed Noah's eyes to meet hers. He looked older than she remembered, somehow. Perhaps it was the dress suit he was wearing, an almost exact copy of his father's. Or maybe it was the silk topper pushed too far down his head, on account of it being slightly too big for him.

'And so, ladies and gentlemen . . . ' Sir John's words drifted into her ears. 'I am most honoured and delighted to declare the Grand Pier of Clevedon open!' A great cheer rose from the crowd. Noah lifted his gloved hands and began to clap. Marnie put her hands together too and mimicked Noah's movements, never taking her eyes off his face. Noah was laughing and cheering and then for a split second his eyes met hers. Marnie's hands paused in mid clap and she drank in the wide smile that broke across Noah's face. The moment passed and Noah's eyes flicked over the crowd before turning at last to Lady de Clevedon. He kissed his mother on the cheek. The pier gates were opened and suddenly Marnie lost sight of him as everybody rushed to be the first to walk the length of the pier.

If she hurried, thought Marnie, she could catch Noah. Maybe they could walk the pier together? 'You coming, Ma?' she shouted. Ma's reply got lost in the sudden blare of trumpets as the band started up again. Marnie was pushed to one side by a sweaty-faced woman in a green velvet gown who seemed determined to crush everyone in her path. Marnie held her stick tight and tried to take a few steps towards the pier entrance. It was no good. Time and time again she was knocked off balance by silk skirts, velvet skirts, knotted bustles and wayward parasols. Finally, she found herself shoulder to shoulder with a couple of elderly matrons walking with steely glares and a determined pace. She let herself be swept along, through the rush of people and chattering voices, until she was past the entrance to the pier and felt the hollow clump of the wooden decking beneath her feet. She looked around desperately. Where was Noah? Surely he couldn't be far away? But one silk topper looked the same as any other and there were so many of them. Then a flash of white caught Marnie's eye and she saw again a plume of feathers bouncing high above the tide of black silk. Lady de Clevedon! And there . . . there was Noah!

'Noah!' she shouted. He was walking towards her, heading off the pier and back on to the esplanade. 'Noah!' she shouted again. A dark-haired girl walking near to Noah turned in Marnie's direction and looked at her in puzzlement. 'Noah!' Marnie tried one last time. But it was too late. Noah was striding off in the wrong direction and, try as she might, Marnie couldn't turn around.

But he *had* seen her. Marnie comforted herself. He'd smiled at her through the crowd. A secret smile, meant only for her. He was busy now, so of course he couldn't come to her. But later . . . they'd be together later. Just as he'd said. *I will meet you here on the beach, the first night I am back!*

49

Marnie

I wait till Ma's snores grow loud and regular. She's had a gut full of beer and she won't wake now till the light of morning strokes her face. I lift the wool blanket that covers us both and slide from the bed. I'm careful to tuck the blanket back around the rising and falling mound of her.

The stone floor is cold on me feet so I quickly slip on me boots, not bothering with any stockings. I leave me bootlaces undone, tucking the loose ends inside so I won't trip. I pull me cotton frock over me shift and grab me shawl before I limp out of the bedchamber into the kitchen. Smoaker will be asleep in the upstairs bedchamber now, with Nep curled up on his feet. Smoaker's empty beer pot is on the table with the remains of the bread and cheese he must have had for his supper. I leave me stick propped up by the fireplace. I want to manage without it. I want to show Noah how strong I can be.

I open the kitchen door and step out into the night.

The March moon is only the white slit of an eye, but the stars wink bright as lanterns in the dark sky. The bells of St Andrew's on the Hill chime the hour of eleven and I stand still for a moment and breathe in the salty air. I taste the tang of seaweed on the back of me tongue and I shiver with pleasure. The echo of the church bells melts away, and instead I hear the gentle swish and slap of the waves as they break on the beach. The tide is in. It's perfect.

Me belly is filled tight with hope, longing and a bubbling excitement. I haven't been able to swallow a bite of food today. I hurry as best as I can across the lane in front of the cottage in Ratcatcher's Row, and down the grassy embankment that leads to the esplanade. All is quiet. The Old Inn has spat out the last of its sots and closed its doors, the excursion trains have taken the last of the visitors back to Bristol and it is hours yet before even the keenest of fishermen will be stirring from their beds. I walk to the railings that run alongside the esplanade and look down on to the beach. The shingle glitters, wet and inviting. Away to me right stands the new pier. Silhouetted against the starry sky, it looks to me like a monstrous insect marching out to sea on long elegant legs. I have still not grown used to the sight of it. The huge arch of flowers and evergreens still hangs over the pier gate and the hundreds of flags that deck the pier from end to end are still waving in the sea wind, as if they don't know yet the celebrations have ended. If I look closely I can just see Smoaker's bathing machines tucked away at the base of the tollhouse, huddled together like some family of giant sea turtles.

I go to the gap in the railings where the stone steps lead

down to the beach. I slip off me boots and carry them in me hand as me feet grip the cold, sandy surface of the steps. I make me way down slowly, me bad leg dragging behind and aching with the effort. I hop down on to the beach and on to the first of the rocks that are jumbled in a pile against the sea wall. I'm careful not to slip as I pick me way across the largest and flattest of the rocks until I reach the shingle.

I dig me toes into the coarse mix of cobbles, pebbles and broken shells. The sand beneath still holds the warmth of the day. It feels wonderful. It's been too long. But I'm here now and I feel like I've come home. The lacy edge of the swash is stretched out before me. The sea is whispering to me. It knows I'm here. It's missed me too, I can tell.

But where is Noah? Me heart tightens into an anxious knot. I look around and peer into the shadows. He's not sitting on our rock. I look up and down the beach, as far as the faint light of the stars will allow. There's no sign of him. I wrap me shawl around me shoulders and kick at the shingle for a while. The minutes pass and still there's no sound of crunching footsteps. He promised he would be here. *I will meet you here on the beach, the first night I am back!* That's what he'd said. And haven't I been waiting patiently for him all these long months? Where is he? I search me memory for the glimpse I had of him today. Stood proud by his father's side, in a new top hat that was slightly too big for him, Noah had smiled at me. I'd caught the smile gladly and eagerly. What can have happened? I try to ignore the worry that's nagging at me insides. I strain me ears, hoping to hear me name being called over the noisy wash of the sea. Still, there's nothing.

I'm cross now; fearful, confused and a bit sick in the belly. I don't know what to do. He has to come! I struggle to imagine the awful possibility that he might never turn up. But me head won't let me think such things. The sea is trying to calm me nerves. I hear its soothing voice reaching out to me. I know I shouldn't; I'd promised meself I wouldn't until Noah was here, but before I can help meself, I'm pulling me dress and shift over me head and placing them on the shingle with me shawl and boots on top. Then I shuffle out of me drawers. The sea breeze lifts a tress of hair off me shoulder and goosebumps run up and down me arms. I walk slowly to the sea's edge. Me skin shrinks as the cold foam breaks over me feet. I gasp, and walk further in until the water reaches under me arms. I take a deep breath and plunge beneath the surface. In just a sliver of a moment I'm back where I belong.

I pull back with me arms and I slice easily through the cold, silky darkness. I swim underwater till me chest feels fit to burst, then I push back up to the surface and take deep swallows of the briny night air. I'm warm now and I lie back on the swell of the waves and paddle with me hands for a while. I look towards the shore and by the light of the stars I can see it's still empty. I'm so scared he won't come, and the feeling weighs heavy in me chest and presses down on me throat.

I don't want to go back home yet. Not to Ma's snores and a restless night. Besides, he might turn up yet, running across the shingle waving his arms at me. He'll have had trouble sneaking out, I think. With his father being here and all. I decide to wait a while longer, so I stay afloat, allowing the waves to dip me up and down.

Time passes slowly as I stay floating on the night sea. It's getting cold now. I can feel me whole body growing stiff with it. I wish Noah was here, Pa, I say. I wish he was floating next to me, holding me hand. We could lie here and count the stars, and the waves could carry us far, far away to where you are.

50

The Journal of Noah de Clevedon

Clevedon. MARCH 29th 1869, Monday

Our first day back in Clevedon has passed very well. We took two carriages and the brougham down to the village this morning and joined in the celebrations for the opening of the Grand Pier. Father made a rousing speech, which was well received by the locals and visitors alike.

The finished pier is magnificent. Father is delighted with it. He says it will certainly prove to be a valuable attraction and will bring more business and visitors to Clevedon (and profit for himself, of course!). Besides affording pleasure to locals and visitors, the pier has made it possible for boats and steamers to discharge their passengers at Clevedon whatever the state of the tides.

At least two thousand people descended on our little village and the air was fizzing with a holiday atmosphere. After Father had spoken, the pier gates were opened and a rush of people clamoured to be the first to walk the wooden decking.

I think I spied the girl, Marnie, in amongst the hordes. It was the briefest of glimpses, but she looked to be well and enjoying the revelry. Although it has only been a matter of months since I was last here, it feels like a lifetime ago. So much has changed for me. I am no longer the boy I was.

As fortune would have it, Cissie and I were pushed together by the crowd and for a blissful few moments, as we walked along the pier, we held hands unnoticed. I say blissful and indeed it was, but I long for the day when I can kiss her sweet, pink mouth. I hope that day is not too far away. I have a feeling there will be plenty of opportunities for Cissie and I to snatch some moments alone while we are here at the manor.

The evening was spent dining and dancing with a few of the more eminent locals. The new pier master, Mr Stiff, attended with his wife, as did the Reverend Strawbridge and chief engineers Messrs Ward and Groaner. The evening was a great success, and of course Cissie danced with me more often than with any other.

Now Father has taken me into the business (as a junior partner of the Clevedon Finance Company, no less!), I think the time has come for me to approach Lord Baird and ask for his daughter's hand in marriage. I can think of no one I would rather spend my life with than Cissie. Father approves wholeheartedly. He has already given me his consent. I need to pick my time carefully, though. Shall I ask for her hand while we are here? Or should I wait until we return to London? What a delicious predicament!

Now to bed! I have stayed too long at my desk already. We are hoping for some fine weather tomorrow, and a picnic, no less.

51

Dippy Go Under, My Dears

By the time I slide back into bed beside Ma it is almost morning. She grunts and shifts in her sleep. I lay still, me damp hair growing cold around me face. I should be tired, but I can't close me eyes. Me heart is thumping deep in me belly and I don't know if it is anger or fear that is making me feel like this.

Noah didn't come.

I waited and waited – alone in the sea – and he didn't come.

He has always come before.

I try to think of all the things that could have stopped him from coming.

His father caught him sneaking out.

He had to go back to London in a hurry and had no time to let me know.

He's been suddenly taken ill.

I can't think of many reasons, but I know there will be a good one. I try to calm meself. He will come to me later today. I know he will. He'll come and explain to me what happened.

He'll be sorry and I'll forgive him and we'll make plans for next time.

I lay still for a while longer, but it's useless to think that sleep will come now.

Smoaker is reopening the bathing machines today, and I'm to help with the dipping. I should be excited but instead I'm fretful. I don't want to be out in the sea all day where Noah can't reach me. I want to stay in the hut with Smoaker. There at least Noah will be able to find me. I dress quietly and, after I've stoked up the kitchen fire, I go outside to look at the sky. I'm glad to see grey clouds rolling over the top of St Andrew's on the Hill. A brisk wind is blowing sand across the lane and the surface of the sea is a mess of grey choppy waves and spitting foam. Only the bravest of ladies will venture out today. I'm happy we won't be too busy.

'I won't be going out there today,' Ma says when I get back inside the cottage. She's slicing bread for breakfast and is wincing with the effort. She is growing worse every day, it seems. It takes her for ever to do anything now. She grunts more often and sits for longer and longer in her chair. I look at her carefully. She takes up the same amount of space, but seems to have shrunk in upon herself. The skin on her arms is looser and her face has sagged.

'It's rough out there, anyway,' I say. 'It'll be a quiet one for certain.'

'Thank the Lord for that,' she says, and sinks down heavily into her chair. 'Couldn't have managed it today, Marnie. I ache so.'

I pass her a cup of tea and she holds it close to her chest and closes her eyes. 'Me and Smoaker will manage today,' I say. 'Tell him I'll open the hut.'

Ma nods at me without opening her eyes and I know I'm free to go.

It's far too early to open the hut – even Smoaker isn't out of bed yet – but I'm desperate to see Noah and I know he'll be feeling the same. He'll come to the beach as soon as he can, and I need to be there for him.

I walk along the esplanade first, towards the pier. I haven't got me stick with me again. I want Noah to see how good I'm getting without it. The wind whips me hair across me face and me skirts stick to me legs. It's empty and wild on the beach. I can spy a few fishing boats in the distance being tossed about on the waves, and there are gulls riding the sky and screeching with excitement. I push me face into the wind and I feel wide awake. The new tollhouse is shuttered; the pier master will be breakfasting, so there is no one to see me walk through the gates and along the wooden decking. I walk right to the pier head, to the back of the pavilion, and look down into the water below. It's dizzying to be standing this far out to sea and this high above the crashing waves. I wonder how the delicate iron legs of the pier can hold up against the power of the ocean. It feels strange out here. I'm not sure I like it. It's too empty and lonely. A person could jump right off the end and no one would notice.

It'll be different when Noah is with me, I think. On a warm day it'll be a good place to take a stroll. We'll sit on the seats

236

by the pavilion and look out to sea.

I turn and look back towards the village. I've never seen it from this way round before. It's all there, spread out before me. I can see Ratcatcher's Row in the distance and the rabble of lanes running behind; I can see the glinting windows of Miss Cranston's Tea House and the bandstand out at Layde's Bay. Best of all I can see the manor, out beyond the cottages, nestled in the dip below the woodlands. If I squint me eyes I can make out the topmost windows. There's Noah's in the middle. I imagine him up there, rushing to get dressed. Leaning over his washstand, brushing his hair with his heavy bone brush. I wrap me arms around meself and squeeze tight. *Hurry up, hurry up*, I whisper.

The pier master has opened the shutters and is standing looking out of his window as I walk by on me way back to the esplanade. He's put out to see me there and opens his mouth to shout. Then he notices me leg and lowers his eyes. Even though he's new in the village, he's just like everyone else.

I make me way to the beach and set out the new signs next to the hut.

Nash's Bathing Machines for Hire
6d for a time not exceeding half an hour.
Two clean towels. One clean gown or other clean and
sufficient covering to prevent indecent exposure of the
person.

I can't stay still. Me fingers are twitching and me feet keep taking me out of the hut so I can look for Noah. Me heart jerks as I see a figure in the distance, but it's only Smoaker. He's holding on to his hat with one hand and balancing the bowl of his pipe with the other. Me heart drops into me boots. It's too late for Noah to come now. Not now I've got me work to do. I pick up a pebble and throw it angrily on to the beach. I don't know how I'll get through the day.

Smoaker stops by the hut and looks out to sea. 'Just you dipping today,' he says. 'No sense in paying the other women to come out.' He licks a finger and holds it up into the wind. 'I'll just bring the two horses for now.' I don't know if he's telling me or the wind. He walks back up the slipway to fetch the horses from the stables at Rock House.

'Please, Noah, please,' I beg out loud. 'Come now!' I stand on the slipway and strain me eyes, looking in all directions. There's nothing to see. I feel tired and heavy already, and me heart stays sulking in me boots.

Smoaker comes back with two horses and busies himself with their harnesses. The wind has calmed now, and out on the horizon the cloudy sky is edged with blue. I sigh. If the weather stays like this, there'll be bathers for certain.

The bathing gowns we keep in the hut are old and stiff. I change into one, in readiness for the first customers. I hate the weight and feel of it and would rather work in me shift, but I know it's 'not decent' and besides, the dark blue alpaca skirt, the knickerbockers and stockings all help to hide me leg. 'We don't want to scare away the customers,' is what Ma would say.

Smoaker sits in the chair in the corner of the hut fiddling with his pipe, and I stand leaning against the doorway and think of Noah. I imagine him lying ill in bed with a fever, or

238

speeding to London in a coach with his father. I know I'll have to go to the manor later. I won't be able to stop meself.

The first bather of the day is a scrawny woman of about sixty who can hardly walk for the gout in her foot. She climbs into the bathing machine with difficulty and I lead the horse and machine into the sea. While I wait for the lady to change, I unhitch the horse and lead it round to the back of the machine, where I hitch it ready to pull the machine back up the beach. Then I wade into the water to wait on the bather. She opens the door eventually and sits on the steps of the bathing machine shivering like a frightened kitten. I take her by the waist and gently guide her into the sea. She squeals loudly and can barely catch her breath as a small wave wets her bosom.

'It's quite safe, Ma'am,' I tell her. 'But I need you to lie back.'

She looks at me as though I am mad.

'It's so I can float you,' I tell her.

'But . . . but I cannot swim,' she stammers.

'That's why I'm here,' I say. 'I'll hold you up. You won't drown, I promise.'

I put me arms under her and lift her like a child. She is as stiff as a plank of wood. She screws her eyes tight shut and clasps her hands across her chest. I feel as though I am bobbing a corpse through the water. She won't last the half-hour; she is not strong enough for a dipping. By the looks of her, I imagine it won't be long before she is gone from this world altogether.

A nursemaid and her two charges are next. The young boys are no more than two or three years of age. She sits on the steps of the bathing machine and passes the wriggling bundles to me. I hold a child under each arm and, as I've heard Ma say

239

so many times, I sing, 'Dippy go under, my dears!' as I plunge them down under the water and hold them there for a second. When I haul them back up they begin to wail and splutter. 'One more to make you hearty!' I shout. Under they go again. Their wailing grows louder, but their nurse seems deaf to the fuss. She is concentrating hard on keeping her skirts dry. I keep on dipping until me arms ache, the boys grow silent and their teeth begin to chatter. Their lips are blue when I hand them back to their nurse.

I know Smoaker has been watching me in me work and I can tell by his face that I've done nothing to cause complaint. I knew I could do the dipping standing on me head. I just knew it. I feel puffed up, like I've just stuffed me face with one of Miss Cranston's creamy pastries. But instead of me belly being full of cake, it's full of pride. I just wish Noah was here to see me.

The lull in the weather hasn't lasted. The wind is whipping up the waves and there is the smell of a storm in the air. When I lead the horse back up the beach, there are no bathers waiting for me. Smoaker is grumbling. 'Not even enough to pay for the horse feed.' The sky is growing darker by the minute. I would be happy for a storm to come now. Smoaker will have to close the hut and I'll be free to go to Noah. Or at least to the manor to see if there is any sign of him. I imagine him lying in his bed; his eyes bright with fever.

There is a deep rumbling from the skies behind the village. Smoaker swears under his breath, but I smile to meself and me belly clenches tight with excitement. As the first fat drops of rain fall on to the slipway outside, I am at the back of the hut taking off me bathing gown and pulling on me frock and boots.

240

52

Apples and Hot Sugar

It's a long walk to the manor. I'm soon soaked to the skin, but I don't mind one bit. I don't mind when me wet hair sticks to me face or when rainwater runs down me neck. I don't mind when the water finds its way into me boots and between me toes. All I care about is getting to Noah as quickly as I can.

I'd forgotten what an effort it takes to walk this road. It's so pitted and rutted by carriage wheels. As I hobble through puddles I pass a small herd of cows sheltering from the storm under an old oak. I am out of breath now. I have tried to walk too quickly and now me leg feels weak and me hip is throbbing. Perhaps I should have brought me stick after all. I rest for a moment by the side of the road and pull a broken branch from the undergrowth. It takes me weight when I lean on it, so I twist and crack off the dried shoots from its length and fashion a walking stick of sorts. It will help get me the rest of the way. I hate to give in to me weakness, but more than anything I need to see Noah.

I begin to walk again, slowly but easily, and soon enough the still, grey walls of the manor come into view. Me heart flutters wildly in me throat. It won't be long now.

I hide me stick in the roots of a horse chestnut tree that stands guarding the entrance gate to the manor. I want to be strong and walk the rest of the way without any help. It's strange to walk up the wide gravelled driveway again. It feels as though eyes are peering at me and watching me closely. Telling me I don't belong. Telling me I'm a trespasser.

The rain has eased now, but the day is still gloomy. I can see candlelight flickering through the manor windows as I walk around the side to the servants' door. I know I must look like a bedraggled urchin, but Noah is used to seeing me fresh from the sea so it will be neither here nor there to him. I expect he'll bring me inside and sit me by a fire to dry. I pass the carriage-house and stables, the coalhouse and the gardener's building. There's no one about.

Then I hear the bang of a door and voices. Steam billows out from behind a low wall. I step closer and hear the sound of clattering pans. I walk past the servants' door to the next one along. It's the kitchen I think, and someone is there, someone who'll fetch Noah for me. The door is ajar and I tap on it lightly, praying that it's not Hetty who answers. The noises inside grow louder, so I knock on the door harder. I jump back when it's suddenly opened by a red-faced woman with her sleeves rolled up to her forearms. She is holding a large spoon in her hand. I wonder if she's Sally the cook.

'Yes?' she snaps at me.

I open me mouth to speak, but before I can get a word out

she says, 'We don't have no beggars here. Get on with you now.' She shakes the spoon at me and moves to close the door.

'No!' I shout. 'Stop! It's the master Noah I'm after.'

She keeps her hand on the door and snorts. 'The master Noah?' she says slowly. 'Now what would you be wanting him for?'

'That's me own business,' I say. I have already decided I don't like this woman. I look her in the eye. 'Please tell Noah that Marnie is here to see him.'

'Marnie, eh?' The woman's eyes glint. She raises her spoon again and points it at me. 'Well, well. I've heard about you and your mad ideas. Master Noah, as you can imagine, is otherwise engaged and I'm sure will not wish to be bothered by the likes of you!'

I don't expect this and panic rises in me like a rolling wave. 'Please,' I say. 'He'll want to see me. I know he will.'

The woman shakes her head. 'I don't have time for this nonsense. We've a dinner to get ready. Now get on your way.' She starts to close the door.

'No!' I shout. 'Wait! He's not ill, is he? Please tell me Noah isn't ill!'

The door shuts hard. I bang on it again. Over and over until me knuckles hurt. It stays closed and I don't know what to do next. I'd like to scream Noah's name at the windows and make him see me. If he knew I was out here, he'd come to me. I'm sure of it. I kick me boot against the wall in frustration.

I close me eyes. I can picture Noah quite clearly. He is lying on his high, soft mattress, his head surrounded by plump pillows. His face is flushed by fever and he is moaning in his sleep. He can't get out of bed, but somehow he knows I'm here. He needs me. I can feel it deep inside of me.

I slump against the wall. I wonder if I should go around to the front of the house and pull the bell of the Grand door. But the thought of it makes me feel stupid and lowly. If the door was shut on me at the back of the house, how much worse would it be at the front? They'll never listen to me, or let me in to see Noah.

The smells of cooking drift out of the manor kitchen and into me nose. Me mouth grows wet as I sniff apples and hot sugar and a rich meaty scent. I remember I've eaten nothing all day and suddenly I feel angry. One day I'll dine with Noah and taste those smells and the nasty hag who shut the door in me face will be sorry she ever did.

I'm tired now, and me disappointment is so heavy it weighs me feet to the ground. I think of the long walk home and the hours that have to pass before I can come here again. Then a thought springs into me head. I'll bring a note tomorrow, I decide. I'll go to the Grand door and pass the note in. I'll say it's an urgent message for Master Noah. Once Noah gets the note, he'll have to tell the servants all about me, and they'll take me up to him. Then I can kiss his hot forehead and hold his hand and make him well again.

This thought calms me and I want to get home now, as quickly as I can, to write the note. I'll have to wait till Ma and Smoaker have gone to bed. Smoaker is precious with his papers and dip pen. He thinks himself a fine gentleman when he fills in his ledgers. He keeps his pen and paper in the dresser drawer and if I'm careful, he'll never know that I've made use of them. I hope I can remember me letters and not smudge the ink too much.

I pull meself away from the wall and stretch the weariness from me shoulders. The day is ending as it began, with dark skies and a gale beginning to wake up again. If I hurry, I can be home before dark. I begin to walk, and as I round the first bend in the path, I pass by a window that is fully lighted now. With the day being so dim outside, I can see into the room beyond, and there is a gathering of people. I see a fire burning in a vast fireplace, a dozen candles in ornate holders and the bright colours of silk dresses. I can count at least five persons standing in the room. The ladies are holding feather fans and the gentlemen are drinking from glasses that sparkle in the candlelight. It all looks so warm and fine. I shiver in me wet frock. I watch as the gentlefolk move around the room slowly and speak words I can't hear. As they move, coming together and parting again, it looks like they're taking part in the most graceful of dances. Then me heart flips and I cry out before I can stop meself.

I can see Noah.

He's at the back of the room. He's dressed in a black suit and white shirt, with a carefully knotted cravat at his throat. The high, stiff collar of the shirt is brushing against his cheeks. His face is flushed in the light. His hair is combed to one side and is shining like the brownest of chestnuts. He's smiling and laughing and is bending his head towards a young lady who is standing next to him.

At first I'm relieved and jubilant. There's Noah, at last. He's not ill and he hasn't gone to London. All I have to do is tap

245

on the window and he'll see me. I lift me hand towards the leaded glass but as I do, a sick and horrible uncertainty crawls through me insides. Me hand drops by me side. I stand and stare, watching the young lady's dark eyes follow Noah's mouth. I see how pretty she looks with her black hair dressed in long ringlets. I see how her rose-coloured gown with its wide ruched skirts curves into her waist and shows off her creamy white shoulders. I see how Noah is looking at her, with his head on one side and his eyes lowered. I've never seen him look like that before. I stand and watch until me teeth are chattering so much that me whole jaw hurts. Only then do I tear me eyes away and turn to go.

53

A Dip Pen and Ink

I don't remember walking home. But I'm here now, sitting at the kitchen table with a plate of bread and bacon in front of me. Smoaker is sitting opposite, picking bacon rind from his teeth. Somehow I know that Ma has taken to her bed early. Smoaker must have told me; but I don't remember when. I take a bite of bread and chew. I try to swallow, but I can't. There's a big lump in me throat. I spit the chewed dough into me hand and pass it under the table to Nep. I had better take some supper through to Ma soon, I think. But I don't move.

Poor Noah. Done up so stiff in all his finery and forced to be polite to his father's friends. Because that's what happened, I tell meself. He couldn't get away from the visitors. The more I think about it, the more I know it must be true. Noah would never have let me down without good reason. I think about the girl he was talking to. I'm sure it was the same one that was on the pier with him yesterday. She might have been pretty, but I imagine her head was as empty as a pauper's purse. She was

247

dull, I know it, and Noah was only doing his duty.

He must be worrying about me, I think; hating himself for not getting a message to me. I'll put him out of his misery. I'll let him know that I'm waiting for him whenever he can get away. I'll write that note and I'll take it to the manor first thing in the morning.

I feel better now and I manage to swallow some bread, though it lands like a rock in me belly. I prepare a plate for Ma and take it through to our bedchamber. She's lying on her back under the blanket, snoring like an old dog. She looks grey in the face and smaller than I'm used to seeing her. I don't wake her, though; me head is too busy with other thoughts. I put her plate on the floor and go back to the kitchen to wait for Smoaker to go to bed. I know it'll be a long wait. Smoaker always stays up late these days, staring into the fire and smoking his pipe. He can while away hours smoking and stroking the cat. He's such a silent man, with never much to say. I'm glad about that tonight, but I do wonder what thoughts fill his head that he can sit so long.

I busy meself washing the supper pots and sweeping the floor. Still Smoaker stays sitting in his chair. He throws another log on the fire and I want to scream. Me fingers are itching to get at his papers and pen. I fold some linen that has been drying by the fire and take up a shirt of Smoaker's that Ma has been mending. It's quiet in the kitchen; only the sucking of Smoaker's lips around his pipe, the spit of the fire and the distant rumble of the sea breaks into the silence. I hope Smoaker can't hear the thoughts in me head, they seem so loud to me.

My dear Noah, I think. *I have missed you these last few days.*

I waited for you at the beach and was worried you had fallen ill when you didn't come. I have something important to tell you.

I write the letter in me head. I try to remember all the words I want to say. I need to get it right so I don't use more than one sheet of Smoaker's paper.

I miss you, Noah. Just send me word when we can meet again. And please let it be soon.

Yours always,

Marnie.

I say the words over and over in me mind and when at long last Smoaker goes to his bed, I rush to the dresser and pull open the middle drawer. I take out Smoaker's dip pen, a brass ink pot and a sheet of yellowed paper. I bring a candle and settle meself at the table with the paper smoothed out before me. I hold the pen between me finger and thumb and try to get used to the feel of it. It's been a long while since I was taught me letters and me hand trembles. The shaft of the pen is smooth, the bone worn to a shine. I like the warm feel of it. I dip the nib in the ink and tap it gently on the side of the pot. I hold me breath as I begin to scratch out me words to Noah. It takes a long while and me arm aches with the effort. It's only when I sign me name at the bottom of the page that the ink drips and marks the paper with a black spot. It's spoiled! The whole thing is spoiled. I want to rip it up and begin again, but me head hurts and me eyes are tired. Noah will forgive me the mess, I think. I blot the ink with the sleeve of me frock and hold the paper over the warmth of the dying fire to dry. I fold the paper carefully and before I place Smoaker's pen and ink back in the drawer, I write Noah's name on the front of the note. It looks good there; the black ink proud against the pale paper. I kiss his name softly before I slip the letter in me pocket and take up the candle to light me way to bed.

'Marnie?' Ma's voice is cracked as I climb into bed beside her. 'I'm so cold, Marnie. The sea has froze my bones. It won't let me go.'

I feel her forehead. It's burning hot. 'Go to sleep, Ma,' I tell her. 'You're just dreaming.'

I turn on me side and Ma's murmurings soon settle to snores as I close me eyes and think of Noah's face lighting up with pleasure when he receives me letter.

54

The Journal of Noah de Clevedon

Clevedon. MARCH 30th 1869, Tuesday

The weather was not kind to us today. The rain-heavy clouds that loured over the manor during breakfast soon burst and put paid to our picnic plans. But the day was not all wasted. Arnold and I took Prince for a long walk through the fields and woods behind the manor. It was exhilarating to tramp through the mud and mists, throwing sticks for Prince and laughing when the beast shook the rain from his coat all over the moth-eaten walking jacket Arnold had borrowed from one of the manor's deep, dark cloakrooms.

We talked of Cissie, of course, and Arnold admitted he is quite envious of me. 'You had better hurry up and propose,' he said, 'or I shall get there first!' Naturally he is joking. Arnold is not the settling type. He is having far too much fun spending his father's money in the whorehouses of London! He regaled me with stories of his most risqué assignations. How much of what he tells me is exaggerated, I cannot tell. But his bawdy tales made me weep with laughter and put me and my one encounter with the dipper's daughter to shame!

It was heaven, then, to return to the manor, kick off our sodden boots and soak in the hot baths that had been prepared for our return. Arnold's London whores put images in my mind that stirred my senses, so I was longing for the sight and touch of Cissie as soon as I was bathed and dressed for dinner.

This evening has been splendid. We congregated in the drawing room after dinner and gathered around the piano. Cissie played and sang for us, very sweetly, then we sat and played a hand of cards. I pressed my knees to Cissie's under the table. She did not pull away, only coloured slightly along her cheekbones. I could smell her breath from across the table and it was sugary and soft like the glacé fruits we had eaten for dessert. I swear I love her madly! I will speak to Lord Baird at the earliest opportunity.

55

The Journal of Noah de Clevedon

Clevedon. MARCH 31st 1869, Wednesday

How very strange. A letter was brought to me on my breakfast tray this morning. It has disturbed me more than I would like to admit. I have had little appetite since. It was from the girl Marnie. The writing inside was crudely formed and the ink was smudged. I am surprised nonetheless that the girl can write at all. The letter was not in an envelope; only folded over with my name on the front. I sincerely hope the servant who delivered it to me did not think to pry. I should not like my boyish dalliances with Marnie ever to be made public. In the letter, the girl begged to meet me again. Of course it is not possible, and nor do I wish to. The time I spent with her last year is best forgotten about.

I decided to destroy the letter, and so burned it in my bedchamber grate.

56

Thin Barley Gruel

I took me letter to Noah up to the manor. It was received at the Grand door by a frosty-faced maid with eyes the colour of mud. She held the letter gingerly, at the very corner, as if it had fallen in a privy and was covered in unspeakable dirt.

'Please see that Master Noah gets it,' I said in me boldest voice. 'It's a matter of great importance.' The corner of the maid's mouth twitched and I thought for a moment she was going to smile. Then, without answering, she turned her head away and closed the door.

That was two days ago and I wonder now if the maid threw the letter straight on the fire, as I've not heard a word from Noah. I feel ill from the want of him. It's as though me heart has been sliced into tiny bits, the pain is so bad. I can't get him out of me head. I think about him so hard that I believe I could make him appear right in front of me. I can see every detail of his face. The pale brown mole under his left eyebrow, the front tooth that hasn't grown quite straight and the twitch that catches the corners of his mouth when he's quiet and thinking. I need to go to the manor again. This time I won't leave until I've seen him. But I can't go yet. Ma has grown worse; with shiverings, pains and a thirst that can't be quenched. Smoaker sent for Doctor Bentley. He was in with Ma a long time.

'A case of severe fatigue,' he announced when he came back to the kitchen to fetch his hat and coat. 'Nourishing broths and bed rest will be best for now, and a spoonful of these powders once a day.'

Now I'm trapped in the cottage trying to get Ma to take mouthfuls of thin barley gruel and beef tea. Most of it dribbles down her chin, so I give up and leave her to sleep. The rain has been lashing down from morning till noon. The bathing machines have stayed sheltered under the pier and Smoaker is cursing the loss of sixpences and the forthcoming doctor's bill. But as he leaves the cottage to tend to the horses, he looks at me and I spy a softening in his pale eyes. 'It's as well the weather has taken a turn for the worse, I suppose. You can be spared from dipping and can mind your ma instead.'

I poke half-heartedly at the fire. The lively flames do nothing to cheer me spirit. I can't settle to any task; I am too restless. Even though the doors are not locked and I've committed no crime, I think I may as well be in Bridewell jail. I press me forehead against the window and watch as raindrops trickle down between the tiny bubbles in the thick glass. I close me eyes and straight away I can see Noah walking towards me. He has on his old blue suit and is waving his hand in greeting. As he comes nearer to me, he begins to run. 'Marnie!' he calls. I wait until he's upon me, then I fling me arms around his neck

255

and he lifts me from the ground. I push me face into his neck and breathe in the damp, salty scent of his skin.

'I'm sorry I've stayed away for so long,' he whispers in me ear. 'I promise it will never happen again, Marnie.'

'Marnie!'

'Marnie!'

I jump back from the window and open me eyes. Ma is calling me. It's just Ma calling me. Me heart sinks like a stone in the ocean, as the ghost of Noah drifts away.

When I go to her, Ma is sitting up in bed with her shawl around her shoulders. Her face looks suddenly ancient and her lips have no colour. For the first time, I wonder what will happen to me if she never gets better.

'How are you feeling, Ma?' I ask. 'Shall I fetch you some broth?'

'I'm parched, Marnie,' she mumbles. 'My throat's so dry. Some beer. Bring some beer to wet my mouth.'

I go to the pantry and pour a beer from the big jug that Smoaker keeps there. Then I go to the fire and push the poker deep into the embers for a moment. I plunge the glowing end of the poker into the pot of beer, and there's a hiss and the yeasty smell of hops. The beer is as hot as blood now and good enough to quench Ma's thirst. I carry it through to her and she grabs it from me and gulps it down so quickly that her face flushes and her eyes shine.

She wipes her mouth with the back of her hand. 'Promise me you'll stick by Smoaker,' she says suddenly.

'What do you mean, Ma?'

'My dipping days are well and truly over, Marnie. I can't do it no more.'

'Don't be daft, Ma. You'll be as right as rain once the doctor's powders get to work.'

'No, Marnie, no.' She coughs a little. 'You don't understand. My bones have grown too cold. I'm weary of it, Marnie. I'm cold and weary.' She coughs again. 'You're a good girl, Marnie. You've been doing well at the dipping, Smoaker says. When you're in the sea, no one knows you're a cripple.' She whispers the last word, *cripple*. 'You can keep the business going, Marnie. It's your turn now. Just you and Smoaker. Stick by him and he'll look after the both of us. Promise me.'

I don't know what to say to her. I hear her words and a part of me can't help but be proud of meself again. This really is me chance now, to be the best dipper in Clevedon; to be better even than Ma. To have the very best of London ladies ask for me by name. It's what I thought I always wanted. Just me and the sea. But that was before Noah. That was before Noah made me feel more alive than the sea ever had.

'Oh Ma, it's not going to come to that,' I say. 'You wait . . . a few days rest and you'll be as good as new.'

Ma shakes her head and slips back down under the blanket. 'Promise me, Marnie,' she whispers.

I don't know what to say. I can't promise her anything. I can't be a dipper for ever. Not now that Noah will want me near him. I want to tell her this. I want to tell her not to worry; that Noah will look after both of us when the time comes. But I know there's no point. She won't believe me yet.

'I promise, Ma,' I lie.

She closes her eyes and I go back to the kitchen to wait for Smoaker's return. I'll go to the manor as soon as he gets back. I sit in his chair by the fire and stare into the centre of it. I stare so hard that soon the shapes of the flames are burned into the back of me eyeballs. I must fall asleep, for the banging of the door wakes me and I open me eyes to see Smoaker hanging up his jacket. I see by the shortness of the candle that it's late and I can tell by the smell of him that Smoaker has been to the inn. Me first thought is that it's too late now for me to go to the manor. Smoaker has spoiled me plans and I curse him under me breath. He turns at the sound of me whisper.

'Marnie,' he slurs. 'Why aren't you in bed? Has your ma got worse?'

'She's asleep,' I force meself to answer. 'I didn't want to rouse her.'

Smoaker takes off his hat and scratches at the bare skin on his head. For a moment I think he's going to want his chair and I'll have to go in with Ma. But instead he puts his hat on the table and says, 'I'll bid you goodnight, then.' His tread is heavy on the stairs as he takes himself to bed and I sigh with relief to be alone again.

I stay in Smoaker's chair and wrap me arms around meself. I rock gently, backwards and forwards, until I am sleepy again. I pretend me arms are Noah's and I hug meself as tight as I can.

57

The Church Bells Chime

It's Sunday now, and still there's been no word from Noah. Every night I've waited on the beach and there's never been a sniff of him. I can't understand why he hasn't come to see me. I've wanted to go to him, but it's been mild these last days and the new pier has brought trainloads of curious visitors to the pier. Smoaker and me and the other dippers have had a job keeping up with the demand. I've never been so weary. By the time it's evening, there's been no strength left in me leg to carry me up to the manor.

I'm sure he can't be ill. He looked the picture of health when I spied him through the manor window the other afternoon. And surely he won't have gone back to London so soon. He wouldn't have left without telling me. But I've been stuck at me work and stuck in the cottage and I've not been able to do a thing about it.

Then, this morning, just as I heard the church bells chime, I had a clever notion. I thought of a way to be certain of seeing Noah. Ma's never bothered with us going to church; she's always scoffed at the idea. She says after working our fingers to the bone all week we deserve a proper day of rest. But all the gentry from round about attend regularly, if only to parade themselves to the locals. The de Clevedons are sure to be churchgoers; I just know it. So that's where I'll go; to the church, to the Sunday service. I'm busting with me own cleverness as I tidy meself up and comb me hair. Smoaker's off busying himself with the horses now and Ma's still in her sick bed, so no one will give a jot where I get to.

I walk through the village and up the hill to St Andrew's church. I need me stick today as me leg is aching bad. I take me time walking so that I can slip into the church after everyone's settled in their pews. It's quiet in the village and I don't pass anyone much on the way. Only the Mistress Miles is outside her cottage, hanging out wet linen in poker-straight lines. She looks down her long nose at me and turns away. She's never forgiven Ma for treading on her toes with the laundry business. I poke me tongue out at her back. She's welcome to rinse out piss stains for ever for all I care.

As I come to the foot of St Andrew's Hill, I see carriages waiting on the pathway. One of them is the gold and black liveried carriage from the manor. Its matching footmen are lolling against the wall. They barely look at me as I limp by and make me way up to the church. The deep echo of organ pipes is fading to nothing as I lift the heavy latch of the huge wooden door and creep inside. I slide into a pew at the very back of the church. No one turns round to look. Reverend Strawbridge is standing up in the pulpit looking very pleased with himself, as though everyone's come to see him and not God. As he starts to speak, I begin to search the pews in front of me for any sign of Noah. There are plenty of bonnets and fancy hats balanced atop towering piles of hair and I have to peer between them to get a better view. I twist and turn and wriggle in me seat as if I've got spiders in me drawers. And then I see him. Right near the front. I want to kneel straight away and thank God!

I can't see much of him; just one shoulder and half of his head. But it's enough. I feel all warm inside now; like everything's all right. I don't listen to a word of the Reverend's sermon or sing a word of the hymns. I just stare hard at the back of Noah's head and pray that he'll turn around and see me. I cough out loud twice, but still he doesn't turn around. A woman right in front of me does, though. She glares at me and tsks, so I cough again. When everyone bows their heads to pray, I tear a corner from a page of a hymn book and quickly roll it into a ball. I keep me eyes on the back of Noah and throw the roll of paper over the top of the bent heads. The paper catches in a strand of his hair and I hold me breath. It trembles for a moment, and then falls on his shoulder. Still I hold me breath. Suddenly, in a tiny movement that I almost miss, Noah brushes the paper from his shoulder. I am staring so hard now that me eyes are watering. But he doesn't turn around and I finally let me breath out in a small whisper of frustration.

I nip out quickly as the service finishes and wait at the back of the churchyard, leaning against the old stone wall. They all come out, the gentlefolk, and gather around each other, parading their finery. Then finally Noah appears, looking like a proper toff in his Sunday-best buttoned-up frock coat. But I drink in the sight of his face. He doesn't see me standing here. He's too busy chattering with his father. The dark-haired girl is standing behind him next to Lady de Clevedon and another gaggle of decorated ladies. I wonder who she is and why she is here. They start to move out of the churchyard. The men place their hats back on their heads and the skirts of the ladies sway and bob over their wide under-cages. I wait to see what Noah is going to do. The churchyard empties. There is only Noah, Sir John, Lady de Clevedon and Reverend Strawbridge left.

Then it happens. Noah glances up and his eyes meet mine. Properly meet mine. His eyes widen and he quickly looks back to where his mother and father are still deep in conversation. He starts to walk slowly away from them, so I peel meself from the wall and begin to dawdle out of the churchyard. I want to rush to him straight away but I can see he is nervous about greeting me in front of his parents. Has he not told them about me yet? I peer at a dog rose and the white blackthorn flowers that are growing in the hedgerow that lines the pathway down the hill from the church to the village. I check behind and Noah is walking towards me. He's not smiling. His face is pink. Sir John and Lady de Clevedon are close on his heels. I move away from the hedgerow and as soon as Noah comes by me side I whisper quickly, 'Noah! I'm so glad to see you home safe. I'll be at the beach tonight, eleven o'clock. Please come!'

Anyone looking will have seen him walk straight past me as though I wasn't there, but I was close enough to hear him whisper back, 'I will bring some wine!'

58

Shadows and Moonbeams

At last! He spoke to me. I put me hand to me chest to calm the clamour inside. I watch him walk the rest of the way back to his carriage and then I crumple to the ground and sit there for an age, not quite believing his words. It'd been a barely there whisper. *'I will bring some wine!'* But I'd caught it all the same. I'm so comforted that I want to stay here for the rest of day and not move till it's time to meet him. But a sudden hunger catches me unawares and I realise I haven't eaten much for days. It's like me belly knows everything is sorted now and it's bellowing for food.

Mistress Miles is nowhere to be seen as I pass by her cottage on me way home. But her whites are still fluttering on their string lines. Just for the devil of it, and partly because I'm feeling in such high spirits, I pick up a handful of earth and fling it over the clean linen. I wish I could stay and see her face when she finds all her hard work spoiled.

Ma's still not up when I get back to Ratcatcher's Row.

Smoaker glowers at me. 'Where've you been?' he asks. 'Your ma's sick. You can't just bugger off like that.'

I think for a moment. 'I've been to church,' I say.

'Church?' Smoaker's eyebrows disappear into the wrinkles on his forehead. 'Now why would you be taking yourself off to church?'

'I've been praying for me ma to get well,' I answer.

Smoaker doesn't know what to say after that, so I busy meself boiling potatoes and fetching the Sunday bacon from the pantry. Me and Smoaker fill our bellies and I take a small dish through to Ma. But she waves it away and asks instead for beer. It stinks in the bedchamber, of old shit and illness. I open the shutters to let the air in. 'Ma, I'll be sleeping in the kitchen tonight,' I say. 'Give you some peace.' I don't think she cares one way or another. She just groans at me.

'Get me that beer, Marnie. And close those shutters. I'm freezing.'

Me mood can't be blackened tonight. Nothing's too much trouble. I fetch Ma her beer and clear away the supper pots. I whistle as I rinse the bowls. 'What you got to be so happy about?' Smoaker asks.

'Nothing to be *un*happy about,' I say. I'm not going to tell him that me heart's skipping inside. That after all these months of waiting and yearning I'm going to be with Noah again. Soon though, I'll be able to tell Smoaker and Ma everything; I'll be able to tell the world everything. Soon as Noah says it's all right.

I get to the beach early. The church bells have only just chimed ten. I couldn't help meself. I'd rather be waiting here than pacing the floor at the cottage. Besides, being on the beach makes me feel closer to Noah somehow, and I want to be here first, to welcome him. There's a light burning in the tollhouse. From down here on the beach it looks like a tiny castle perched on the edge of a dark cliff. The pier stands haughty next to it, its long length disappearing into the darkness out at sea.

Steamers, all the way from Wales, have been landing at the pier's jetty all week now, bringing more and more visitors to the beach. Smoaker reckons if it carries on like this we'll have to get some more bathing machines built. The jetty'll make it easier for me pa to land now, I think. I find meself a comfy spot next to mine and Noah's rock and settle down to wait.

As I stare out to sea and watch the stars kissing the horizon, I realise I haven't thought of me pa in ages. For the first time ever I imagine how I'd feel if he never came back. I think about it slowly and carefully, going this way and that way in me head. Always I come back to Noah. As long as Noah is with me, I think, maybe I could let me pa stay away. It doesn't feel too bad when I think of it like that. Maybe Pa's happy where he is, and maybe it's time I let him stay there.

Me backside starts to bruise where it's been resting on the shingle. I stand and stretch meself. It must be nearly eleven by now. Noah'll be on his way, hurrying down the esplanade. The hairs on me arms start to prickle and stiffen, like they're readying themselves for his embrace. I walk up and down the beach for a while, humming anxiously. I hear the distant chimes of the church bells and I stop and count. One . . . Two . . . Three . . . Four . . . Five . . . Six . . . Seven . . . Eight . . . Nine . . . Ten . . . Eleven. Then there's nothing. Only the sound of the sea rolling impatiently on to the shingle.

I can't believe he won't come. Me teeth start knocking together, even though I don't feel cold. I rub me arms and pull me shawl tighter across me shoulders. I keep looking back at the beach steps, expecting to see the shape of Noah standing at the top.

Then the light goes out at the tollhouse. The pier master must have taken to his bed. I'm alone now. Just me; standing on the beach while the rest of the world sleeps. Is that where you are, Noah? I ask him. Have you forgotten about me? Are you curled up under your blankets dreaming of things I don't know about? A sudden sadness washes over me. It starts at me toes and sweeps up through me legs and belly till it's filling me head. But I hold it back. I won't let it turn to tears.

Something or someone has stopped him from coming. He wouldn't leave me on me own like this. I know it. I can feel in me heart how much he wants to be with me. If I close me eyes tight, I swear I can hear his thoughts. *I am sorry, Marnie*, he's saying. *I tried to get there. I really did*. He's looking out from his window, I'm sure of it. From high up there at the edge of the village, he's looking down on to the beach trying to catch sight of me. But it's too far away in the darkness for him to see anything other than shadows and moonbeams. I'm comforted by his words though, and something inside me hardens. I'll be strong for you, Noah, I tell him.

I won't let you be taken from me.

59

The Journal of Noah de Clevedon

Clevedon. APRIL 4th 1869, Sunday

Today passed pleasantly enough. Spring has well and truly come to Clevedon and our merry party spent the afternoon in the gardens. I walked with Cissie along the upper terraces and we watched the jackdaws croaking around the crumbling chimney pots of the manor. Afternoon tea was served in the orangery, after which we played a few rounds of croquet. It has become quite a craze of late and is most popular with the ladies. Arnold showed me how to send a ball into the bushes as an excuse to search the undergrowth with Cissie (with no chaperone at our heels!). He is a devil indeed. But I did steal a kiss from my love and we were deemed rotten at the game as we managed to lose our balls three times in a row!

One thing that marred the day, though – the girl Marnie was waiting outside church after service had finished this morning. It was a shock to see her there, especially as Cissie and Mother and Father were close by. Luckily I think she sensed my embarrassment and did not approach me directly. As I walked past her to get to the carriage she issued an invitation for me to meet her on the beach. For one terrible moment I thought Mother and Father should hear as they were walking close behind. I hissed at her to 'leave me alone!' and I hope that will be the end of the matter.

60

A Metal Hoop and a Hammer

I haven't slept well. Ma called for me three times in the night and then every time I tried to close me eyes all I could see was the back of Noah's head. No matter how much shouting and pleading I did, he wouldn't turn around and look at me. Now me own head's banging with tiredness.

So, I'm telling the truth when I complain to Smoaker of not feeling too good. 'I'm not right today,' I tell him. 'I'd best have a day out of the sea to shake it off. I know we can't afford another doctor's bill.'

Smoaker's not happy and he'll give the other dippers a hard time today, I know. But it's just how it is, and I don't care too much. It's a warm day, fresh and clean, and I can hear the lambs bleating on the hills behind when I go outside to empty Ma's chamber pot in the privy. It's a pity I won't be on the beach today. Before Noah, I wouldn't have missed a day like this for the world. But he's under me skin now; buried there deep. He's stolen me heart away from the sea.

I see to it that Ma is comfy. She won't have the shutters open, so all I can do is tuck her blanket around her and leave a bowl of broth and a pot of beer by her side. 'Be a good girl, Marnie,' she murmurs to me.

'I always am,' I say. I put on a clean apron and lace me boots up tight. I've got the whole day to meself now and there's only one thing I want to do with it.

The village is thronging with strangers. They're parading purposefully up and down the esplanade; gentlemen in straw boaters and caps and ladies in cumbersome gowns and fanciful hats. Miss Cranston's is bulging at the seams with matrons taking tea and nibbling fine pastries, dropping their crumbs on to lace tablecloths. I can already see five or six bathing machines dotted along the shoreline. A band of rusty fishermen in their smocks and heavy blanket trousers are leaning over the railings puffing slowly on their pipes. Their wives have set up stalls along the way and are screeching, 'Mackerel! Fresh mackerel!' at every passer-by. For a few pence they are splitting and grilling the fish with a little butter and salt. Me mouth waters at the smell. The pier seems to be swaying under the weight of people tramping up and down its decking and I can see white clouds sailing from the funnel of the steamer that's docked at the end.

I walk by it all and out of the village. The crowds thin out and soon there's only the odd farmer and cart, so no one sees me as I begin the climb up the road to the manor. I go careful and take me time. I've got all day, and I know the road well enough by now to mind the biggest pits and rocks. When I finally reach the gates to the manor, they're open. I stand at the bottom of the driveway looking up at the soft grey walls and at the windows blinking at me in the spring sunshine. I stare up at Noah's window. If he's there now, looking down at me, I won't have to go any further. He'll come running out to me and at last he can tell me himself of the troubles he's been having. But he doesn't come running. No one comes running. The manor just stands there silently, mocking me and sneering. I toss me head at it and begin to walk up the driveway. I'm not sure what me plan is, but I know I'm not going to the Grand door. I go around the side of the manor, the way I always go, and I keep me eyes and ears open for any sight or sound of anyone. I hear horses snuffling in the stables and whistling coming from inside the gardener's building. I pass by the servants' entrance and come to the kitchen door. It's half open and I hear voices and low laughter. I wonder for a moment if I should go inside. With me apron on, maybe I'd be mistaken for a maid. I could keep me head down and search the whole place for Noah. But then a voice from inside the kitchen grows louder and I'm afraid someone's coming out and I'll be caught before I've even begun. 'Hetty!' a voice shouts. 'Hurry up with them papers and camphor. I ain't got till Christmas!'

I hasten away and hide meself behind a small bush. I stand there a while until the voices from the kitchen fade away and I'm certain there's no one about. I part the bush with me fingers and between the sprigs of green I see the edge of the gardens disappearing around the back of the manor. I take a deep breath to steady meself and I limp as fast as I can to the wall opposite and press meself against it. I edge along it, one

271

step at a time, until I reach the end. I poke me head around the corner and I gasp at how lovely the gardens are. The lawn is emerald green and smooth as pond water. It stretches up to the woods behind and there are stone steps that lead to another garden, high up under the trees, with a house made of glass, twinkling in the sun. I've never seen anything like it. I want to pull off me boots and run across the grass and feel it tickle between me toes. I wish, I wish, I *wish* I could do that. I grip me stick in me hand and swear to meself that one day I will. One day me leg will be strong and straight and me and Noah will run across the grass together and nobody'll be able to catch us.

I hear a noise and I look back to the manor and see some large glass doors being opened on to the garden. Two maids walk out carrying a table. Others follow with chairs and trays laden with jugs and plates of food. They carry everything to the far end of the garden and arrange it all underneath the shade of an oak tree. As they walk back towards the manor, more people spill out of the glass doors. There's the girl with the dark hair again. She floats over the lawn, the hem of her white lace dress trailing along behind her. A white parasol dangles from her wrist and she holds her head high. Some gentlemen follow behind her. They are hatless and wearing fancy silk vests in jewelled reds, greens and blues. They're carrying small balls and metal hoops and large hammers. Two other girls in wide-brimmed hats and crinolines flounce out on to the lawn too and then, just as I'm wondering where Noah can be, he's there, walking out of the glass doors with Prince by his side and another young man; a good-looking young man with fair hair and a pale moustache lounging across his upper lip. Noah and the fair-haired man are laughing at something. Noah punches him on the shoulder. 'Arnold!' he shouts. 'You are incorrigible!'

I don't know what the word means, but I can see how happy Noah looks. I want to go and join him, but it doesn't feel right somehow with all those others there. So I stay where I am and watch awhile. At least I have him in me sights now.

One of the gentlemen hammers the metal hoops into the lawn. Then one by one, each person holds on to a hammer and tries, it seems, to hit a ball through a hoop. It seems a strange way to pass the day, but I'm sure if *I* was to have a go I'd knock a ball straight through the middle of one of those hoops. Prince runs from one person to another, stealing a rub behind the ears or a pat on the head. The girl with the dark hair can barely hold her hammer straight. Noah goes to her and stands behind her. He reaches his arms around her waist and places his hands next to hers on the hammer. They take a swing together and the girl laughs when the ball rolls slowly through the middle of a hoop. As Noah steps away his hand brushes a curl of hair from off her neck. Me mouth's gone dry and me legs are shaking. I try to shout his name but only a thin croak comes out.

It's Noah's turn with the hammer now. He grips the handle and smiles at the girl with the dark hair before he swings his arms back and hits the ball hard. I watch it roll quickly across the lawn. It's coming towards me. Noah shrugs his shoulders and lifts his hands in defeat. He drops the hammer on the lawn and begins loping across the lawn after the ball. Prince is running ahead of him. Strings of drool are flapping against his muzzle. The ball rolls to the edge of the lawn and stops just inches from me feet. In another moment Noah will be here. He'll see I've come to find him. A picture flashes through me head. I'm out there with the rest of them, on the lawn, and I'm knocking balls through all the hoops and Noah's got his arms around me waist and he's whispering in me ear how much he's missed me. Me tongue's sticking to the roof of me mouth now and the palms of me hands are damp.

Prince stops by the ball and sniffs at it. He pushes at it with his wet snout, then his ears prick and the ball is forgotten as he sees me hiding around the corner. He barks once and wags his tail furiously. He leaps to greet me and his fat paws land square on me chest. Then suddenly Noah's here too and he's standing staring at me with an odd look on his face. I think if I open me mouth me heart will leap straight out of it.

'What are you doing here?' he hisses at me. He takes a handkerchief from his vest pocket and wipes it across his forehead. He looks back quickly over his shoulder. Prince whines and drops back to the ground to go and sit at Noah's heel.

I take a deep swallow to loosen me tongue. 'You . . . you never came,' I whisper. 'I waited for you. I . . . I waited for you. I knew something was wrong. So . . . so I came to you instead.'

Noah frowns. Someone shouts his name. 'I'm coming!' he yells back.

Noah shakes his head at me. 'Look. I don't know what you want. But you can't stay here. Please. Go, before somebody sees you.'

Poor Noah. He's panicking and scared. Frightened his father

will see us together, I expect. 'This isn't what you want,' I say quickly. 'I know it's not.' I smile at him and hold out me hand to touch his arm. He flinches and moves back a step. Poor thing. He's as nervous as a rabbit. I can't go yet. There's too much left to say. I want to tell him that we're safe for a moment. No one can see us here. 'Is it your father?' I say gently. 'Has he forbidden you to see me? We can go to him together, you know. I'll help you to change his mind. He'll soon see sense. Especially when we tell him about the baby.' I know there isn't a baby any more, but I'm not ashamed of me lie.

'I have no idea what you are talking about.' A flush of pink is creeping up Noah's neck from under his starched white collar.

'Noah! Have you got lost?' a voice shouts in the distance. Prince barks excitedly and bounds off back to the gardens.

Noah stuffs his handkerchief back in his vest pocket and bends to pick up the ball. 'I want you to go now, Marnie,' he says stiffly. 'You have no business being here. Go now. Before you get thrown out for trespassing.'

'But Noah!' I reach me hand out to him again, but he's turned and is heading away from me. 'Noah!' I urge. I manage to grab his shoulder, but he shrugs me off and as he walks away his handkerchief falls at me feet.

'Just go!' he pleads.

And then he's gone. I hear a babble of voices and Prince barking and I'm ready to go after him, to show me face in front of all the others. But instead I bend down and pick up Noah's handkerchief. Did he mean to drop it there for me? To give me something else of his while we can't be together? This handkerchief is made of the finest silk. I smooth it in me hands, then I lift it to me nose and breathe in Noah's scent. I've never smelled anything like it before. It's sweeter than Miss Cranston's on baking day or wet grass on a spring morning. It smells fresher than a stack of clean linen or a spray of sea foam. It's better than all the good things I've ever smelled in me whole life, all mixed up together. I fold it carefully and tuck it in me apron pocket. 'Thank you, Noah,' I whisper.

I make me way back down the road to the village. I feel lighter now and contented. It'll take some time, but at least I know what's wrong now. We'll make it right with Sir John somehow. He wouldn't see his son unhappy, I'm certain of it. But for now, I've another piece of Noah safe in me pocket and the sun is shining brighter than a new penny.

61

The Journal of Noah de Clevedon

Clevedon. APRIL 5th 1869, Monday

What is that girl thinking? Coming here and telling me she is with child? Lord above, is she completely insane? She had no belly that I could see, and if she is with child I am certain it can't be mine. Heaven knows how many other men she has lain with, she is such a wild one. Why oh why did I ever befriend her?

I must shake her off. I cannot have our association brought to Father's attention or indeed to Cissie's. The nerve of her! To come to the manor like that, and to sneak around spying! I've a mind to confide in Arnold. He will know what to do. It is an annoyance I could do without, as I am quite intent on asking Lord Baird for his daughter's hand in marriage before the week is out!

62

Red-Hot Angry Words

It's been busy this last week. Everyone in the world wants to be in Clevedon, promenading on the pier or bathing in the sea. From early morning to late in the afternoon the bathing machines are trundled to the water's edge. I've dipped so many fragile and paper-light ladies that their faces and bodies look and feel all the same to me now. They scrunch up their features and mewl like babies; until I plunge them under, that is. That's the best part of all. When I see their eyes grow big as saucers and their chicken-bone fingers grasp at the air, I want to laugh out loud. I don't of course. I just murmur niceties to them, like, '*There, that wasn't too bad, was it?*' or, '*My, my, madam, your complexion looks much improved already.*'

They come to the sea for strength, but not one of them knows the true might of the ocean. They would all drown in an instant if I was to let go of their bony waists. It's a strange thing to hold their lives in me hand, to have them cling to me and trust me, when out of their bathing gowns they wouldn't give me the time of day.

Noah's on me mind the whole time. Every time I close me eyes I see his face; his perfect face: his pale smooth skin, the turn of his mouth and the despair in his eyes that I want to kiss away. I've put his handkerchief with the other one under the firebrick in the backyard. I try not to smell it too often as I don't want to sniff the scent of him away.

I'm thinking of him now, as me last customer of the day climbs up the steps back into the bathing machine. She's panting like a dog, but just like all the rest of the bathers, she's trying to keep hold of her dignity despite being as wet and bedraggled as an old dishcloth. I wade out of the sea and round the machine to lead the horse back up the beach. This is the worst bit. Me costume is so heavy with water it feels the weight of a suit of armour and me stockings fall down me legs like wrinkles of leathery skin. It's a struggle without me stick and I'm glad I've got the horse's harness to hold on to. Me leg's feeling stronger these days though, I'm sure of it. I'm scared to think it in case it's not true, but what if working in the sea all day is curing me at last? I wish I could tell this to Noah, and not just in a letter.

But I will write him another one tonight, like I've done every day this week. I don't care if Smoaker notices his paper missing; I have to let Noah know how much I love him.

There's still customers waiting at the hut when I get there. But none of them are mine. I finish earlier than the other dippers, so I can go back to Ratcatcher's Row and mind Ma. Smoaker doesn't know it, but once I've changed back into me frock, I don't go straight to Ma. I walk up to the manor first and take the letter I wrote the night before. It's always the same maid who answers the door, and now she just snatches the letters from me hand without hardly looking at me. The letter I wrote last night is in the pocket of me frock. As I walk the road to the manor, I think about the words I wrote and hope they'll bring some comfort to Noah.

> My love Noah,
> I'm still here waiting for you. Our child is growing bigger by the day. Have you spoken to your father yet? Be brave and do it soon. We are meant to be together. We both know it to be true. Send word to me soon.
> Remember how much I love you.
> Marnie

As I near the Grand door of the manor, I take the letter from me pocket and as always I look around me and up at Noah's chamber window, hoping to catch a glimpse of him. I'm sure Sir John must be keeping him prisoner in there. But I'm puzzled as to why Noah is never at his window looking out for me, when he must know by now I always deliver his letter at this time of day.

I pull the old rope of the doorbell and it clangs loudly in the still air of early evening. A moment passes and I hear footsteps echoing from inside. There's the clank of metal latches and the door swings open. I hold the letter out in front of me and set a smile on me lips. Then the best thing in the world happens. It's not the hard-faced maid peering out me from the shadows of the manor, but Noah himself. Me hand drops to me side.

'Noah!' I gasp.

Noah stands for a moment, like he's so glad to see me he doesn't know what to say.

'I knew if I kept coming I'd soon see you,' I say. I start to climb the few steps towards him. 'Oh, Noah! What are we going to do? I can't bear it much longer.'

Noah takes me arm and leads me back down the steps. His grip is tight. He turns me to face him and looks straight in me eyes. When he begins to talk, his voice is low and slow and deliberate. 'I have no idea what is going on in your head, Marnie. But you have to stop this now. If you ever thought there was anything between us, you were wrong. Stop sending me letters. Stop coming to the manor. There can *never* be anything between us. Do you understand?'

I watch his mouth move and I hear the sounds he's making. His face is so earnest and I want to hold it in me hands. I remember the touch of *his* hands on me twisted foot: the shock of it, the warmth of it and the rightness of it. And I remember how our bodies were together on the beach and how he made me his. I want to keep the memory of it all for ever. I hear his words all right. But I don't want to. He put these feelings in me and it's too much for me to bear on me own. It's not fair if he won't share. I stick me chin out at him. 'You don't mean what you're saying. I don't believe you.'

'Marnie, I cannot say it any clearer.' He lowers his voice and clenches his teeth. 'You are just a village girl and I am the son of Sir John de Clevedon. What happened between us should never have been. You must leave me alone now or I shall be forced to call upon the law. I shall deny ever knowing you and no one will believe anything you say. Leave now. Please.'

He walks up the steps to the Grand door and as he steps into the manor he turns his head. 'Go now, Marnie, and don't ever bother me again.'

As he starts to close the door, red-hot angry words bubble up me throat and fly from me mouth. 'I don't care for your fancy words, Noah de Clevedon!' I shout. 'But I know you love me!' The door closes with a bang and a rattle. 'I know you love me! I know you love me!' I scream at the blank wood. I can't believe he's done that. I can't believe he's shut the door in me face. I stand where I am for an age, thinking all sorts and nothing at the same time. Eventually all the anger runs out of me and I sag in the middle like an old straw mattress.

I limp back down the driveway and out on to the road. Me leg is shaking so much it can't hold me up any more. I sit on the side of the road propped up against the flaking bark of a beech tree. I stare down at the ground and before long I'm watching a line of black ants scurry through the dust from one small rock to another. They don't seem to know where they're going. I poke me stick into the midst of them and they scatter in panic, in every direction. But a moment later they've found each other again and they carry on as before, as though nothing has happened.

I stay sitting until me muscles ache and the sky turns dirty orange. Then, slowly and stiffly, I stand and walk back down the road, leaning heavily on me stick. When I get back to the cottage, Smoaker is boiling mad at me. 'Where've you been, girl?' he shouts. 'Your ma's been laid out on the floor all afternoon thanks to you!'

'What do you mean?' I ask.

'You never came back, did you?' Smoaker yells. 'And your ma got so parched she got out of bed to fetch some water and fell flat on her back.'

'Oh,' I say. 'Is she all right?'

'Well, she's back in bed. As for the rest of it, you'd better go and see for yourself.'

I start walking towards the bedchamber. 'Oi!' shouts Smoaker. 'Where *have* you been? Answer me that.'

'I haven't been nowhere, Smoaker,' I answer dully. 'Nowhere.'

'Hey! Come back here!' Smoaker's voice lands hard on me back, but I take no notice of it as I open the door to Ma's room and then close it behind me.

'You all right, Ma?' I say as I sit on the edge of the bed. There's a candle flickering on the bed stand next to her. The flame lights up the new white streaks in her hair and throws shadows in the hollows of her shrunken cheeks. Her arms lie outside the blanket, like raw beef sausages.

'Marnie?' she says. Her voice is sleep-thick and blurred around the edges.

'It's me,' I say. There's a brown bottle and a spoon lying next to the candle. Smoaker must have given her a dose of her laudanum.

'How was the sea today, Marnie?' she murmurs.

'It was warm, Ma,' I tell her. 'Plenty of bathers.'

'That's good.' She sighs deeply and I think she's dropped back to sleep. I listen to her breathing and the rattle in her chest. I wonder for a moment what Noah's doing right now. But it hurts so much to think it that I stop and I shake Ma's shoulder instead. 'Ma? Ma? You're not sleeping, are you?' She

283

stirs and groans. 'I'm still here, Ma,' I say. 'And I want to know something. I want to know about me pa.'

'You don't have a pa,' Ma slurs. 'Told you, Marnie. Found you in a seashell.'

'You told me that when I was little, Ma. I'm fifteen now and I need to know. I need to know the truth. Who was he? Who was me pa?' Ma mumbles something I can't hear. 'What did you say, Ma? What did you say?' I ask her.

Her eyes flick open and she looks at me. I keep quiet and wait for her answer.

'He gave you your name, you know.'

'Who did? Me pa?'

'It was him that wanted to call you Marnie.'

'Me pa wanted to call me Marnie? But who was he, Ma? Where is he now?'

'Means from the sea, it does. That's why he wanted to name you Marnie . . . Marnie from the sea . . . ' Ma's voice trails off. She takes a shuddering breath and closes her eyes.

'Ma?' I shake her shoulder again. 'Ma! Tell me!' She's breathing heavily now. A snore rumbles from her throat. I shake her again, but I know it's useless. The laudanum's got her now. She's fast asleep and I've got no more chance than a cat in hell without claws of waking her.

Back in the kitchen, Smoaker glowers at me over the bowl of his pipe. 'She's asleep now,' I offer. Smoaker doesn't reply. I think his anger at me has taken away what few words he has. He knocks the ashes from his pipe into the red embers of the fire and places his pipe on the mantelpiece. He leaves the kitchen and I hear his footsteps tread wearily up the stairs.

I drag me mattress in front of what remains of the fire. I lay down on me side and curl up as small as I can. I press me hands on me belly to where the pain is worse. It's like there's a rat inside me gnawing at me guts. There is no baby, I know that, but I won't let Noah do this to me. He can't make me love him like this and then toss me aside like a rotten fish. I'll make him see that he loves me. He doesn't need anyone else. He only needs me. It's as simple as that.

The night passes slowly. I watch the thick black of it change to a milky grey and then to a dull yellow before I leave me mattress to build the fire and set the kettle to boil.

63

The Journal of Noah de Clevedon

Clevedon. APRIL 10th 1869, Saturday

I hope I have put the matter of Marnie to rest now. I showed Arnold her letters declaring her passion for me. He found the whole situation highly amusing of course, until I pressed upon him the potential for disaster should Father, Cissie or indeed Lord Baird hear word of it. He was uncharacteristically serious for a moment, for which I am grateful. 'It is simple, my dear fellow,' he said. 'You must station yourself within earshot of the Grand door. When the bell rings you must answer the door while I distract whichever maid is hurrying there herself. You tell this wench, in no uncertain terms, to put a stop to her nonsense or you will have no choice but to set the authorities upon her.'

I have to say his plan worked beautifully and the girl eventually left. As luck would have it, everyone was in the garden when she screamed at the door. Thank God! I don't know how I would have explained that away. They say we are all entitled to a few mistakes in life. I hope I make no more like that. I will wait with apprehension to see if another letter arrives before I can fully congratulate Arnold and myself.

We organised a sketching party this afternoon. A picnic was laid out for us in the meadow by the top woods. Paper, paints, pencils and easels were set out for our convenience and a more pleasant few hours you could not have wished for. Cissie insisted on using me as her subject. I did not complain of course, for it was the perfect excuse for me to stare at her beautiful face and milky shoulders without interruption.

I am to speak to Lord Baird tomorrow. The time has come, and although I am sure the outcome will be successful, I cannot help the nerves that are churning in my stomach. A glass of wine before bed to settle my thoughts, I think!

64

Broken Shells

It's quiet this Sunday morning. There are few people about. The air seems hushed, the sea is calm. Maybe it's because it's early or maybe it's because I'm calm meself. I know now that I haven't tried hard enough to reach into Noah's heart. I have to do better. I can't let anything get between us, not even Noah's own words. I've got to be the strong one now.

The sea has tossed its memories up on the tide line; broken shells, twisted salt-bleached wood, brittle fish bones, a dead gull and tangles of black seaweed. Me heart tugs as I look at the mess of it. Me own memories are down there on the beach too: me screams when Ma dipped me under the waves for the first time, the mark of me stick deep in the shingle, me sandy footprints on the stone steps, the salt of me sweat melted into the ocean, strands of me hair floating on the surface, mine and Noah's laughter blowing in the wind and the sweet, sweet taste of him on me lips.

I feel like I'm saying me goodbyes to the best friend I've

ever had. But me heart lies another way now. It doesn't belong under the glossy surface of the sea any more or in the spit of foam in the curl of a wave. It belongs in another place, away from the sea, past the esplanade, beyond the village and as far away from the sea as you can be in Clevedon. It belongs up at the manor with Noah. So I turn me back on the ocean and I walk away.

I let meself quietly into the church. The congregation are seated and I check for the gleam of Noah's hair amongst the Sunday bonnets and oiled heads. He is seated at the end of the third pew from the front. I step back out of the church and close the door behind me. I am content he is there.

I stand in the churchyard listening to the din of voices from inside singing hymns. I wait quietly and patiently and soon the wooden doors swing open and the God-fearing of Clevedon waft out into the spring sunshine. I stand with me hands clasped in front of me and I lean gently on the cracked stone of a moss-covered grave. I see the girl with the dark hair first, then Sir John and Lady de Clevedon and Noah's friend – the one with the fair hair and wicked glint in his eye. Then I see Noah. But I don't move. I stand still as the gravestone with me gaze fixed upon him. I know he sees me when his face flushes red and he presses himself to his fair-haired friend and whispers something in his ear. The friend darts a look at me and hurries Noah away down the pathway towards the waiting carriages. Poor Noah. He thinks he doesn't want me, but I know he does.

I pull meself away from the gravestone and limp past Reverend Strawbridge, who is deep in conversation with Sir John. I let meself back into the church and breathe in the dank stone smell of it. It's empty now and the tap of me stick echoes in the silence. I walk as far as the third pew from the front and pick up the hymn book that's resting on the small shelf in front. The book Noah's just been holding. I press me hands around it, sensing the touch of him flowing into me. I slip the hymn book into me pocket and smile. It's comforting to feel the book bang against me leg as I walk back to Ratcatcher's Row.

I go to the backyard first and take Noah's handkerchiefs from under the firebrick. I slip the squares of cotton and silk between the pages of the hymn book and put it back in me pocket. It's good to have these parts of him so close to me.

I go about me chores quietly. I give Ma an extra dose of laudanum. I think as it's Sunday she deserves some proper rest. I boil some potatoes and put some bacon to spit in a pan of fat. I sweep the kitchen floor and sew a patch on one of Smoaker's shirts. He sits in his chair by the fire and sucks on his pipe. We don't speak. With Ma away in the bedchamber there isn't anything to say between us.

We eat our supper in silence and then I take some broth through to Ma. She manages a few mouthfuls, but most of it dribbles from her chin on to the blanket underneath, which is already crusty with past meals. 'I got meself a man, Ma,' I say. Her eyeballs roll under her thinly stretched eyelids. I think she's listening. 'I got meself a proper man, Ma,' I say again. 'He's handsome and kind and he loves me. Did you hear me? He loves me. He don't care about me leg. He just loves *me*.' I pick up her hand. It's cold and clammy. 'Are you listening, Ma?' I ask. Her fingers twitch and I know from somewhere deep inside of her she can hear me. 'I told you about him before, Ma, but you didn't believe me. It's Noah, Ma, from up at the manor. Do you remember me telling you? He's a proper gent. I thought I was with child. Cos we did it, Ma, right on the beach, we did. I'm not, though. Having a baby, that is. But it makes no difference to anything.' I let go of her hand and put me fingers on me lips. If I close me eyes and think hard enough I can remember exactly how his kiss felt. Soft and warm. Like going home to somewhere I never knew I had. I shiver and open me eyes. 'Anyway, Ma,' I say, 'you'd best get yourself better. I'll be bringing him here to meet you soon.' Her eyes flicker again under her closed lids. But this time I think she's just dreaming.

When I go back to the kitchen, Smoaker has taken himself to bed, leaving behind only the whiff of his pipe smoke. It's not quite dark yet. When I go outside the air is trembling silver under the freshly risen moon. It makes for an easy walk up the road to the manor. I pass through the iron gates and keep to the shadows as I near the old stone walls. Me heart is thudding hard. Not because I'm afraid of being caught, but because I'm near to where Noah is. Round the side of the manor, just past the door to the kitchen, there's a line of washing hanging limply in the late evening air. Someone will get into trouble for not taking that in. I move away quickly, leaving behind the sounds of servants hard at work. I know exactly where to go, and soon I'm there, by the big lighted window. I hold me breath as I peer inside and I'm not disappointed. They're all in there; the fancy ladies and the dapper gentlemen. Some are gathered by the fire, others are lounging in soft velvet chairs. There's the girl with the dark hair. This time she's dressed in a

291

powdery-blue silk with a cascade of white flowers in her hair. She looks a vision and a shard of envy stabs into me heart. There's the fair-haired young man. He's leaning against the fireplace stroking his moustache. His mouth is stretched into a silent laugh. And there's Noah. I lean against the cold stone and fix me eyes on him. All the others fade to nothing; their faces, their jewelled gowns. Even the glow of the fire becomes a distant haze. There's only Noah now. Noah and me. Just being here, being this close to him, is enough for now.

I stand there for an age. There's nowhere else I'd rather be. I watch Noah's mouth move. I watch how the candlelight turns the brown of his hair a coppery orange. I watch him tuck a lock of his hair behind his ear. I watch him take a sip of golden liquid from a glass. He seems as happy as I have ever seen him. I watch his hand holding the glass and his other one reach down to rub the top of his wolfhound's head. I see how his face softens and his eyes shine as he bends his head to murmur something to the hound. Me hands clench into angry fists. I want to go in there and shove the thing out of the way. Noah's smiles and caresses are only for me. It makes me skin crawl to see that animal taking what is mine. I'm glad when it finally sidles off and moves out of me sight. I stay there, close to Noah, until a door in the room opens and Noah and the rest of them leave. I want to hurry and check the other windows to see where they've moved to, but I know it's time I should go back now. It's late and the skies have darkened. But it's of no matter. I'll be back tomorrow night and the next and every night after that. I'll keep on coming until Noah belongs to me.

As I pass by the forgotten washing again, I pull a pair of

white silk stockings from the line. They're Noah's for certain. I push them into me pocket and all the way back to Ratcatcher's Row I smile to meself as I remember how, on the beach, he'd rolled them off his lily-white legs. I'm halfway down the road when I hear barking in the distance. I picture Noah standing by an open door while his hound takes a last run in the grounds. He'll be to his bed soon and it comforts me to think of him away from all the others. It's best to imagine him alone in his room, where I know where he is and that he's thinking of me.

65

The Journal of Noah de Clevedon

Clevedon. APRIL 11th 1869, Sunday

It has been a day of mixed emotions. What should have been the happiest day of my life has been spoiled by that damn girl. She was outside the church again today, despite my words of yesterday. Granted, she did not approach me or speak to me, but somehow that has made my unease even greater. Arnold was interested to see her in the flesh and I had to convince him that despite her unusual beauty I did nothing to encourage her in any way. He said that despite her deformity he would have found her hard to resist himself. But then he is Arnold.

After we returned to the manor I tried to push the hateful encounter from my mind and I met with Lord Baird in the library and asked him for the honour of his daughter's hand in marriage. I think I kept my voice steady and I looked him in the eye when I spoke. He paused for a moment and stroked his great white beard. I am sure my own heart stopped at that moment. But then he clasped my hand in both of his and shook it so hard I thought my whole arm should fall off! 'I am delighted. I am delighted,' he kept saying. I am sure I detected a tear in his wise old eyes. He is a warm-hearted man and I shall be very lucky indeed to have him as my father-in-law.

I went straight to Cissie then. I took her to the gardens and on to the upper terrace by the orangery. The view from up there is magnificent. As we stood gazing over the roofs of the manor, the village below and at the sea spread like a gossamer blanket in the distance, I fell on one knee and asked the most important question of my life. She had no hesitation in consenting to be my wife, and as I have wanted to do for the longest time, I took her perfect face in my hands and kissed her full on the lips. It was as delicious as I had hoped and I can only imagine the greater joys that will soon follow.

I announced our engagement at dinner this evening and the toasts were loud and long. Later, Mother took me to one side and confessed she was saddened to be losing her boy to another woman and asked that I should not neglect her. Poor Mother. I kissed her dear cheek and told her I should never love any woman as I love her and that she should be glad to be gaining a daughter. I think she was consoled.

It is past one in the morning now and my head is spinning with one too many brandies. We shall be returning to London at the end of April. I hope to God the girl stays away until then.

66

A Piece of Bacon

It's a slow day. It's early afternoon and only a handful of bathers have been to hire a machine. I'm minding the hut for Smoaker while he's off to speak to Doctor Bentley. Ma's started babbling nonsense. We can't get a word of sense out of her. Smoaker's put it off for too long, but I knew he'd have to swallow another doctor's bill sooner or later.

I'm sitting out on the slipway watching a straggle of children messing about on the water's edge. The boys have rolled up their britches and are kicking at breaking waves and sending showers of foam over each other. The girls are squealing like eager piglets. They're running in and out of the water, their bare feet slapping hard on the wet sand. For a moment I'm envious of them. They're running so free, with not a care in the world. They're doing what I could never do and always wished I could.

I finger Noah's stockings, hidden deep in me pocket. They're cool and smooth and just the touch of them soothes me mood.

Every night this last week I've been back to the manor. Every night I've stood outside the big window and watched Noah. I couldn't go a day without him now. He'll come to me soon. I know he will. If I just wait for long enough.

Me eyes wander over to the esplanade and I watch the buttoned-up gentry stroll aimlessly up and down. I see a girl carrying a heavy basket over her arm. She's wearing a small straw bonnet balanced proudly on the back of her head. She stops at the railings and rests her basket on the floor. She looks down on to the beach and I can see she is watching the children too. There's something familiar about her. Then she turns her face towards me and straight away I see that it's Hetty.

Without stopping to think, I close the door to the hut and walk up the slipway to the esplanade. I go straight to her and tap her on the shoulder. She jumps and turns to me with a guilty look on her face, as though she's been caught being idle. 'Hetty,' I say, and the guilty look on her face changes to annoyance.

'What do you want?' she asks. She stoops to pick up her basket.

'How . . . how is Noah?' I ask.

Hetty raises her eyebrows. 'Not again! Don't you ever give up?' She snorts loudly.

'It was him that brought me to the manor that time, you know. The time you saw me in the kitchen with him. He's brought me there other times too.'

Hetty smiles widely. 'You're a right case, you are,' she says. 'Belong in Bristol Asylum, I reckon.' She adjusts her basket on her arm and begins to walk away from me.

'Why don't you believe me?' I call after her. 'It's true. Me and Noah are going to be together. You wait and see!'

She stops and turns. 'Oh, really?' She fixes me with spiteful eyes. 'Then how come Master Noah has just got engaged. To Lady Cissie Baird. To be married in the summer, they are.' She grins at me like a cat with a fat mouse in its jaws, and then turns on her heel.

It's like I've been hit in the face with a rock. I hold tight to the railings. 'You're a liar!' I shout after her. 'You're a liar!'

She laughs. It's a merry tinkling sound. 'Master Noah de Clevedon and a dipper's daughter!' she calls back in a sing-song voice. 'Whatever will you come up with next?'

The rest of the day passes in a blur of sea and sand, wet and dry, noise and quiet. I dip a woman who's hoping the sea will cure the affliction that has her skin falling off her in thick yellow flakes. I dip a young girl whose mother tells me is suffering from terrible hysteria. And I dip an old crone who stinks of sweet rotting meat and who wants to live out the rest of the year to annoy her son. The whole time me belly is churning with a mess of anger and hatred and terror and envy. I don't want to believe Hetty's words. But why would she say them if they weren't true?

Back at Ratcatcher's Row, I boil up some supper, but me mind's not on it and the potatoes are as hard as pebbles. Smoaker pushes his bowl away in disgust. 'Your ma's not good, Marnie,' he says to me. 'The doctor can't do no more for her. Says we're to keep her comfy with the shutters closed and feed her as much broth as she'll take. Oh, and I had to pay out for more powders too. But I don't know why if they ain't doing her no good.'

I nod at him and gather the pots for rinsing. I can't think about Ma just now. It's only Noah on me mind. I need to know if what Hetty said is true. I need to know so much that once Smoaker's retired to his bed, I don't even poke me nose around Ma's door before I'm off out the cottage and on me way up to the manor.

I'm breathless and hot by the time I get to the manor gates. It's not quite dark yet, so I keep away from the driveway and walk close to the manor walls till I've passed the Grand door. I go to the first window and peer inside. No candles have been lit. It's shadowy and dim and empty of people. The next window is the same, although I can see a long table set with white plates and glasses and piles of fruit and flowers. The next window I peer into is lit and a fire is burning in an ornate marble fireplace. There's a large oak desk and cushioned chairs and Sir John de Clevedon is sitting in one with a book open on his lap. But there's no Noah. I'm worried now I won't find him. Sweat is trickling down me back and me hands are clammy. There's a clattering from the stables and a young boy comes out carrying a bundle of straw in his arms. I duck down under the window and press meself against the wall. But he's so intent on his task that he doesn't think to look me way, and after he's thrown the straw into the back of a cart he goes back inside the stables. I wipe me hands on me frock and brush the damp hair from me face before I push meself back up on me feet. There's one more window on this side of the manor and I hurry to it, being careful not to tap me stick too loud on the stone pavings.

There's a glow coming from this window. A pool of light is dripping on to the ledge, so I know already the candles have been lit. I balance meself carefully and slowly lift me face to peer through the bottom pane of glass. There are books everywhere, on shelves on every wall. I've never seen so many. There's red ones, green ones, gold and black ones. There's fat ones, thin ones, short ones and tall ones. Seems there's as many sorts of books in the world as there are sorts of people. But it's not them I've come to look at.

I peer deeper into the room and at last me heart is rewarded. There's Noah sitting on the arm of a dark green velvet chair. He's leaning forward and his hair is flopping over the side of his face. Prince is sitting at his feet with his muzzle resting in Noah's lap. But it's who is *sitting* in the chair that makes me belly tighten. It's the dark-haired girl again. Her face is tilted up towards Noah's and she's biting the pink of her bottom lip with a little row of pearly teeth. Lady Cissie Baird. I hate the name already and I've only heard it the once today. She laughs at something Noah says and he cups her chin in his hand. I want to close me eyes now. I don't want to see any more. Already I'm breathing fast and there's an anger bubbling away inside me that's bigger and hotter than I've ever known before. But I keep watching. I can't tear me eyes away.

Noah bends his head closer to the girl's uplifted face. He puts his hand on the back of her head now and before I can even blink, he's kissing her on the mouth. There's a scream pushing its way out of me throat. I want to yell and shout and tell him to stop. I bite me arm instead, hard enough to taste

300

blood, and the pain is nothing to the pain that's tearing at me insides.

It's true then. It's true what Hetty said. Noah is engaged to be married.

I don't remember getting back to the cottage, though I must have fallen at some point because the hem of me frock is all muddied. Me head's so full of black thoughts that I think they might start pouring out me mouth and ears, all thick and sticky as tar. I don't understand why he'd do this to me. If he loves me why would he hurt me so much? He must love me, I think. I remember how it felt on the beach that night. He showed me his love then and it was real and powerful and true. Me head's on fire with anger. How dare he do this to me? Haven't I waited for him all these long months? Haven't I stayed true to *him*? I'm boiling inside. I'm boiling so fast and hard I think I might burst. I want to hurt him now. I want to hurt him as much as he's hurt me. I want Noah to feel the dreadfulness of this much pain. That much he deserves.

It's dark now and I'm going to need a candle. There's one still burning on the mantelpiece in the cottage, so I carry it with me to the pantry and fetch a piece of bacon left over from supper. I wrap the bacon in a cloth and put it safe in me pocket. That was easy. The next part is the hardest. I light Smoaker's lantern and take it with me next door to the rat-catcher's cottage. I check there's no candles still burning in the windows. I'm glad to see it's all in darkness. I open the gate as quietly as I can, making sure not to let it bang back on itself, and I make me way round to the rat-catcher's backyard. There's a small hut

301

at the back of his yard where I know he keeps his poisons. 'Me pa's got buckets full of arsenic!' Ambrose used to boast to me. I'm glad that at last Ambrose has been good for something.

It smells strange inside the hut, like old oil and wet fur. But at least I know there'll be no rats. I lift me lamp up high and shine it on the boxes and tins that line the shelves. I'm not sure where I'll find it or even what it looks like. But I needn't have worried. Me light has caught the red painted letters on an old wooden box stored right near the door. A R S N I K. I lift the lid of the box and see that it's full of tiny grains of white powder. I'm not sure how much I'll need, but I'm sure I shouldn't touch it. There's an old spoon on the shelf above the box, so I pick it up and after I've taken the bacon out of me pocket and undone the cloth, I sprinkle two large spoonfuls of the powder over the meat. Then I add another one just for good measure. I close the lid of the box and wrap the bacon back up carefully, taking care not to spill any of the powder. Then the bacon goes back safe in me pocket.

For the second time today I'm back at the manor. I'm hiding in the bushes at the back, just waiting and listening. Even this far out of the village I can still hear the sea whispering in the distance. The moon is bright tonight and the lawns of the manor look as rich and soft as velvet. I wait for what seems an age. Me legs grow stiff from standing so long and I wriggle me toes in me boots impatiently. Then at last I hear sounds; a door opening and voices murmuring.

'Go on, boy!' I hear Noah shout. Me heart lurches at the sound of his voice. There's a short bark and a whine. The voices by the door are low again and I take the bacon from me pocket to be ready. I hear Prince snuffling near to the right of me and I whistle short and sharp. He barks loudly and comes running to the bushes. Before he reaches me, I throw the bacon out on to the lawn and as I knew he would, he rushes to it and snaps it up in his jaws. He chews fast on the meat, one end of it hanging out the side of his mouth. While he's busy eating, I creep out of the bushes and hurry as best I can back towards the manor gates. Before I've gone halfway, the hound starts barking again and I know he's going to come after me. But so be it. He's eaten the meat now. I hear him bounding towards me and I ready meself for his paws on me back. But then Noah's shouting, 'Prince! Here, boy! Come on. What have you found? A rabbit?' At the sound of his master's voice, Prince yelps excitedly and turns tail back to the manor.

I'm shaking now and I just want to get back to me bed. But I can still smile. And I do, when I think that not long from now Noah will know exactly how much love can really hurt.

67

The Journal of Noah de Clevedon

Clevedon. APRIL 17th 1869, Saturday

Prince is dead. There. I've written the words on paper. But it still doesn't seem real. I can't believe he has gone. I keep seeing the shadow of him at my heel and I keep reaching down to stroke his head. But he's not here any more. We buried him this evening, just before sundown, under the old oak at the bottom of the gardens. It was his favourite place when the days were hot.

I am bereft without him. Poor boy. He died in such agony. Howling all night long. The whole manor was awake suffering along with him. We fear he was poisoned, but the gardener has sworn that he keeps nothing that would inflict so much harm.

The whole place has been quiet today. Even the servants have been mourning him. Poor Hetty could barely serve breakfast this morning for her sobbing. Not that any of us had an appetite. Cissie has done her best to comfort me, the sweet girl. But I fear I will feel this loss for a long time to come.

68

The Journal of Noah de Clevedon

Clevedon. APRIL 18th 1869, Sunday

As we were leaving for church this morning, the gardener brought to me a piece of cloth he found in the gardens under some bushes. 'It has the whiff of the butcher about it, sir,' he said to me. 'And look, see, there are grains of arsenic stuck to it.'

'Are you sure about that?' I asked him. He looked most offended. 'Sir. I know me poisons, and I assure you that is most certainly arsenic. It's what did for your hound, sir,' he said. 'We can be certain of that much.'

Who would do such a thing to poor Prince? To inflict such pain upon an innocent animal? And for what purpose? It is beyond me.

It was with a heavy heart that I attended the morning service. And I couldn't help but look around me at the other churchgoers. Would anyone so wicked as to kill poor Prince dare to enter God's house?

It was only after the service finished, as we gathered in the churchyard and I saw the girl Marnie standing there yet again, that true fear pricked at my heart. She stood there so brazenly, her blue eyes so cold and staring. And she was smiling at me! But it wasn't just any smile. It was a triumphant smile, and it sent a shiver running down my back.

I asked Arnold if he thought she could be capable of poisoning Prince, but he assured me that grief was allowing my imagination to run wild. I am not so sure. There is something about that girl. She won't take no for an answer. And I feel her eyes on me all the time.

69

The Journal of Noah de Clevedon

Clevedon. APRIL 25th 1869, Sunday

It has been a dreadful week. Every day there has been a letter from that girl. It is what she writes that frightens me the most.

I am certain now that she is responsible for poisoning my poor Prince. She writes such strange things. She asks me how much it hurts to lose a loved one. How would she know to ask that if it was not her hand that fed Prince the poisoned meat? She says that now I have learned my lesson perhaps I should be kinder to her. But worst of all she declares her undying love for me and says that nothing will get in the way of us being together. I swear she is quite mad and I am only glad that we are leaving for London next week.

I wish the servants would not bring the letters to me. It is becoming harder and harder to conceal them from Cissie when they are delivered to me in her presence. She is naturally curious as to who is writing to me so often. I have told her they are from friends in London. I am so ashamed to lie. I wish I could tell the servants to send Marnie on her way without accepting her letters, but I am worried she would find another way of getting them to me. I am afraid that soon the truth will come out, for it must surely be the subject of much gossip in the servants' hall.

She was there in the churchyard again today. I tried not to look her way. I tried to keep my head down. But I swear I could feel her eyes burning black holes in my back.

I have confided in Arnold again and shown him the contents of the letters. He takes it all lightly, as is his way, and assures me that a girl like her could not possibly harm me in any way. But I am not so sure. I am keeping Cissie close by me and I will not sleep well again until we are back in London.

70

Tiny Pieces

Word has spread throughout the village that Noah is to be married. I hear the women at the water pump in the morning, tattling about it.

'*Will they wed here in Clevedon?*'

'*Has anybody seen her yet?*'

'*Is she very beautiful?*'

'Don't believe what you hear,' I tell them. 'The girl you are talking about is plain and dull. There'll be no wedding. You wait and see.'

They give each other knowing looks and I hear them whisper as I walk away.

'*She is worse now her mother is so ill.*'

'*What will happen to the girl if her mother dies?*'

'*There'll be no one to keep her from the madhouse then.*'

They know nothing and their gossip means nothing to me either.

Back at the cottage, Smoaker is waiting for me at the kitchen table. His eyes are red-rimmed and I wonder if he's been crying for Ma. I don't care enough to ask. I set his bread and tea in front of him and take a bowl of broth through to Ma. I know I should try and get some down her, but I can't be bothered with the effort. Noah is taking up all me thoughts and strength and all I can think is, it is a shame that Ma will never get to see inside the manor. She would have liked it.

Smoaker shouts out that he's off to the beach now, to open up. I shout back that I'll see him there. I tuck Ma's blanket in, tight around her. I don't like to touch her now she's so shrivelled and sickly. She doesn't look like Ma any more and she doesn't smell like Ma either. I'll tell Smoaker that she took some broth. It'll stop him fretting for a while. I leave Ma to her dreams, whatever they may be, and I take her broth to the kitchen and tip it back into the pot by the fire.

The day is fine and blustery. It'll be a busy one, but at least I only have the morning shift to get through before Smoaker sends me back to the cottage to look after Ma. He still has no idea that I take meself up to the manor instead. I have to be near Noah, though. Anybody would understand that.

I won't give up on him. I'm so close to making him see that he doesn't have a choice. Noah and Marnie. It was always meant to be. He knows now what it's like to hurt good and proper. I taught him that when I got rid of the wolfhound. He won't want to hurt like that again. I'm thinking all this as I leave the cottage and make my way to the beach. As I look towards the sea I'm startled yet again by the sight of the pier. Will I ever get used to it? It's not that I mind it. In a strange way it's what brought me and Noah together. I think it just scares me somehow. It looks so fragile, stretching out to sea like that with only its spindly legs for support. I'm afraid the sea will keep bashing at it and bashing at it until one day it will be smashed into tiny pieces and be washed away.

There are a handful of customers milling about outside the hut. I go inside to change and Smoaker looks at me questioningly. 'She's fine,' I tell him. 'She had half a bowl of broth.'

Smoaker's face relaxes and he nods towards a very plump woman whose bosom looks like it's fighting to escape the confines of her fancy frilled bodice. 'She's your first,' he says. 'Hurry up.'

I feel the cold of the sea more than usual today. I'm irritated by the weight of my bathing gown, and everything that used to thrill me is now just an annoyance and a waste of precious time that could be spent near Noah. But I go through the motions anyway. The plump lady shrieks loudly when I plunge her under.

I've done three customers and I'm leading the horse and bathing machine back up the beach to collect another when I see them in the distance. I stop where I am, hardly believing my eyes. The horse is confused and nudges at my shoulder. But still I don't move. There's the Bath chair, a footman, a maid and someone else. The blood rushes to me head so fast that it's only the harness I'm holding on to that stops me from falling.

71

The Journal of Noah de Clevedon

Clevedon. APRIL 26th 1869, Monday

I am elated! Father has just informed me over breakfast that we are to leave for London early. There are new business matters to attend to and we are to leave tomorrow! Already the servants are rushing around in a panic. Cissie is thrilled too. She says she can start our wedding plans in earnest now. I feel a great weight has been lifted from me.

It is a beautiful day outside. A last stroll in the gardens with Cissie would be a fine idea for this afternoon. I would like to take a happy memory away with me when we leave Clevedon tomorrow . . .

Hetty has just brought me a letter. I of course thought it was from the girl and my throat went dry. But I am happy to report, as my heart is calming, that it is from my darling Cissie and I am going to open it now and scribe her words on this very page as I read them. It is my first letter from my wife-to-be and I should like never to forget it.

Darling Noah,

I know you are busy in your chamber, and I have been busy in mine too, of course, instructing the maids on how to pack my trunk! As it is our last day here, your mother has asked if I would care to accompany her for a walk along the pier. I said that I would like to very much as we have not made as much use of it as we perhaps should have whilst we have been here. I was thinking also, that while we are there, I might sample the delights of sea-bathing. Your mother is quite sceptical as to the benefits. I know she did not fare too well herself, but she has nevertheless kindly lent me the use of her bathing gown—

72

As Blue as Hedgerow Cornflowers

'Miss.' I greet her as she opens the bathing-machine door. Her sleek black hair is tucked inside a large blue bathing cap that's edged with lace. It makes her look younger somehow, like a pale, nervous child. She smiles at me nervously. 'Will it be very cold?' she asks.

'The quicker you're in the better it is,' I say, giving her me usual answer.

She places her stockinged feet on the first step down. Her ankles are small and delicate, but the bloomers she is wearing conceal the rest of her legs. Her heavy wool bathing gown is belted tightly around her tiny waist. I can see the gown has weights sewn into the hem of it, so it doesn't billow around her when she enters the water. Only the finest of ladies go to this kind of trouble. I reach me hands up to her and she holds on to them as I guide her down the rest of the steps. 'Take a deep breath,' I say as she reaches the last step and her feet dip into the chill shock of the sea. She gasps and her hands grip tight on mine. I let her stay there awhile till she is used to the sensation, then I take me hands from hers and place them around her waist. I remember seeing Noah's hands in the very same place. I wish I'd never seen it. I want to wipe the picture out of me head for ever. But it stays all the same, hot and throbbing, taunting me and filling me belly with a thick black envy.

Cissie Baird trembles in me hands as I lift her from the steps and lower her into the sea. She squeaks like a baby mouse and her black eyes grow wide and shiny with tears. She blinks hard and the tears catch on her lashes and thicken them so they frame her eyes like painted strokes on a porcelain doll. I can see why Noah thinks he loves her. Who wouldn't want to love such a fragile and delicate creature? But he doesn't need her. She will never love him as much as I do and one day her beauty will fade and Noah will be left alone with a feeble and ugly wife. I'm the only one who can make him truly happy. He'll soon see that when she's not here any more.

I lay Cissie Baird back on to the surface of the ocean. I hold her afloat by placing one hand between her shoulders and the other on her lower back. The sea is being kind to us today. It's tired and sleepy and there are no sudden waves to catch us unawares. Cissie has crossed her hands and placed them over her bosom. I think she will look well in a coffin. 'I hear you're to be married,' I say to her. She nods her head, too afraid I think to open her mouth lest it's filled with seawater. 'I'm to be married too,' I say, 'to a wonderful man who loves me more than life itself.' She lifts her lips into the smallest and briefest of smiles. It's not a real smile. Why should she care less about me? Why should she even take notice of me? If only she could see inside me head, *then* she would notice me, *then* she would care more about me than anything she has ever cared for in her whole life.

I keep floating her, gently bobbing her up and down to the rhythm of the sea. I slowly move further away from the shoreline. I move deeper and deeper into the sleepy green water until me costume is sticking to me ribs. 'Me fellow's very handsome,' I tell her. 'He's got thick brown hair. Shiny as a chestnut, it is.' Again, she just throws me her pretend smile. 'Are you ready for your dipping now?' I ask her.

'I think so,' she whispers. 'I am warmer now, at least.' She takes her hands from her bosom and trails her fingers in the water. 'I am surprised,' she says. 'It is far pleasanter than I imagined.'

I look to the shore to see how far out we've come. We are further away than I thought. But Cissie Baird doesn't seem to have noticed. There are other bathers back there, closer to their bathing machines, and I can just see the reddish gleam of Smoaker's head as he stands outside the hut puffing on his pipe. I move me hands from Cissie Baird's back and put them under her arms. She's heavier now her costume is soaked, but still she weighs no more than a child. I turn her around so her back is to the shore. 'I was telling you about me fellow,' I say. 'How handsome he is.'

'You are lucky,' she says. 'My fiancé is handsome too. And the kindest man I could wish to find.'

I see Smoaker is talking to someone now. It's a gentleman in a suit. Not a local in rolled-up shirt sleeves. They are both pointing to the sea and waving their arms in the air. I squint me eyes and with a shock that squeezes tight the roots of me hair, I realise it's Noah. What's he doing here? He's running on to the beach now. Smoaker is lumbering behind him, his belly bouncing over his belt.

'Is everything all right?' Cissie Baird asks.

'It's fine,' I tell her. She's paddling the water with her hands now.

'This really is most refreshing,' she sighs.

Noah is standing at the water's edge. He's waving his hands madly over his head. It seems that everybody on the beach, every man, woman and child, has stopped whatever they're doing. They've all turned towards the sea and there are dozens of faces staring out at me.

'One of the things I love most about me fellow,' I say to Cissie Baird, 'is his eyes. One of them's blue, you see, like a summer's day. And the other's grey. Like a winter's day.'

She looks straight at me and her mouth drops open.

Noah has taken his jacket off and he's wading into the sea. 'Cissie!' he yells. 'Cissie!'

Cissie Baird tries to twist her head around. 'Who . . . ' she begins to say. I grip hard on to her shoulders and with a quick shove I push her head under.

Noah's swimming now. Just how I taught him to. His arms are splashing clumsily through the water. The shoreline behind him has filled with people, and there are dozens more gathered on the Grand Pier. I pull Cissie Baird to the surface and she lets out a choking gasp. Water shoots from her nose and her eyes are huge and wild with terror. Her bathing cap falls from her

317

head and sets loose a tumble of black hair. I catch the lavender scent of it before it drops heavily into the sea and fans out around her shoulders.

'Cissie!' Noah yells again, his voice breathless but closer. Why does he keep calling out *her* name? It's me he wants. It's *my* name he should be shouting out. I push Cissie Baird under the water again. She struggles against me now, kicking out with her legs and pulling on me wrists as I press down hard on her shoulders. She doesn't look much like a lady now. Noah will soon see. Once she's not here whispering lies into his ears, tricking him into thinking he loves her, once she's gone for good, he'll come back to me. He'll finally see that it was only ever him and me. Noah and Marnie. He's coming closer so I smile at him, hoping he'll see that everything will be all right. Cissie Baird kicks me hard in the belly. I'm not expecting it and for a moment me grip loosens and her head rushes back to the surface. This time she roars like some demented dog and vomits seawater all over me arm. She's stronger than she looks. But no matter. I'm stronger still. Of course I am. I'll have arms like me ma's before too long. I grip Cissie Baird by the shoulders again. She's screaming now.

'Shush,' I say to her. 'The sooner you're in the better it is.'

Noah's almost upon us. I can see his face clearly. His mouth is twisted into a strange shape. His hair is sticking to his forehead. He's struggling through the water, half walking, half swimming. 'Cissie!' he shouts again. But this time his voice is breathless and weak.

I push Cissie Baird back under the sea for the final time. The air around us heaves a sigh of relief as her screams are silenced. I look down at her face. It's so pale. The sea veils it in a shimmer of green and blue. Her eyes are staring up at me, huge and round and bulging. Tendrils of black hair are caught around her neck, but the rest of it is trailing behind her, floating on the surface of the sea. I remember Ambrose after he'd drowned; how his hair spread out like black feathers in the shallows and how he wouldn't stop staring. She's not kicking any more and her arms have gone limp by her sides. It won't be long now.

'Marnie!'

He's said me name! I lift me head. Noah's so close that a few strokes would bring me to him. 'It's almost over,' I call to him. 'A moment more and then nothing can stop us from being together!'

'Marnie. No,' he gasps. 'Let her go. Let Cissie go.'

'No!' I shake me head. 'I can't. We can never be together while *she's* in the way.' I'm trembling now. It's hard to be so close to him.

'We can,' he gasps. 'Let her go. And I promise. We'll be together.'

'No,' I mumble. 'You're lying.' I want to believe him but me head's all in a mess now. I just want to go to him and be in his arms and for everything to be all right.

'We can't be together if you drown her!' he shouts. 'Let her go!'

He's right by me now. I can see his eyes; one a fierce blue, the other a hard cold grey. If I reach out I could almost touch him. I could be in his arms in the blink of an eye. I take me hands from Cissie Baird's shoulders and move towards him.

But next to me there's a great whoosh and a gasp as Cissie Baird bursts from the sea. She's gulping down more air than a floundered fish. Before I can reach him, Noah's got to her. He's gathered her in his arms and he's wiping the wet hair off her face. 'Cissie,' he's saying. 'My love, my love. I have got you now. You are safe. You are safe.' She's retching and howling and coughing and Noah's chest-deep in the water, carrying her back to the shallows.

He's forgotten I'm here. Already I've disappeared. I watch the back of him moving further and further away. It's like the whole world is moving away from me. He was lying. Of course he was lying. I think I knew it all along. But I just wanted the touch of him for one last time. Now me arms and me heart are aching with the loss. It hurts more than anything ever has. It hurts more than all those weeks and months in the yellow room when sickness was prowling round me body. It hurts more than all the sharp words and looks that have ever been thrown me way. It hurts more than the thought of Ma lying on her deathbed.

The sea laps around me waist, tiny little licks as though it's trying to comfort me. Noah's back on the beach now. I can see him laying Cissie on the shingle. A crowd gathers round them and hides them from sight. Bathers and dippers have left the sea and the machines are empty and abandoned. People are hurrying along the pier. Gentlemen are holding on to their toppers as they rush to see what all the fuss is about. Crinoline-clad ladies are moving slower, their great skirts bobbing and swaying around their ankles. A parasol is blown over the side of the pier and lands upside down in the sea. It's caught by a passing breeze and sails quickly out beyond the pier head. There's only one person left looking out to sea. It's Smoaker. He looks so sad and lonely standing there all by himself. But I'm glad at least there's someone who hasn't forgotten me. He lifts his hand to me and I do the same. I think it's a farewell.

I can't go back there. Besides, I don't want to. There's nothing left for me. The sea nudges me again, sending a small wave over me bosom. I take a long, slow breath and gather all the hurt inside me into a small, tightly wrapped bundle. I pack it away deep inside me heart and look for one last time towards the shore. There's me beach, full of people and bathing machines, just as it should be. There's Smoaker's hut standing proudly next to the grandest pier of all. There's the esplanade snaking its way along behind the sea wall. There's the muddle of cottages and chimneys, and although I can't see it from here, I know that Ratcatcher's Row is there beyond the grassy embankment, with Ma tucked up in bed inside our cottage. I peer into the distance, up to where the woods disappear into the hills. I think I can just make out the sturdy walls of the manor, with its windows glinting in the sun.

I turn me back on it all and begin to swim. Me arms are strong and I pull back long and hard. I push through the water easily and me heart begins to lift as the sea soothes me and whispers comforts. I've been away from it for too long. I should have known never to turn me back on the only friend I've ever had. Soon I'm past the pier head and further out than I've ever been. I can sense the ocean floor dropping away beneath me. But the sea is holding me safe. Its colours are changing the further out I swim. Its greys and greens are now blues and dark blues and puddles of black. I'm past the jagged edge of the land now and even though the sea is calm today there are still waves crashing and smashing into the tumble of rocks at the foot of the cliffs. I swim hard and long and when I quickly look back, the pier has grown tiny and Smoaker is only a dot on the shore.

The sea has grown blacker and blacker. It's rougher too. Even the gulls haven't flown out this far. Me legs are growing tired, me bad leg is losing its strength. Me bathing gown is weighing me down and I wish I'd taken it off. I stop swimming and just paddle for a moment. I try to undo me buttons and wriggle me arms out, but me gown is too cumbersome and I'm swallowing too much water. I start swimming again but much slower than before. I can see the black line of the horizon stretched out before me. It goes on for ever and ever.

The waves are getting bigger. They keep breaking over me head, and although I know the sea is only playing with me, I wish it wouldn't. I'm losing me breath and I can't spit out the water fast enough. The sea is so heavy now. It weighs a ton and I can hardly push me arms through it any more. I close me eyes for a moment, just for a little rest. But the sea grabs me legs and tries to pull me under. Stop it! I shout. Just let me be!

Then, just when I think I can't swim an inch further, I see something in the distance. It comes closer, flying fast over the waves. I can hardly believe me eyes. It's a green fishing boat with a white cotton sail flapping madly in the wind. It's right there, like it's just popped up from over the horizon. Another wave closes over me head, but I don't mind any more because I know me pa's coming to get me. I can see him now; he's waving to me and beckoning with his hand. Come here, he's saying. Come on. Swim to me. He looks just like I knew he would. Matted yellow hair and a brown leathery face with a beard right down to his knees. I'm coming, Pa, I shout. Seawater pours into me mouth; there's too much of it to spit out, but it doesn't matter because suddenly I'm swimming faster than I've ever swum before. I'm whipping through the waves. I look behind and I see a flash of gold and the quick flip of me tail. Me heart feels fit to burst with happiness. It's me and the sea and me pa. The three of us together. It's what was always meant to be. Pa's reaching out his hand to me and I'm swimming nearer and nearer. I see the old green paint peeling off the side of the boat and I can smell warm fish and seaweed. The sea is rolling over me and it's cold and beautiful and it's washing away all me hurt. I stretch me hand up out of the water. Pa! I shout. Then I feel his warm rough fingers on mine and as he grips me hand tightly and pulls me into his boat I see that his eyes are as blue as hedgerow cornflowers.

Alison Rattle

Alison grew up in Liverpool, and now lives in a medieval house in Somerset with her three teenage children, her husband – a carpenter – an extremely naughty Jack Russell and a ghost cat. She has co-authored a number of non-fiction titles on subjects as diverse as growing old, mad monarchs, how to boil a flamingo, the history of America and the biography of a nineteenth-century baby killer. She has worked as a fashion designer, a production controller, a painter and decorator, a barmaid, and now owns and runs a vintage tea room. THE MADNESS is Alison's second novel for young adult readers. Her first, THE QUIETNESS, explored the relationship between two girls caught in the dark underbelly of Victorian London.

Follow Alison at www.alisonrattle.com or on Twitter: @alisonrattle

@HotKeyBooks Come & here from young peop
talking about books and their own creative wor
at @LiftandPlatform next Tuesday 21st
platformislington.org.uk/express-yourse...
May 15, 2013 | 02:38 PM

@HotKeyBooks We are coo-ing over the latest
Hot Key Baby (3rd so far since we were born!)
ee @saramoohead & little Drew (on
old!)

@Isobel Journal @Isarahbento
t is great isn't it!?

.iving (rooms) throu
istory
ollowing on from Becca's
esterday about history's
ore

Discover more at hotkeybooks.com!

Now you've finished, why not delve into a whole new world of books online?

- Find out more about the author, and ask them that question you can't stop thinking about!

- Get recommendations for other brilliant books – you can even download excerpts and extra content!

- Make a reading list, or browse ours for inspiration – and look out for special guests' reading lists too...

- Follow our blog and sign up to our newsletter for sneak peeks into future Hot Key releases, tips for aspiring writers and exclusive cover reveals.

- Talk to us! We'd love to hear what you thought about the book.

And don't forget you can also find us online on Twitter, Facebook, Instagram, Pinterest and YouTube! Just search for Hot Key Books